The Long Patrol

The Long Patrol

A Story of Light Horsemen from
Gallipoli to the Palestine Campaign
of the First World War

George Berrie

LEONAUR

The Long Patrol: A Story of Light Horsemen from Gallipoli to the Palestine Campaign of the First World War

Originally published in 1949 under the
title *Morale*

Copyright © 1949 George Berrie

Published by Leonaur Ltd

Material original to this edition and its origination in
this form copyright © 2005 Leonaur Ltd

ISBN (10 digit): 1-84677-033-5 (hardcover)
ISBN (13 digit): 978-1-84677-033-3 (hardcover)

ISBN (10 digit): 1-84677-026-2 (softcover)
ISBN (13 digit): 978-1-84677-026-5 (softcover)

http://www.leonaur.com

Publishers Notes

Contents

Chapter One
The Bush - January 1915

The little waterhole lay in the centre of a natural clearing, an acre of the soil which grows scattered grey-box trees in a thick brigalow scrub. The moon was nearly down, but it still threw streaks of light across the pool as the Bushman, riding bareback, came quietly from a cattle pad through the tall dead timber. He had a job to do there that night and, as he got near the pool, he felt anxious. He had delayed his coming as long as he thought he could with safety, but the December night was hot, and he might have overdone it.

He edged his mare close to the water, but before he let her drink, he rode slowly round it, leaning over and looking carefully for fresh tracks in the mud. There was still enough light to satisfy his eye, and he felt relieved when he saw that, so far, no dingo had been for a drink that night. But it would, for no dog with a full belly would face the heat of a midsummer day thirsty. There were a few other waterholes scattered through the scrub, but they were drying up fast. The Bushman knew them all, and he had taken good care that no dingo would go near any of them that night. This one was a favourite and closest to the outlaw's daylight home in the Booraba range. At some moment before daylight the dingo would drink.

He let the mare have all she wanted before he reined her back. A grey-box tree stood some twenty yards from the water's edge. It was not tall, straight and slim-trunked like its fellows. In its infancy something had twisted off its top close to the ground, and is a result, eight feet up, three stout branches made a perfect seat. The Bushman rode alongside and put his gun carefully in the fork. Then he balanced himself on the mare's back, and drew himself up after it, still holding the end of the reins. Once in the tree fork, he made the gun's position secure and, leaning down, he pulled the bridle from the mare's head. For some moments she stood there, then, in obedience to a soft tongue click, she moved away and grazed for awhile in the clearing before she disappeared along the track by which they had come. In the morning she would be standing at the horse-paddock gate.

The Bushman settled himself comfortably with the gun across his knees. Several times he put it to his shoulder to practise a noiseless movement and to satisfy himself that his position commanded the pool thoroughly. Several dingoes might drink that night, and his bushcraft told him that the one he specially wanted would circle the clearing at some distance first, and he knew, too, that its cunning was more than a match for his own. To get a killing shot he would need to wait until its greedy gulping masked the sound of his slightest movement. He would have starlight only to aim by, but he meant to kill, for this would be his last chance—the last shot of his civilian life. The next one might even be in action, and he wanted fervently to cry quits with this particular enemy before he crossed the world looking for others.

And *what* a dog!—if only one had him trained to obey a whistle. The Bushman had trapped a few dingoes, but a toe was all he had to show after a long- battle with this one. Laying baits was only a waste of time and poison, and nothing could persuade him to cross the wire of a spring gun. Fifty men had once assembled and driven ten thousand acres of thick forest. They had bagged several, but not the arch-outlaw, although they knew he was there. He knew too much to be driven on to waiting shotguns. What could you do with a dog that dug his way under high netting fences, but never came out where he went in? What he had cost the neighbourhood in slaughtered sheep couldn't be calculated. Well, *he* was off to camp in the morning, so if the dingo won that night, someone else could take on the job of getting him.

It was rather a nuisance all the same—the Bushman thought—this war. For six years he had been trying to knock four thousand acres of scrub into shape, fencing, ringbarking, and clearing prickly pear, and living in a bark hut like a blackfellow. For a few months after war broke out he had carried on as usual, but cursing the Kaiser all the same. Then, suddenly, he realised that the First Division of the Australian army had sailed and that most of his friends had gone with it. The knowledge brought something like panic, and he lost no time in clearing everything of any value off the place. When he climbed into the tree there was nothing on it but himself, his mare, and enough tucker in the camp safe for breakfast—after he had given the dingo his in the shape of a charge of shot. Then he would be free for a fifty-mile ride to the railway and a four-hundred-mile train journey to Sydney.

He moved in his seat to ease a slightly cramped muscle, and began wondering what a soldier's life would be like. He'd heard a lot about the South African war from fellows who'd been through it. They'd had it rough, seldom out of the saddle for weeks at a stretch except for a bit of sleep, and the tucker had been pretty poor. They didn't talk much about the actual fighting, but he remembered hearing one chap say that the worst thing about shell-fire was its moral effect He had an idea that artillery had altered since then.

He would have to learn to drill, of course; he wasn't at all sure that he knew even how to stand to attention, let alone salute; Then there was army discipline. He had a vague idea that it meant strict obedience—saying "Sir" to all sorts of strange birds and keeping your mouth shut when they told you off. If others could manage that part of it, he supposed he could, too. The thing was to get into camp without delay and find some way of catching up those who had already gone. It was possible that no more might be sent; the Kaiser's alleged pedigree— "Out of Europe by Christmas"—might be accurate. He had missed being' one of the First Division because he had had this blessed patch of scrub round his neck; even now he'd wasted an additional week trying to get square with a dingo. He wished he had given the whole outfit—dingo and all—to the Red Cross, and joined in the rush to the Barracks on August the fourth.

The parade-ground stuff was one side of soldiering, but what about the real thing? He had read somewhere that, you might know the drill book backwards but be quite useless in the firing line. He'd heard a South African chap say that the true spit-and-polish fiends were often the most gun-shy, and that no one really knew if he would suit the game until he tried himself out under fire. This war, too, seemed a bit different to any other. You might have to sit down and be pounded to bits, unable to hit back, the rifle in your hand about as useless as a boomerang. You would have to look on that as all in the day's work, and back yourself not to be one of those sent for.

The moon had all but disappeared and the mixed light made the shadows indistinct. When its glow faded away the Bushman felt easier in his mind, as his eyes became accustomed to the starlight. In less than an hour the first streaks of day would show, and he knew he hadn't long to wait. The pool was distinct enough—nothing could break its circle of light without offering a good target. A shadow passed across it, and he felt his scalp bristle, but it was only a night-bird. At the edge of the thick standing timber there was a fringe of green hopbush, and he thought he saw something fawn-coloured come partly out and draw back quickly. For a moment he dared not move; then, very slowly, he drew the gun upwards. He must make sure that he fired at nothing but the arch-outlaw. If he could get *him*, the rest of the pack could carry on the good work with his blessing.

Ah! His eyes hadn't let him down. A small yellow shape came quickly to the water's edge and stood there, lapping greedily. It was a half-grown dog—a veteran would have been less confident. It would have been an easy shot, but the Bushman mastered the temptation. The other would come in his turn, and it was something to know that his presence in the tree was unsuspected. The pup was very thirsty—that, too, was a good sign, but he was glad to see it slink back into the gloom of the hopbush. He felt quite confident now, for the pup had left behind the scent of security which would go far to lull the suspicion of the older dog.

A stick cracked in the thick undergrowth to the right of the waterhole, and the Bushman's heart first missed a beat and then banged hard against his ribs. A wallaby came out and drew itself slowly to the water. Suddenly it sat up alertly, then with thudding tail it hurtled across the open ground and vanished. It could only be a matter of seconds now, and the Bushman, the gun already to his shoulder, covered the section of the water *opposite* the wallaby's point of exit. It was, he knew, an almost certain guide if the the dog ran true to form and circled the pool at least once.

Then the dingo came—so stealthily that it was right out on the clearing before the Bushman saw it. He took note of a slight limp and drew a long breath to steady himself as it stopped a few yards from the water and listened. Almost any sound now would ruin his chance. He was aiming at the spot where the pup had drunk, and he knew that the slightest movement he made, although inaudible to himself, would be a danger signal to the outlaw unless it were gulping greedily. At last the dingo circled the pool and turned to the water in the tracks made by the pup. It put down its head and began to drink. The sound of the gunshot rang over the dead tree-tops, and mingled with its echoes came the flapping of startled birds and the thudding of wallabies.

The Bushman slid to the ground, broke his gun and put the second cartridge into his pocket. Then he walked to the quivering body and stood looking at it, quietly exultant. He had won at last in a long battle of human wit against animal subtlety. It was a good omen—surely. He pulled the dead dingo some little distance from the water's edge and set to work with his knife. The skin was of no value to him now—he meant to give it to a neighbour whose place he would pass on his way to town. He threw the carcase up into the tree fork, seated himself on a log, and pulled out his pipe.

After all, he thought, in the bigger game ahead he would meet men just as crafty as any dingo, and just as fond of killing for sport. They would meet him with his own weapons, and they would strike first unless his alertness surpassed theirs. He felt an added eagerness to be off, to try with others of his countrymen the mettle and wits of the new world against the pick of the old. He got up from his seat, threw the skin over his shoulder and disappeared along the narrow pad through the hopbush.

It was daylight when the Bushman reached the bark hut on the edge of the open downs. The fire was still smouldering in the cooking galley. He kicked the ends of the brigalow log together and hung a billycan of water over the flame. While it boiled he strapped the dingo skin on to the front of his saddle, and nailed up the door of the hut. It had been a camp, but not a home. Since boyhood had never had one, and he wondered if the war would provide it. He took a piece of charcoal from the galley and scratched a notice on the door: "Gone to Berlin."

Chapter Two
Liverpool Camp - February 1915

"More marmalade!" "You'll be sorry!" "You had a good home, but you left—left—left—pick it up there!"

The Bushman, dressed in dungarees, stood in a group watching the day's catch of recruits marching in column of lumps towards the Quarter Master's store. As a soldier of at least seven days' standing, he felt entitled to criticise. He had passed his tests easily enough and had spent the week going through the preliminary agonies of "sections right" and "slope arms," but for him seven days in Liverpool Camp were seven too many. A blind man could see that it was being run by the rejects of the regiments that had sailed. The problem was how to get out of it! There was one easy way, but it led in the wrong direction. You only needed to give Lip to an Acting-Temporary Sergeant Major, and you went over the High Jump without ceremony. The Bushman had a sense of humour and six years battle with scrub and dingoes had taught him self-control. The swelling chests of certain budding Napoleons didn't trouble him.

Still, it was maddening to think that he would have to wait for the formation of another regiment. His heart sank at the prospect of months modelled on the previous week, and he cursed himself once more for being four months behind in enlisting. He walked across to the Post Office, and as he passed the Q.M.'s store someone hailed him.

"Mr. Roberts would like to see you for a few minutes." Roberts! At first the Bushman couldn't place the name, then he remembered the clerk in the country Stock Office where he had sometimes done business. There he had usually handed the Bushman a chair while the latter was waiting to see the boss, but positions were reversed now. The land-owner saluted the one-time office boy with appropriate deference.

It seemed that there was a vacancy on the staff which was helping to win the war by giving out blankets, with promises of boots and trousers later on. Would he care about the job? No drill or other duties. The Bushman was cautious. Little as he liked the parade ground, he knew that a certain amount of it had to be endured, but it occurred to him that a friend amongst the officers might be useful.

"Is there any chance of getting away before a new regiment is formed?" he asked. "Most of my pals have gone. I'd give a lot to be able to join the 6th Regiment."

"You *might*, wangle a place in one of the reinforcement drafts," replied his friend. "They're supposed to be sailing any day. If you like I'll give you a note to the officer in charge of the lot you want to get with. There may be a vacancy between now and sailing, and if so you'll probably get it, I'll pile it on a bit since you're so anxious to get to holts with the Kaiser."

He wrote the letter there and then. The Bushman took it gratefully and made at once for the draft headquarters. He found that there was already a waiting list, and the best he could get was a promise of chance number six. He left the tent hoping fervently that an epidemic of thirst or insubordination would break out in that draft before it sailed. It *did* seem a bit queer, though, that if they wanted to punish a man for getting boozed or giving cheek, they stopped him from going where he might cease to be a nuisance permanently.

In answer to his prayers, most of the draft did get on the spree, and five of the worst offenders were hunted back to the depot. That left the Bushman with one to go. He spent his spare time for the next two weeks wondering how he could chisel that one limpet from its rock. He made the acquaintance of several members of the draft, and threw out hints of a swap, but they fell on deaf ears, and the Bushman grew desperate.

He went off parade one afternoon very downhearted, and, having a leave pass, wandered off into Liverpool and into the nearest pub. The only other uniformed man in the bar proved to be one of the draft, but it took five beers—for all of which the Bushman paid—to make him confidential.

"Wish I'd never "joined that draft," he mumbled. "I'm not keen on it. If a man waits for the new regiment it might be all over. That'd do me."

The Bushman's heart thumped harder than it had while he'd been waiting for the dingo. What a dingo this one was! He replied casually:

"Why don't you go A.W.L.? That'd do the trick. Or tell the Sergeant off!"

The man of the draft eyed him craftily, "Go A.W.L. when I'm broke? I might if I had a fiver. What's *your* game, old man, anyhow?"

The Bushman plunged.

"Well, it's this way. I've got a lot of pals in that regiment and my name's down for the next vacancy in the draft. If you like to work it so that I get your place, you're on a fiver."

He spoke a bit too eagerly. The other's eyes glistened with cunning and cupidity.

"Make it a tenner, mate, and its a bet."

That would leave the Bushman with a bare five pounds to see him across the ocean, but he was prepared to embark at a pinch without sixpence. For a moment he played with the idea of getting this bird so drunk that his arrest would be a certainty. A few whiskies on top of the beer would do it, but even that might not cost him his place in the draft. He cursed himself inwardly for being so precipitate. It was useless to try and call the other's bluff after he had shown his own hand w freely—all he could do was to "see" him.

"All right—that's a bet," he said. "The day my name goes on the draft's roll, the tenner's yours."

"Half of it down now," insisted the other.

The Bushman choked back his rising temper. Time enough to tell this cold-footed Shylock off when his place was certain.

"No, you don't," he said. "Not a bob till it's all O.K."

"And how do I know you won't bilk me?" retorted the other. "Think I'm going to take your word for it when you won't take mine?"

There was reason in that.

"Look here," said the Bushman. "Tell you what I'll do. I'll bet you a tenner to nothing that I don't sail with the draft. We'll tell Roberts, the Q.M., about it; you can see me give him the cash and you collect as soon as my name's on the roll. What about that?"

"All right—that's a bet. But how's it for a quid now, old man I'm stone-motherless broke."

The idea appealed to the Bushman. It was getting late and a quid now might do the trick and save him the other nine. The bet wasn't good until Roberts held the stake. He handed over the quid promptly.

He left very soon afterwards, and once out in the night air he knew that he had been in that pub long enough. His head was swimming. Then he looked at his watch and began to run for the bridge in a panic. He got to the gates just in time and waited awhile inside to see if his benefactor had followed. There was no sign of him.

To get to his lines the Bushman had to pass the draft headquarters. As he came opposite its orderly-room the clerk saw him and darted out.

"I've been trying to find you all the evening," he said. "You've damned near missed your chance. One of the fellows has gone sick and you're in in his place. We're sailing on Wednesday, so report here first thing in the morning."

The Bushman let out a yell of joy at his luck. Besides finding him a place in the draft it had saved him nine pounds. He did not leave as its junior member either, for another vacancy occurred next day. His acquaintance of the Liverpool pub was given the "High Jump" for being drunk and overstaying leave.

Chapter Three
Cario - March 1915

The *Marere* lay at anchor a little distance from Fort Macquarie Steps. She was a small tub-like looking vessel of some six thousand tons, and where she had been picked up by the British Government, no one seemed to know. Her officers were English, her crew Maltese. From her deck downwards to her hold she was fitted to carry horses and fodder. The draft—fifty-two strong—sat on its kit bags on the wharf waiting for the lighter to take them aboard. The main subject for speculation was, would she provide a better home than Liverpool Camp? Only those uncertain of the behaviour of their stomachs in rough weather doubted that she couldn't be worse. At least at Liverpool they were on solid ground. The Bushman, for one, felt quite happy. He had tried himself out a couple of times across the Bight, and was satisfied that not even mucking out below deck in the tropics would affect him. He felt sorry for a young Scotsman in the draft, who admitted that he'd never left his cabin on the luxury liner which brought him to Australia,

Besides the draft there were some odds and ends of infantry and artillery on board, and the Bushman's spirits dropped a bit when he saw the hammocks swung on the small troop deck. They were almost touching—it meant crowding much the same as it had in a bell tent in Liverpool camp. Then he remembered the row of horse-boxes on the forrard deck, and at the first opportunity made a careful reconnaissance. It might have been against Ship's Orders, but a couple of half-filled chaff bags on top of the most secluded box provided him with as perfect a camp under the stars as he could wish for. He scrounged a small tarpaulin as an insurance against rain, and not even a tropical downpour succeeded in driving him down into the musty atmosphere of the troop deck.

The *Marere* took on five hundred horses at Newcastle and plunged southward into the Pacific. Each man on board had an average of seven to look after. They had to be fed and watered, their stalls had to be mucked out, and each had to get a mile of exercise daily. That programme didn't leave the draft with much spare time, and most of that it put in on its rifles and ammunition. It worked in sections of four, with one of the section in charge—more or less. The rations were reasonably good—certainly an improvement on Liverpool, and there was a dry canteen on board. The few inevitable pinpricks of army life were almost unnoticed. By taking them as a matter of course the draft felt it was helping to win the war, and the *Marere* might have finished her voyage without a major incident only for the unfortunate fact that the draft included an "Old Soldier."

How he ever got in always puzzled the Bushman. His general appearance was considerably against him, but his row of service ribbons and his proficiency on the parade ground, where he made the rest of the draft look like the raw recruits they were. had evidently told heavily in his favour. He might of course, as a man who had seen service, have been useful amongst a lot of young soldiers; on the other hand, he probably knew all the points of King's Regulations backwards, a doubtful qualification when not one of the officers on board could have passed in their A.B.C.

For the first three weeks of the *Marere's* voyage the Old Soldier was a model of behaviour and did, if anything, more than his whack of his section's work. It was bad luck, and worse management, that he personally should have been told off over some badly cleaned stalls by the Orderly Officer, and, smarting under a sense of injustice, his feelings got the better of him. He relieved them by throwing down his broom and refusing duty. Further, he let that officer know exactly what he thought of him, of the other officers on board, and of their ancestors, male and female, into the bargain. Those members of the draft within hearing put their fingers in their ears, not because of the profanity of the Old Soldier's outpourings, but because, if called to give evidence at a court-martial—which surely must end in a firing party—they could truthfully say they had heard nothing. Their sympathy, too, went to the Old Soldier, but much of it evaporated when they found he had been placed under close arrest and they had to find a guard over him in addition to horse pickets and other duties. The only possible clink was a small and flimsy wooden structure on the boat deck. It had a door, but no window. The guard, with his fixed bayonet exposed to the rusting influence of the Indian Ocean spray, stood a few feet away, mostly gazing firmly in the other direction and praying that if the Old Soldier did run amuck it would happen during someone else's turn of duty.

There were six officers on board, including the M.O. and the Vet. In an unlucky moment they decided to court-martial the prisoner. An uneasy escort saw him safely to the orderly-room, and there he gave the court a brief lesson in military law. He refused to plead on the grounds of an improperly constituted tribunal. He was marched back to his eyrie on the boat deck, while the members of the court scratched their heads and consulted various textbooks to find out why.

The Bushman was doing his turn of guard duty when the mess orderly came along with his prisoner's dinner. Its meat ration had obviously been cut by nearly half. He looked firmly to his front while the mess orderly heard a fresh instalment of the *Marere's* pedigree and that of every officer on her. Out of the tail of his eye he saw the dixie flying overboard, followed by a plate, knife and fork and a couple of army blankets. Then came the sound of splintering wood, and this time he had to look round. The wall had a hole in it where the window should have been, and the door was hanging on one hinge. The look on the Old Soldier's face would have frightened the Kaiser. It certainly frightened the Bushman. He prayed inwardly that his prisoner wouldn't try to break guard. He couldn't have stopped him even if he'd been game to use his bayonet—which he wasn't.

The next court was differently constituted. It consisted of an

21

Artillery Captain, the Vet. and the M.O. When asked to plead, the prisoner said he would this time, if only for the information of the ignoramuses who thought that a cod-crusher and a linseed lancer were entitled to sit on a court-martial trying a soldier on active service. Once more he let himself go, this time about the capabilities of the Vet. and the M.O. The latter wouldn't get a job bandage-rolling once off the *Marere*; in the interests of posterity, the former should have had his cods crushed in infancy. The uproar brought the ship's captain on the scene, and the change wrought by his presence was magical. The Old soldier stood rigidly to attention, answered "Yes, Sir," and "No, Sir," to a few curt questions, and turned about in his best style when his escort was ordered to take him back to his domicile. He knew better than to risk spending the rest of the voyage in irons. Next day he was under open instead of close arrest.

The *Marere* took in coal at Aden, otherwise she made a non-stop run from Newcastle to Suez, and was five weeks doing it. The unshipping of the horses was not without incident. One broke away and took to the waters of Fort Tewfik, but eventually after a long swim it was headed back, lassoed, and brought once more to earth on the end of a couple of the *Marere's* winch ropes. The draft's train trip to Cairo was not without its share of incidents either. The Old Soldier, once more under close arrest, broke loose from his guard, severely handled a couple of possible witnesses to his *Marere* performances, and capped everything by smashing a train window. The draft drew a long collective sigh of relief when it saw him handed over to an escort in Cairo who would, as he well knew, use bayonets without any compunction. It expected only to hear of him when his sentence—to be shot at dawn—was announced, and certainly never to see him again; but it did.

The Bushman missed the excitement of that train trip. To his delight he was included in a small advance party which left for Cairo as soon as the *Marere* berthed. Through the Khamsin which chased the train all the way he caught sight of the sandy desolation he was to know so well in subsequent years. At

Heliopolis he saw bright lights, gay cafes, crowded streets, beskirted men and trousered women, and in the morning he woke in a camp on the sand of Abbassia.

Early in the next forenoon the whole draft was given leave—and pay. With a hundred "disasters" in his pocket, the Bushman soon made one of a crowd, walking, running or urging slow donkeys towards the mysterious looking domes and minarets of Heliopolis. By the time he'd had a haircut, a boot clean, several drinks and a civilised feed, he'd mastered the coinage problem and two necessary passwords—"igri" and "imshi." Heliopolis was, however, only the gateway to Cairo, the city of mysterious legend. The Bushman had heard many hair-raising stories of Cairo, but had always put them down as travellers' tales. His pass was for Heliopolis only, but the lure of Cairo was too powerful, especially when, later in the afternoon, he failed to find one member of his draft about the streets. He decided then to be in whatever might be doing, and boarded a tram for Cairo,

The city was crammed with men in Australian uniform, and the sight of them reassured him in his lack of a proper pass. There seemed to be little chance of finding trouble if you didn't go looking for it, so he saluted all the Sam Brownes he saw— carefully. He wasn't to know then that that was the surest way of attracting attention.

He took a gharri to Opera Square and found a few of his fellow reinforcements in a cafe there. None of them had been asked to show leave passes, but they had been warned by some older hands not to make it too hot for the first night, and to get back to camp early. The Bushman made the acquaintance of a Tommy Sergeant at dinner-time, and the latter suggested taking a look round Cairo's underworld. With the moral support of an N.C.O. the Bushman felt reasonably safe from getting into trouble, so he accepted the offer.

Where they went he never exactly knew, but more than once he felt thankful that he wasn't alone. The streets were narrow, dark, and particularly filthy; the inhabitants were evil-looking to the last degree. Women, young and old, of various nationalities, bailed them up from every doorway. The Sergeant used his cane vigorously at times to clear a passage, and he had to come to the Bushman's rescue when two women tried to drag him up a stairway. Before long the latter hadn't the faintest notion where he was, or of the way out of the human cesspool, and by the time the Sergeant had shown him a "half-piastre can can" he decided that, for the first night, he had seen enough. The Sergeant, however, intimated that, for him, it was only the evening's prelude, and described the shortest way back to Opera Square.

The more the Bushman tried to follow his directions the more he became hopelessly lost. All the streets were alike, and all seemed to come to a dead end sooner or later. At last, when he found himself in one where he could see no sign of a uniform, he began to get windy. He stopped to light a cigarette and narrowly escaped being brained by an article of bedroom furniture thrown from a window two storeys up. He dodged across the street and looked for the zone of fire. Through a window which fronted a narrow balcony he caught glimpses of a full-size "rough house" in progress. Shouts and screams followed a fresh downward stream of furniture. First chairs, then a table, and lastly a small piano came crashing to the footpath. Several screaming women—partly naked—climbed from the window and raced along the balcony. Ominous clouds of smoke drifted after them, and by that time the packed street was in an uproar. Shouting natives ran to and fro, and like magic swarms of uniformed men appeared. The warning signals of a fire engine sounded close at hand as flames began to lick the walls outside the window and fresh clouds of smoke came from the rooms adjoining.

Then the Bushman woke to the fact that there was nothing accidental about either the row or the fire. A number of men rushed from the burning building and joined those who had already attacked the fire engine. As fast as a hose was directed at the flame it was slashed into pieces, and the protesting firemen hustled into the crowd. The Bushman decided that, for his first night in Cairo—and that without a pass—it wasn't healthy. He pushed his way through the throng behind a tall, fair-haired boy in Light Horse uniform. On the outskirts of the crowd they stopped to draw breath, and the Bushman asked: "What's the strong of all this?"

"Don't know quite," the boy replied; "but the yarn is that an Enzed got stabbed in that brothel last night, so his mates came along to clean it up. They've made a job of the whole street while they were at it. Gawd Didn't those "bints" squeal! Look out!"

Another fire engine dashed by; just missing the Bushman.

"This isn't on *my* programme," continued his acquaintance. "I'm for camp as quick as I can beat it. You got a pass?"

The Bushman admitted that he hadn't.

"Better get out of it too, then," said the other; "it's a wonder the Jacks haven't been along before this. There'll be a round-up in an hour or so. Where are you camped? Abbassia, eh? Oh, you're one of our new draft then—s'pose you'll be over to join us before long. Ma'adi's a great little joint—the best in Cairo. I'm a driver. Christ! I can see some Jacks now. S'long, mate."

"Here—hold on." The Bushman grabbed his arm. "I'm clean slewed. Which way do I go to get the tram for Abbassia?"

"Come on with me," replied the other. "I'll show you as we go."

They ran and, before long, the Bushman could see that apparently thousands of others—some with their tongues out—were running too, in any direction that led out of Cairo. He didn't slacken speed himself until he was safely on a tram bound for Heliopolis.

Chapter Four
Alexandria - April 1915

The draft spent a week at Abbassia, none too happily, The camp was rough and the food worse. There were certainly the attractions of Heliopolis, but they soon emptied pockets of the few piastres they contained. The Khamsin continued to add to the general gloom for several days, but the uncertainty as to what lay ahead was the chief worry, and the rumours circulating were always those of extreme pessimism.

The Regiment had no room for additions to its strength—it was already over establishment. So said one or two who came over from Ma'adi to look up pals in the draft. In any case, if room was found for it there, its main jobs—apart from the severe training it needed to fit it for absorption in *the* Regiment—would be fatigues, pickets and cleaning horse-lines. Of course, when action made gaps in the Regiment's ranks, reinforcements' claims for absorption might be considered, but until then—well, they would have to pay a just penalty for taking so long to find out there was a war on. The Bushman began to wonder if, after all, he had been lucky in fluking a place in a draft of reinforcements.

Meanwhile the Old Soldier—guarded by other old soldiers—had been securely caged behind barbed wire. When his case, for preliminary investigation, came before the O.C. of the camp—a Colonel of the Regular Army—that official raised his eyebrows when he glanced over the Charge Sheet There were enough crimes on it to warrant half-a-dozen courts-martial, but there wasn't a solitary witness in support of them. He remanded the case for a few days and sent a curt "please explain" to the officer in command of the draft, who had been placed in a difficult position. The personnel of the *Marere's* abortive courts had scattered, taking good care to leave no addresses behind. Not for them the certain derision the Old Soldier's story would let loose over their heads—sleeping dogs were best let lie. The O.C. of the draft came to the same conclusion, with the result that the Old Soldier appeared in the camp orderly-room for the second time alone. In a temper at such a puerile waste of his time, the Camp Commandant tore up the charge sheet and dismissed the case. The draft decided that, after all, army discipline wasn't what it was cracked up to be. Given certain circumstances, you could get away with almost anything in the shape of insubordination.

The draft eventually moved to Ma'adi feeling not unlike dogs going into a new kennel, but it found that the alleged prejudice against reinforcements had been much exaggerated. It was at once split up and attached in small groups to troops in each of the three squadrons. Someone early in the game had christened A. the Squatters, B. the Navvies, and C. the Cockles, and the Bushman, appropriately enough, found his way into C. along with several of those with whom he had palled up in the draft. It was true that often enough the parade for stables consisted mainly of reinforcements, but the Bushman for one didn't object, such was his relief at being at last attached to a regiment.

The camp was ideally placed, on flat sand alongside the pleasant suburb of Ma'adi, with its English residents, its tree-lined streets, its well-built dwellings with their luxurious lawns and gardens. There was a cinema, a recreation room, and a wet canteen, also a stadium. For those who had piastres to spend, the Nile Cafe was within easy walking distance, and official leave to Cairo was reasonably frequent. Unofficial leave was safe enough provided its taker used ordinary common sense. There was no need to get back to camp by the main gate when there were miles of desert joining the horse-lines at the back. The Regiment did its mounted and tactical work on that stretch of desert, and fought mock battles over the Mokattam Hills and the remains of the petrified forest.

There had to be a blot on the Ma'adi landscape—and inevitably it was the regimental cookhouse. Compared to it those of both the Marere and Liverpool were reasonably satisfying restaurants. Loads of rations could be seen going into it daily, but little enough ever came out. What became of it inside the cookhouse, was a mystery, since it was accepted that even the greediest sergeant-cook couldn't eat it all. The Bushman cut down his tobacco consumption, kept out of the canteen and Cairo, and spent the bulk of his fortnightly pay on tomato omelettes in the Nile Cafe, and oranges. But before long the camp at Ma'adi had something else to think about. Rumours spread that the infantry division was going—somewhere; then that it had gone, and finally that the advance guard of the Australian Army was in action. Then there was only one topic of conversation in the camp from canteen to cookhouse, and men became restless with suspense. Were the mounted units going too?

Even signallers, who could usually be depended on for more or less reliable information, confessed to knowing nothing, and the orderly trooper resting in the shade of the big tent overheard nothing worth passing on.

The Bushman had an additional reason for worry. He was still attached to a troop merely as a reinforcement and he was doubtful about his position if the regiment moved. That it would sail before long, he felt pretty sure. By the time the Landing was a week old, and from the news which had leaked through, it looked as if even the mounted units would be needed to give a hand. The horses would be left behind and some would have to stay to look after them. He could scarcely expect to be given precedence over original hands, and could only hope for another issue of the luck of Liverpool Camp.

He wandered over to the transport lines as soon as the evening meal ended, looking for his acquaintance of that first historic night in Cairo. He found Snow in a very despondent mood, cursing a certain Sergeant-major and his own quick temper.

"Was that why you shifted to the Transport?"

"That was it," replied the dejected Snow. "The swine made it so hot for me that I put in for a driver's job. I wish to Gawd

I'd stood it now."

"Couldn't you swap back again?"

"I've been trying that all the week, but he's poisoned every troop leader against me. Come on, let's get round to the stadium. There's an Irish middleweight—a Tommy from the prison guard camp—fighting Cameron the Queenslander. The whole of the First Brigade will be there."

They were none too early. The open-air stadium was three parts filled when they got there, with an hour to go before the preliminary events. Snow and the Bushman forgot their forebodings in the excitement of a willing four-round contest which the Irishman won on points. The excitement of the crowd reached its height when the Brigadier, who refereed, walked to the edge of the ring and held up his hand for silence.

He was a fighting man in every sense, that Brigadier. He had been an amateur heavyweight champion in his day, and even when long past that day he would have made most men sorry if they had taken him on in a serious contest. He wore the ribbons and carried the scars of the South African war, and he was about to lead a brigade through stirring years, to earn its love and admiration and the deep regard of every man who took the field in a saddle. Australia has never bred manhood to surpass that of the "Old Brig."

For a few seconds he stood watching his silent men, his hand still raised. Then he spoke, and his great voice boomed over the stadium.

"You've seen a good fight tonight, lads," he said; "but there's a better one going on just over the way. I want you to give three cheers for our Infantry, the men who have blazed the track and made a name for Australia. Now!"

The cheers came with a vigour from a thousand throats, but silence fell again as quickly when the Brigadier held up his hand.

"I know that you are all anxious to lend them a hand, and I can tell you on the best authority that before many days pass we shall be alongside them."

A mighty shout burst from the gathering. Hats were hurled

skyward and hands shaken. The cheers at last died down to a babel of excited talk and laughter, but two men at least sat in moody silence. One knew that there was no place for him. The other was uncertain.

For the Bushman the suspense ended the next morning. He was picked for the team, but there was no reprieve for Snow. A few days later, when the Regiment marched out of camp in the silence of the spring night, there was no excitement; nothing but the unusual hour and the full marching order to show that the movement differed from any other. A few civilians lined the streets of Ma'adi and shouted good-bye to individual friends, but those of the Regiment detailed to stay behind remained in their tents or on the horse-lines. No—not all of them. Snow stood in the tree shadows near the railway station and watched the Regiment entrain with a grin on his face.

About an hour before the parade fell in, the Bushman had gone across to say good-bye to him, but when he quietly poked his head through the tent flaps he was greeted by some startled oaths. Snow was kneeling on the sand and dredging in a kitbag.

"Oh—it's you. Come on in then, and tie those flaps behind you."

The Bushman did so and eyed him curiously. There was an air of defiant determination about the tall, fair headed boy.

"What are you up to?" the Bushman asked.

Snow lowered his voice.

"This is no good to me." He began to chuckle, "I'm wondering what old four-eyes will say when he sees me the day after tomorrow. He can't put me overboard, anyway. I'm going to be well planted on that boat when she pulls out from Alex."

"They might send you back," the Bushman replied. "It'd be worse than ever then."

"Not they," said Snow emphatically. "They'll be thinking of something else, long before we hit that peninsula. There's others going to give it a fly besides me. Anyway, I'll chance it. I'll go 'magnoon' if I stop here."

"How'll you get on the boat?"

"Don't know yet, but I'll find a way." Snow grinned and pulled a fat wad of notes from his pocket. "Feloos keteer. It talks. I did a trot at the school two nights ago."

The Bushman put out his hand silently. Snow gripped it hard, and for those two men mateship was born, a bond which would carry them through Life and Beyond.

"It'll be dead easy," Snow whispered. "You're going to march from Bab-el-Louk to Cairo and get a train there for Alex. I'll be on that train, too, and I'll follow the crowd down to the boat—I'll see you there. Clear out now."

From the shadows of a vantage point near Bab-el-Louk station Snow watched the Regiment move off through the silent streets, but the silence was soon broken. Before the marching men bad gone far, cheer after cheer came from the native onlookers. For awhile Snow followed at a convenient interval, then his pace grew with his confidence, and he kept abreast of the column, but on the footpath. Others, too, were moving along. A few of these stragglers seemed different. Their clothes were stained, their hats battered—one man had bloodstains on his tunic. Snow saw him edge near the marching column and slip quietly into & broken section. He had been there, and he was going back—for more.

When the column got near Cairo station, Snow hurried ahead and hid behind a pillar near the entrance. He watched the Regiment move slowly on to a platform, but too many men who knew him were passing backwards and forwards to make boldness a safe policy. He edged sufficiently close to the barrier to locate the position of the baggage trucks. He could only reach them with safety from the farther side, and that meant finding a way on to the opposite platform. A redcap stood near the barrier, but Snow saw with relief that he wore no stripes. He slipped back again behind the pillar, and when he reappeared his sleeve carried three stripes and a red armlet band. He walked past the "Jack" with the unconcern of an A.P.M., and through the barrier on to the platform. There he reduced himself to the ranks again and passed quickly to the far end of the carriages. Once safely in an empty one, the rest was easy. He climbed through the window and dropped on to the line between the two trains. Crouching low, he made his way slowly and noiselessly back to the baggage vans.

As he climbed into one, he thought he had lost the game, for two Gyppo porters appeared. Before they could raise an alarm, Snow pushed two fifty-piastre notes into their hands and burrowed his way under some kitbags in the darkest corner of the truck, but he scarcely dared to breathe freely until the wheels began to grind beneath him.

Once more he stood in the shadows of a building, this time within a few yards of a ship's gangway. In semi- darkness he had prowled about the wharf looking for any spot where he might sneak on board, but the boat stood too far out even if ropes had been banging or doorways left conveniently open. He watched the Regiment file up the gangway, followed at short intervals by the rest of the brigade. Even with full equipment he had no chance of brushing by the guard posted at the deck entrance. As time passed and daylight came, he grew desperate. At any moment the gangway might be hoisted and the boat move out into the stream. Then, as a line of heavily loaded trucks drew on to the wharf, he gave a sigh of relief.

In a few moments a fatigue party came down the gangway and began carrying away the baggage. Snow was soon amongst them, with his hat pulled well down. He dived on to the biggest bundle he could find, and followed the rear file closely up the ladder. Somewhere amidship he dumped his load and mingled with the crowd. There seemed to be little more than standing room on the boat, and he brushed past men of his own squadron unrecognised as he made for the nearest ladder leading below deck. For a while he searched swiftly but vainly for a safe hiding place, and after a couple of narrow escapes he climbed in desperation down into the engine room, A gruff voice hailed him at once.

"Now then, lad, clear out of here. No one allowed—"

Snow stopped him urgently.

"Find me a place where I can plant for a day or two, mate— for Christ's sake don't give me away. I'll make it worth your while."

The engineer looked at him suspiciously.

"What's the game, son?" he said. "I've had about half-a-dozen of your mob come at me with the same yarn already. You want to stow?"

"Only till she's well out to sea and they can't put me off," whispered Snow. "They left me behind and I want to go. Look here—"

He held out a couple of notes, but the engineer waved them aside. He began to laugh.

"I wonder how many more bloody lunatics you've bred in your country. You want to go to Gallipoli? Here— come along o' me."

Somewhere in the bowels of the boat he opened a small door, and Snow stumbled through into thick air and pitch darkness. He turned round to thank his benefactor and crammed the notes into his hand.

"Fetch us some tucker, old man, and a candle, and let's know when she's a day out. A man'll lose track of time in here."

The door closed behind him, and Snow, as he felt for matches, thought he heard sounds of stifled laughter. A voice drawled:

"Snow's spin. Fifty wanted in the centre."

Then several matches were struck at once and Snow discovered the other half-dozen lunatics who had been ahead of him.

Chapter Five
Gallipoli - May 1915

The transport lay anchored some miles from the shore, but the blurred line of the inland ridges showed irregularly even through distance and darkness. During the night the intermittent crackle of line fire was punctuated by a shell burst and periods of silence; The Bushman and Snow, before they dossed down near the deckrail, listened with speculative interest and mild contempt. Call *that* a war? After the yarns they'd heard it sounded tame.

Snow had made his peace with Authority after a bad quarter of an hour in the orderly-room, and during the short voyage his behaviour was circumspect. The sergeant-major had other things to worry him besides stowaways. The troop sergeant's grip was already in pieces and a corporal was doing most of his work. Luckily the voyage was short and the weather fine, for the congestion on board was terrific, and with the sergeant slipping on his job it meant every man fending for himself.

"We'll soon know who's who," chuckled Snow to his mate as they burrowed side by side into their blankets, "These parade ground Napoleons will be more below ground than above it."

The Bushman was of the same opinion, but he was more concerned about it.

"They'll have plenty of time to do some damage, all the same, before they fade away," he replied. "What a nerve a man has to take on stars or stripes unless he's been at the game before and knows he won't let men down."

Snow chuckled again.

"It's the 'feloos,' " he said; "Think how handy ten-and-six a day would have been to us back there in Cairo. And no picquets or fatigues. You only want a bit of bluff to put it over. Tell you what"—he snuggled a bit closer to his mate—"I'm getting windy myself. I mean—can a bloke stand getting badly knocked without squealing? I'm going into action gagged."

The Bushman turned in his blankets. The hardest ground he had ever camped on was a feather bed compared to the iron deck of the *Lutzow*. He said; "Well, gag yourself now and get to sleep. Chances are it's the last we'll ever get. Christ! Listen to that!"

In a moment they were on their feet and fighting for places on the rails with others equally anxious to see and hear. The ridges had suddenly erupted a continuous roar of rifle fire. The crackling sounded so close that no one doubted that the Infantry were making a last stand on the water's edge. Until daylight the incessant firing scarcely slackened. The Bushman grew tired of speculating after awhile and returned to his blankets, but Snow stayed at the deck-rail, fascinated.

"Come and get some sleep, you fool," urged the Bushman. "You'll know all about it soon enough. We'll both wish we were back in the horse-lines this time to-morrow—if we aren't pushing up daisies."

"Well," decided Snow, as he reluctantly took his mate's, advice, "I want a run for my money, anyway. If I tail 'em first throw, I'll burst out crying"

As the forenoon passed, things on land seemed to become normal. An occasional shell burst over the beach, and the more the Bushman looked at the ridges the more amazed he felt at the work of the Infantry, At last a tug drew alongside the transport and men and baggage were crowded below its decks. For more than a mile of the slow journey shoreward the tug moved unchallenged, and at last curiosity got the better of many of the men. The Bushman and Snow were amongst a few who made their way on deck. They stood for awhile on the safe side of the smoke stack, listening to the "plonk" which occasionally broke the smooth surface of the water.

"Spent bullets," remarked one man with an air of unconcern. He wore a South African ribbon and gave the impression that all this was like old times to him.

"Well, if they are," replied the sceptical Snow, "you can have these and I'll try the other sort."

Then, to their right and in the far distance, they heard four reports in quick succession, and the sky above the ridges began to scream as if in torture. Surely it must be in flames, thought the Bushman—something must be visible. His feeling was one of intense curiosity—the screaming was now nearly overhead, and the impulse to have a look was irresistible. He poked his head round the smoke stack just in time to see the last of the four shells burst, and its aim had been fairly good. With a venomous swish a shower of pellets rattled against the funnel and on the iron decking. The water showed a pretty pattern. A cheer came from below deck as Snow grabbed the tails of the Bushman's tunic and dragged him down.

"If you want to get cracked here, I don't," he said. "What did you want to put your head round there for, you bloody old fool?"

The Bushman was apologetic, but he was quite satisfied. He said: "I simply had to watch that one bust, old chap, but you won't catch me doing it again. They hit hard all right."

No further shots were fired. The Turkish battery had christened the new arrivals and kept its shells for better results later on. With no more than a couple of casualties, the Regiment landed and reached the reasonably safe side of a hill in Shrapnel Gully. There men dug in and waited for two days. Then, one afternoon they took over a sector of the front line, and a few infantrymen kept them company for the first night.

The Bushman and Snow sat on the firestep listening reverently to an infantryman's account of the big attack. He might have been describing a football match, so casual was his tone, and it wasn't specially put on for the benefit of the newcomers, either.

"Jacko told us over our own telephone lines that what was left of us would be swimming to Imbros next morning, and he was so cocksure about it that he even started his cooks over with dixies to give 'em breakfast on the beach. Most of 'em got the last breakfast they'll ever want till Allah cooks 'em one. You can see 'em lying out there now—thick, and ripe as cherries. There's two of 'em right under the parapet."

"Let's have a look, mate," begged the Bushman. The infantryman handed over the periscope with the indulgent air of a grown-up giving a child a completely new toy.

"Keep it moving, mind," he said; but the Bushman soon forgot the warning in his first look at No-man's Land and some of the realities of war. The infantryman hadn't boasted. Two bodies lay together not three feet from his face. Eighty yards away he could see the earthworks of the Turkish trenches, and the intervening ground was dotted with still figures—most of them on the Australian side of half-way. In a deep gully turning diagonally to his right they lay piled in heaps—they had been caught there trying to take refuge whilst retreating. The Bushman smelt something new, and something he would never forget—dead men. Not one of the attacking army had set foot in the Australian trenches. He wondered if any troops in the world could have broken through that First, Infantry Division, and he felt a thrill of gratitude at the prospect of following where it had led. And how very nearly he had missed the chance! But for his own persistence and Snow's determination, both of them would still be in a camp—somewhere.

A terrific explosion hit his eardrums, and his face began to sting as if scratched by a dozen razor blades at once. He jumped off the firestep nearly on top of the two men below. Snow began to laugh and the infantryman to curse.

"You bloody fool," he roared. "Didn't I tell you to keep it moving? D'you think periscopes are made to give Jacko practice? Put your thick head up there and let him knock some sense into it—he couldn't knock any out."

Snow examined the Bushman's face carefully. He fished out a few flecks of glass with a pin, and carefully smudged a drop of blood to make it look like the real thing,

"There y'are," he said proudly. "Wounded in action, and

fined a week's pay for careless use of periscopes. Wait till that gets back to the scrub!"

After four nights of incessant firing, and days of sniping, the silence of the armistice seemed unnatural. The Bushman and Snow sat on the firestep and cursed their luck at not being selected for the burial party. There were strict orders against any man showing himself, but from an invisible position behind sandbags they had a peep, and so had nearly everyone else. After several narrow escapes from being caught they gave it up. Then they heard someone bellowing a message further along the trench: "Anyone here Interpret French? Anyone here who understands French?"

Snow hopped down at once.

"That'll do me," he told the Bushman. "Parlee-vous Francy? Mayswee Mopsoo! Yes, I can."

"You liar," expostulated the Bushman. "You know no more French than my boot."

Snow grinned.

"What odds," he said "They don't, either. What's the job, Corporal?"

If the corporal had belonged to the Regiment he would have told Snow to. go to hell and not waste their time. But he didn't, and for all he knew Snow might have been a crack linguist. He said: "There's a Jacko general out there trying to tell them something, and they think he's talking French. Come on, then, if you can speak the lingo. There'll be a hell of a row, mind, if you can't."

Snow was quite prepared to chance a row for the sake of getting a good look at what was going on. Anyway, he did know a few words of French—he had picked them up from a mademoiselle in Cairo, though it was unlikely that the Jacko general would talk on any of the topics *she* had.

They scrambled over the parapet, and as they moved across No-man's Land Snow got a full view of one of the war's unique happenings. A rough boundary line had been pegged half-way between the two trench systems, and stretcher bearers were busy carrying bodies from the Australian side where most of them had fallen. Some were being buried where they lay—they had been there since the Landing. At the half-way boundary the bodies were handed over to Turkish stretcher-bearers, but, apart from them and the grave-diggers, there were few men to be seen. The Turkish lines showed no signs of life, but below ground men waited with their fingers to the trigger.

The corporal took Snow to a little group of officers standing near a green crescent flag at the half-way line. A stout figure in Turkish uniform was trying hard to explain something in what sounded like several languages at once. Even if Snow had taken Sydney University honours in French he would have soon found that they taught it differently in Turkey. He guessed that, anyway, and explained the handicap to a colonel in the group of officers.

"I'm sorry, Sir," he said, "but I'm afraid I can't make head or tail of him."

The colonel eyed him with suspicious disgust. He said: "What the hell did you come out here for, if you couldn't speak French? This is no place to play the fool."

"I can speak it," retorted Snow. "It's this old Abdul that can't—not the French I learnt at school, anyway." He took a long shot. "It might be his Constantinople accent that's got me beat, Sir. Get him to write it down."

For all Snow knew—or cared—the general's accent might have been pure Parisian, but after wasting a good deal more time he had to admit that the French exercise had him beaten too.

"I'm afraid it's no use, Sir," he told the colonel sorrowfully, after pretending to study the document carefully. "That's not french French, whatever it is,"

The colonel turned to the corporal.

"Take this man back to the trenches at once, and take his name, number and unit too. We'll find out tomorrow if he understands orderly-room English. And see if you can find someone else."

39

Snow retreated in good order. What he had seen was worth a week's pay, especially in a place where you couldn't spend it even if you got it. Before he slid over the parapet he turned for a last look at a picture of history in the making. On that little plateau the New World had tested itself in pitched battle against the Old. And it had won.

Chapter Six
Gallipoli - June 1915

The sap was in semi-darkness, and traffic was congested by relays of tunnellers carrying filled sandbags to the back areas. The Bushman dodged his way through to a spot where the evening- rations were usually given out. He was running a bit late—the official reason was the shelling of the beach; the real one, the swim he had indulged in after the fatigue ended. He found the dixies empty, as he expected;, but the sergeant's voice reassured him from the depths of a dugout.

"Snow drew yours," he said. "You'll find him in the front line. What kept you?"

"Beachy Bill," replied the Bushman. "The cow pasted the pier for nearly an hour. Four infantry coves got knocked."

"Better get a move on then. You and Snow go on shift in about half-an-hour."

"Where's the night post camping?"

"Some of them are on the firestep and the rest in the possies along the sap. There's only the 'Green Stripe' empty."

The Bushman passed the Green Stripe possy on his way to the firing line. Everyone dodged sleeping there if he could, for it had acquired it's name from something vastly different to a brand of whisky. On the ground level above, several feet of loose earth covered the body of someone who had fallen there during the Landing. The position was too exposed to make re-burial possible, and somehow the opportunity: offered by the armistice had been neglected.

The possy had been dug in the sap wall directly below, and now green liquid was oozing out and seeping slowly downwards. The Bushman held his breath as he passed, but the only alternative to camping there that night was to stretch out along the trench wall in the firing line—a football for the clumsy feet of everyone passing.

He found Snow waiting for him in the front line with a pint of tea, a dixie lid containing a few spoonfuls of—something. It had, been potatoes and onions before the cooks had been let loose on it. The Bushman got a tin of Fray Bentos and some biscuits from his haversack and sat on the firestep. He seldom grumbled at the tucker, but when he tasted the tea he cursed and threw it, as he thought, over the parapet. As it happened, he had momentarily lost his sense of direction and the tea found its way on to the heads of the occupants of the next bay. When their healthy curses, and laughter, had died down, the Bushman relieved his feelings by letting go about the cooks.

"Wouldn't you think that, for all they've got to do, the useless cows would give the onion dixie a lick out before they made tea in it?"

"What'd you order now, if you walked into the Australia?" asked Snow. "A ten-course feed . . ."

Several voices interrupted him.

"I'd have a pound of chocolates first."

"I wouldn't," replied the Bushman. "I'd like to be able to go out to the killing pen where there was a bullock hanging up, and before I started to grill him whole I'd drink every drop of his blood. They took good care to leave none in this briny string. Why can't we have a bully beef stew? If the sergeant cook was worth a curse—"

"The bastard went sick to-day," interrupted Snow, "and the quack put him on light duty."

"Light duty! I wonder when he ever did anything, even in Ma'adi. Any jam, Snow"

"New brand," replied Snow, handing over an unopened tin. "Deakin's apricot. Hope's there less kerosene in it than Robertson's marmalade. I'm going to Dundee specially some day to tell him off."

The Bushman dug his bayonet point into the tin and found that that was all the opening it needed. Whatever the contents were, they poured as freely as condensed milk. Snow began to laugh.

"Useless cooks-windy sergeants-briny beef-lance-corporal bacon, mouldy cheese, watery jam, and iron biscuits," he recited. "Not a drop of blood in the whole issue! Let's catch a Jacko to-night, you old blood-drinker, and hang him up for the morning."

The Bushman stopped eating, but not because he wasn't hungry. His stomach felt far from comfortable, and it worried him, for he had always prided himself on having one like an emu. At home he had worked and thrived on the hardest tucker. He packed his gear away, and followed Snow to the observation post where they took over from two others. The shift lasted an hour, and they halved it at the loophole. While one tried to piece together what he could see of No-man's Land, and took the chance of a bullet in the face, the other stood with fixed bayonet in the trench bottom. The loophole was a small slit, about two inches by one, in a stout iron plate hidden by sandbags in the parapet. By day it was carefully covered, and periscope observers took up other positions. Still, far too many bullets flattened on the plate during the night. They weren't all fluke shots. That was the Bushman's opinion as he took first shift.

After a few nights of it they decided that it was better to chance being potted during a quick look over than to undergo the continued strain of loophole observation only. The uncertainty of accurately placing anything they did see through the narrow slit was nerve-wracking. The sudden gleam of light on a tin, the movement of a shadow, the swaying of grass or scrub—anything or nothing at all was likely to be magnified into a mass attack if an observer got windy. Unless the firing made it too dangerous, they took a look over every few minutes. A couple of seconds was enough to bring reassurance and continued confidence.

The next observation post was some twenty yards-along the trench. Suddenly the Bushman and Snow heard sounds of scuffling and blasphemy. Snow darted round the traverse and came back in a few moments shaking with laughter.

"What's up round there?" asked the Bushman. He kept his

eye to the loophole, for at the moment he thought he saw something suspicious. Snow explained with bursts of mirth.

"Chummy went to sleep at the loophole and slipped off the step right on top of Dick—nearly on his bayonet. Dick thought he'd been potted, yelled for stretcher-bearers, and started to pick him up. Soon as Chummy got on his pins he wanted to know why the hell Dick knocked his knees under him, and hoed into him right and left."

The Bushman wasn't paying much attention.

"Snow," he whispered, "come up here."

Snow was beside him in a second, "What is it, Blood?"

"There's a sniper planted somewhere a bit to the left—think he's lying near that grave, but I can't see any flame from the loophole. He knows where it is, though; he's put his last three shots right on to the plate. I'll have to chance it or he'll get one of us."

He pushed his head above the parapet for a split second only, but it was nearly his last. He saw the flame, heard the report and felt the bullet hiss past his cheek. Some clods rolled off the parados behind him. He was breathing hard as Snow crowded against him.

"Didn't get you?" he muttered anxiously. "Shouldn't have done that."

"No, he didn't; but we'll make him wish he had yet. All right, Jacko, my son, you've had your shot; you wait there till we've had ours."

"D'you know just where he is?" asked Snow. "Too far for a bomb?"

"Bomb! No, they're harmless anyway, except to the chaps that throw 'em. We'll give him another shot—at a dummy this time. Tell Dick to come here for a minute."

The Bushman explained his trap for young Jackos. When he signalled by throwing a clod, Dick was to put his hat up slowly on his bayonet point, and give the sniper time for two shots. The name of the first would give them his position. They went round into the next bay, and there, with slow caution, they pushed their rifles over the sandbags.

"We'll have to get well up," whispered the Bushman. "Wait for his second shot, and aim well behind the flame. We'll chance three rounds rapid each. Got the clod? All right then—now."

The trick worked. The first spurt of flame showed the shallow pit where the sniper lay. Simultaneously with the second they pulled their triggers—once, twice, thrice, and dropped down from the parapet in high hopes. Dick gleefully showed them a bullet hole in his hat. They tried the bait again, but this time there was no response.

"He might be lying low for awhile," muttered Snow. "We'll know in the morning if we got him. Here's our relief coming."

They handed over and the Bushman picked his way through the figures asleep on the trench floor. Generally he was a good sleeper and used every minute of those two precious hours off, but this time he spent part of them at the latrine, and finally crept into the smellful depths of the Green Stripe possy with feelings bordering on fear. Surely his guts, of all things, weren't going to let him down after a bare month of it? He turned uneasily and moved his cartridge pouches further round. To make matters worse, the tunnellers were passing and repassing the possy, and he couldn't settle down to sleep. He cursed when he looked at his watch and found that one of his two hours had already been wasted. His thoughts kept going back to the duel on the parapet; somehow he couldn't compose them; it scarcely seemed worth while trying to sleep.

Someone tugged at his arm. It was Snow.

"Wake up. Blood," he said. "Our shift. Gosh! The blowflies must be worse here than out in that scrub. You're lyin' in a nest of squashed maggots."

Chapter Seven
Gallipoli - June 1915

From a dugout near the top of Rest Gully the Bushman watched the Regiment falling in on one of the lower terraces. It had come out of the front line that morning after twenty eight days there, and everyone was hoping for a real spell, however brief. Moving had meant heavy fatigues, and they had lasted until well into the afternoon. The Bushman had been one of a party carrying Headquarters stuff, and while bringing a certain case, wrapped carefully in a blanket, he had been escorted by one of the senior officers every step of the way. When he stopped for a rest the officer stopped too and yarned affably, but he kept a watchful eye on the case.

The Bushman was in the grip of diarrhoea and feeling rocky. He didn't mind sweating with pick and shovel, or even risking a sniper's bullet if it helped to win the war, but he couldn't see that knocking himself up carrying booze for dugout kings was going to help much. He wished that one of Beachy Bill's observers could see them, and he was quite prepared to take his chance of coming down whole if a shell sent them both skyward. He took a pious and silent vow that, if by any weird fluke, he ever wore stars, no ranker would have reason to curse him for a windy booze artist.

That afternoon Snow had pestered him to go sick and he had gone—for the first time. The M.O. gave him some dope and put him off duty, A real spell and soft food might have put him right, but there was no chance of either. Evidently you only rested in Rest Gully when you were under its soil, for here was the Regiment getting ready for an all-night digging stunt.

From where he sat, the Bushman could hear one of the senior officers talking. It seemed that a new position was in course of construction on the extreme right flank. A complete trench system had to be established there, and when it was finished the brigade was to occupy it. "Dangerous job." "Likely to be working under fire." "No one else game to tackle it." "We'll show 'em"—and a good deal more of the same sort of "bulsh."

Just after sundown the Regiment moved on. For a few seconds the Bushman sat where he was; then he put on his gear, picked up his rifle and went quietly down to the roadway. At heart he knew that he was a fool, that a night's hard digging might land him in hospital; but stay behind he couldn't. He shouldered a pick and shovel as he passed the spot where the Regiment had loaded up, and he overtook the tail of the slowly moving column as it was winding up the hillside. He lost count of the ridges it crossed before it came to a final halt.

A line had been pegged out on a narrow strip of land running parallel to the ocean and not very far from the water's edge. The ground was hard—a mixture of clay and pebbles— and the roots of the low scrub made shovelling tediously slow. Placed a few feet apart, the men began to dig. All night they toiled, and they needed no urging. Gradually the line lowered, and by midnight the sap was deep enough to give cover from casual fire. Once when the hail from a machine-gun pattered on the long heap of dirt, the diggers crouched low, but when it slackened they leaped again to the job.

The Bushman worked doggedly. He called up every scrap of his resources of nerve and grit, and so did the man behind him. His energy nearly ended the Bushman's career as a soldier or anything else. In the dim light he underestimated the distance between them, and he landed the point of his pick in the pocket of the Bushman's tunic. It left a skin graze on his hip, but it scattered the contents of the pocket far and wide, and a precious tin of tobacco into the clay. To its owner that was the night's real tragedy.

Just before daylight the tired men filed back along the sap they had dug, and stacked their tools in a deep gully near its entrance. The Bushman, dazed with exhaustion, sat there for a few minutes before he felt game to tackle the track back to Rest Gully. It was there that Snow found him. Until then he had imagined him having for once a real sleep, sound and unbroken, and he cursed his stupidity with all the fervour of mateship. He threatened to go straight to their troop leader when they got back to camp if he wouldn't obey orders and stay off duty when he was put off. The Bushman grinned.

"You'll need a windlass to find him," he said, "They tell me he's struck water at fifty feet." Then he got up. "I'm all right now. Snow. Let's get on back."

They followed the shadowy line, now filing across the flat ground of Shell Green. Snow carried both rifles and made the Bushman rest again before they climbed the steep ridge beyond Clark's Gully. From the trenches to their right came occasional bursts of fire and bullets hissed and whined high overhead on their way to the ocean. The Bushman felt that wounds would have all been in the day's work—at least they wouldn't have been as demoralising as this filthy disease which threatened to destroy them. Men were being evacuated daily. That looked like being his fate—to be counted out in the first round. As they climbed the winding roadway leading up to the dugout's, he shut his teeth and vowed to drop before he went sick again. Perhaps the disease would run its course if he took a spell off duty and gave it a chance.

They passed by dugout's where other men already lay in the sleep of exhaustion. Some had not even taken off their bandoliers. At the cookhouse in the bottom of the gully a light from a fire glowed, and it gave Snow an idea. He began groping at once amongst their gear as the Bushman subsided thankfully on the floor of the dugout.

"What are you looking for?" he asked.

"Quart-pot," answered Snow. "I'll make a drop of tea."

"Where'll you get the water, anyhow?"

"Up at the soakage. Drop of tea'll do you good."

"And where's the tea? We haven't got any."

"Haven't we?" retorted Snow. "I wasn't on cookhouse fatigue yesterday for nothing. Tea and sugar. I'll boil up at the fire down there—I'm pretty good with greasy Joe. You have a sleep while I'm away."

Tired though he was, the Bushman wasn't sleepy, and in his state sleep was far from safe. He made up his blankets and watched Snow sliding down the gully side and bounding up the opposite slope. He had seen others making for the soak and he wanted to get there first. The boy was tireless—a blend of wire and whipcord—but so had he been until this cursed disease had gripped him. At last he dozed off, but woke again at once as Snow crawled into the dugout.

"Have a go at this, Blood," he said. "It's worth all the tea."

The Bushman took the bottle from him and felt a different man at once.

"Where th' hell did you score this?" he asked.

"Never mind," chuckled Snow. "I'd have brought the whole jar if I'd been game. 'Tisn't such a bad old war after all."

The fiery spirit soothed both mind and stomach; it gave the Bushman fresh heart. Then he lay back on his blanket and slept again as the sickly light stealing over the hills brought another day to Rest Gully.

Chapter Eight
Gallipoli - July 1915

For awhile the Regiment's new home was a good one—too good to be lasting. Jacko was so far away that from certain well concealed spots observation could be done without a periscope; but the Heads wouldn't leave well alone. They set their hearts on occupying a ridge running parallel, and began by ordering the digging of a tunnel to the bottom of the gully and a sap up the slope. A support line came next, and while communication trenches were being pushed on to what would eventually be the front line, the diggers had to be guarded against surprise.

By day parties of men lay motionless amongst the prickly scrub and endured torments of heat and thirst. By night they crouched lower still, for sniper's came close enough for them to hear the click of bolts after every shot. Gradually the new post became habitable, and gradually the Regiment learned to help itself, for no one else would. Food was still bad, and neglect worse. The climax came on the day of the rice issue.

The Bushman was doing light duty as permanent mess orderly. His disease, had become chronic, and he was gradually wasting. He was one of the Diarrhoea Kings who were seldom game to sleep anywhere but handy to the latrine. In spite of Snow's remonstrances, he refused to go sick again. Those who did were put on light diet—an extra ration of condensed milk and a cupful of rice. You could cook it yourself, or eat it raw, but on this particular day rice was actually on issue and the mess orderlies made special trips from the cookhouse to the support line to break such incredibly good news. A dixie of rice for each troop! to be used as a vegetable to help down the saline Fray Bentos, or kept as a second course topped up with Ideal milk. Rice! The Regiment waited for those dixies with drooling mouths.

The Bushman collected his two—one of tea, the other of rice—and staggered with them up the back terraces. He sat down for a few minutes before he continued his journey through the low tunnel, and along the twisting sap leading up to the support trenches. He had very little strength in his legs or wind in his lungs, for he had developed a dry cough. His arrival was greeted with cheers, and the squadron crowded round him eagerly. He felt a glow of satisfaction when he began to dish out the contents of the dixie, but he very soon saw rice being scattered everywhere, and heard mutinous curses.

"What's up with it?" he asked in concern, with a ridiculous feeling of personal responsibility. He had just served Snow, who said nothing but put a spoonful of grey coloured grains into his mouth. Instead of closing his teeth on something soft and melting—as he had fondly hoped—he bit something hard. The outside of the grain was soft, the inside was as hard as it had been when it left China. He was just in time to stop several exasperated rice-lovers from kicking the dixie to death.

"What *ought* a man do with those cooks?" he asked in bitter disgust. Here—give us that dixie! I'm taking it to the first officer I can find above ground."

"You can save yourself the trouble. Blood," replied Snow. "They won't do anything, you know that well enough."

"I don't care," he answered obstinately. "I'm going to make one of them eat a spoonful if I have to jam it down his neck."

He did persuade a lieutenant to put some rice into his mouth, but it went no further. He spat, sympathised, and made the usual pie-crust promises to take the matter up. The Bushman returned to the squadron and found it topping up on biscuits and liquid apricot.

"How'd you get on?" asked Snow.

"Oh, he's going to play hell, of course. We do our job—I wonder why they can't do theirs. They could give orders and see they were carried out in camp all right."

"Yes, but this isn't camp," replied Snow. "There was nothing-to be windy about there; here they're worrying more about whether their dugout's are deep enough than about the Q.M. washing in the water we ought to be getting. And the higher up you go, it's worse. Anyway, what happened to the Captain who did kick up a row and told the Q.M. off?"

The Bushman moodily opened a tin of beef and tried to force some of it down, but his stomach rebelled. He had no better luck with a biscuit and jam, and yet he felt desperately hungry. Hungry for anything with flavour and taste, anything without the deadly sameness of the stringy, fatless beef or the liquid apricot jam. He carried his dixies to the cookhouse and relieved his feelings by telling one of the "greasies" what he thought of him. On his way back he stopped at the signallers' dugout on the top terrace. They were lunching on bully beef rissoles—piping hot—and their fragrance made him feel faint. The signallers drew the ordinary issue rations, but they handled them themselves, which made all the difference between full stomachs and empty ones. The rissoles were fathered by Fray Bentos at his worst—they were spiced by doubtful onions and fried in rank bacon fat, but served with a spoonful of properly boiled rice they were tasty enough to win a war on. The Bushman cadged a pint of flour, a couple of onions, a jam tin of fat, and hurried back to the valley.

He collected all the dry twigs he could find near the sap and lit his fire well out of the way of traffic, vowing that if anyone tried to stop him there would be trouble in the orderly-room or anywhere else they liked to take him. The smell of those fried rissoles had made him ravenous, and desperate. He opened three tins of beef, minced the contents up with the onions, and rolled them well in the flour. Then he flattened the mixture and fried bits of it at a time in his dixie. The fame of his enterprise soon spread as the noses of passers-by smelt him out, and when he carried the piled-up dixie into the supports, his section was waiting for him gog-eyed and open-mouthed. By the time the last rissole crumb had disappeared, the whole troop was imploring the Bushman to take on the cooking", and to win the war by saving their lives instead of trying to take Jackos. There might have been something in that, but the Bushman wouldn't see it.

"No," he replied; "let someone make those malingerers at the cookhouse do their job."

He felt more cheerful after his feed, and forgot about the rice sufficiently to challenge Snow to a louse hunt. Snow always won, but the Bushman suspected the accuracy of his count. He accused him of rejecting all that didn't crack with sufficient emphasis.

"We'll swap to-day," he said, and threw his trousers across the dugout to Snow. They had been riding breeches originally, but by the time they had seen a few weeks' service in the trenches their thick seams had made a perfect incubator. July had come, but not even midsummer could persuade the Brass Hats responsible into issuing khaki shorts. They had, it is true, made an effort to conform to Indian traditions by issuing helmets during the Egyptian summer. The helmets disappeared unanimously—kicked into the desert by the horses? There had been a serious row over the wholesale destruction of Government property, and there was another when the legs were cut off twenty thousand pairs of breeches; but it was impossible to crime a whole army.

Snow killed steadily and exhibited a few choice specimens proudly. The score was still two to one in favour of the Bushman. It seemed unaccountable, for they were always side by side, asleep or awake. They came to the conclusion that Blood was sweeter than Snow.

"Only you haven't got any," remarked Snow, looking critically at the Bushman's skinny legs and emaciated rib?.

"It beats me what this mob finds to live on, on your carcase."

The Bushman scratched at a row of scabs round his middle. "This is where they get you," he said, "under your belt. They like to be able to get their backs up against something". I tried some of that powder on a big fat cove yesterday, and he turned handsprings through it."

"I'm going to try that South African stunt with them," said Snow. "You turn your trousers inside out every day, and going from the outside to the inside soon breaks their hearts. Tell you what, Blood, you'd better shave that beard off. You'll make a horrible looking corpse even without it, and you'll be one soon if you don't get away."

"Bit harder today," replied the Bushman. "I think that cholera inoculation did me good. You'd have laughed at poor old Frank this morning". He had a new pipe in his pocket—got it in a parcel yesterday—and in it went plonk!"

"You *ought* to go. Blood," urged Snow earnestly.

"What's the sense of waiting-till you're carted off on a stretcher?"

"I might be like old Dave, not half as bad as I think I am. They started off yesterday with him on a stretcher, and just before they got to Clark's Gully, Beachy Bill opened up. Dave hopped off and beat the stretcher-bearers to the dugout's by fifty yards. There's a big move coming off soon; I got the oil from the signallers. They're going to dish out white rags to sew on our backs and arms so as we'll know who's who in the dark."

"What good'll you be in a charge?" asked Snow. "You're as weak as a kitten now. Look here, if you don't go sick tomorrow I'm going to parade to the major."

"Don't be a bloody fool," replied the Bushman roughly. "Think I'm going sick with a stunt coming off? I'll see it out till I drop. Then—they can do what they like with me."

Chapter Nine
Gallipoli - August 1915

Midnight stars threw a fitful light over the deep scrublined valley, but none reached the bottom of the front-line trench. Sleeping men stretched along its rear wall, lying" stiff and straight to guard themselves from careless feet. Others, with drawn-up knees and outflung arms, lay huddled on the broad firestep and one, cursing" softly, turned in his blanket. A stifled voice muttered: "What in hell's up with you now?"

"These *bloody* chats—"

"Well, let 'em eat you, but for Christ's sake lie still. I want some sleep."

The officer in charge of the post moved slowly and carefully along the trench. High above, bullets whined on their way to the ocean, and sharp crackling sounds followed them closely. The "dicky-birds" hissed by like tiny indrawn breath gasps. Distant artillery belched sullenly with drawn-out screams and muffled explosion, but in the trench all was still. On the firestep figures crouched at intervals with their faces to the loopholes, trying to piece together the shapes and shadows of No-man's Land, and flinching as bullets thudded against the sandbags above their heads.

As the officer passed one post the observer reeled backwards and half-fell, half jumped to the trench floor. He staggered about holding his head, and blood from both sides of his face trickled through his hands. Expecting to see him collapse, the officer caught his arm and flashed his torch alternately on cheek and temple. They carried long shallow scratches through skin and surface flesh, and in a few minutes the wounded man had recovered from the shock and was suffering mostly from smart.

"By Gawd your luck's in," the officer told him. "That bullet must have split on the edge of the loophole. It got you on one side, and a bit of nickel on the other."

"Don't you believe it, Sir." It was Snow who spoke. He had come from a post further along to see what the commotion was about. "It split on his dial—wish mine was as hard."

"Take him through to the dressing station," said the officer to the sergeant, "and put another man on the post."

He started to continue along the trench, but Snow stopped him urgently.

"I wish you'd make my mate go sick, Sir," he said in a low voice. "He's been doing half-a-dozen trips a day to the latrine for the last two months, and he's got a hell of a cough too. He can just about stand up, but he won't go sick. I can't make him, but *you* could."

"Where is he?" asked the officer. "I'll soon fix him."

"He's on post with me now. Wait a minute till I get back, and for Gawd's sake don't tell him I said anything."

He darted off, and the officer gave him a few minutes' grace. As he moved towards the post he heard sounds of low stifled coughing. The Bushman was leaning against the trench wall, swaying in his effort to fight down the choke in his throat. Snow stood at the loophole.

"Doesn't sound too good, that cough of yours," remarked the officer, "you'll let every Jacko know where an observer is. Have you seen the M.O.?"

"No, Sir."

"What, not at all?"

"I was on sick parade some weeks ago."

"You haven't had that cough for weeks. What did you parade with?"

"Diarrhoea."

"And you've still got it, haven't you?" The officer's nose had been well educated.

"Yes."

"Why the hell don't you go sick then?" he snapped. "You ought to have been evacuated weeks ago."

"I *was* going sick," replied the Bushman, "but I thought I'd wait till the stunt was over."

"Well, it is over, and I can't see what use you'd have been in a hop-over with a cough like that. Anyway, you go sick on the early parade, and don't come back. I'll give you a special chit to the M.O."

He moved away and the Bushman subsided on to a sandbag seat. He was nearly all in, and, sick at heart as he felt at the thought of being beaten, he knew now that he had been a fool. Snow's first comment summed up the position accurately.

"You'll be worth more to the Regiment in a few months alive, Blood, old man, than you will in a few weeks dead. Don't worry about us. We'll be here when you come back."

But would they? That was what troubled the Bushman most as he staggered off slowly to the support trenches. Someone relieved him at the end of his shift, and he stood for awhile at his dugout before he decided that it was only waste of time to make his camp there. He picked up his blankets and climbed drearily down the sap leading to the back areas. From the sap he went up some rough steps to level ground, to spend what was left of his last night with the rest of the "Diarrhoea Kings." They lay wrapped in their blankets around the latrine. The pains in his stomach were shooting severely, and he felt afraid to stoop while making his doss. With his feet he scraped away the clods and prickly holly leaves arid went down on his knees carefully to place his folded blankets in position. At last he sat down and leaned back against the sandbagged dugout.

What a fool he had been! After all his efforts, the disease had beaten him. He might have been back by now, cured, if he had gone away when he first got bad. Now it would take months at least, and where would the Regiment, or what was left of it, be by then? What would become of Snow? He lay down carefully on his blanket, but began to cough again, and fresh pains shot through his body. He got up and shuffled slowly towards the latrine, but someone passed him, running. After all, the Bushman won the race, for the other man fell suddenly, and lay still.

In the morning the Bushman followed a couple of stretcher-bearers away from the M.O.'s dugout. Near Headquarters they rested a moment and put down their burden.

"Who've you got there now?" asked a sleepy signaller.

"Don't know who he is," answered one. "They found him flat out to it alongside the latrine in the Valley. He's still out."

"What's up with him?"

"What's up with him?" repeated the bearer. "Haven't you got a bloody nose? Get hold of this stretcher for a few yards and you won't want to ask. Blimey, he must think Jacko's winning all right, he keeps muttering 'beaten—beaten—beaten.' It's a pity the bastards wouldn't win, we'd all get out of this then, somehow."

Chapter Ten

The Hospital Ship - August 1915

The hospital transport lay at anchor in Mudros Bay. Its deck space was crowded by men. They lay or sat about in huddled groups, neither knowing nor caring about the outcome of an appaling muddle. The medical authorities were quite unable to grapple with it, but they were not to blame for the colossal casualty list of sick. The crime of sending unacclimatised men——men who knew nothing of heat or thirst—to the inferno of Suvla was not theirs. The Turk had wonderful allies—the deadly fly and the even more deadly War Office. The few doctors on the transport did their best, but they had little or nothing to do anything with. A few of the worst cases were taken ashore, but the Lemnos hospitals were already overflowing. There were no nurses on board and there was little food. The transport was a dying ground floating above a cemetery.

The Bushman lay on the far end of the deck and watched an orderly bringing a dixie of porridge through the groups of listless men. He knew it would be empty long before it reached him. After his evacuation he had spent two days at Imbros, and he began to rally at once when freed from the continued strain of duty. Then be had been bundled on board the transport with a thousand others—mostly Tommies—and at the moment his one craving was for food. He waited awhile, hoping that the orderly might come back with another dixie; then he roused himself and determined to get a square feed somewhere—if it killed him. The moral effect of a wash would be another tonic, if he could only find a fresh-water tap. He took his rucksack down to the lower deck, and after a short search he found one. By good luck he still had the piece of soap he had taken to Gallipoli thirteen weeks previously, and he blessed Snow for putting it and his battered quartpot into his haversack before he had staggered off to the beach.

He examined his naked body with critical interest. His knees were as knobby as those of a newly-born draught foal, and his ribs like those of a blackfellow's kangaroo dog. He ran his knuckles over them smartly and fancied they rang like guitar strings. His collarbones were nearly raw from bandolier pressure, and round his middle he wore a belt of neat little scabs.

Fresh water and soap after thirteen weeks! The Bushman lathered himself until he looked like a snowstorm. He found a tolerably clean singlet, but his tunic was filthy—it still carried the white rags sewn on for the hop-over which the Regiment had been spared. His shorts were badly frayed where the ends had been hacked off. When he looked at himself in a pocket mirror he decided that his beard would come off as soon as he could get hold of some boiling water.

One of the ship's crew, passing by, saw him and stopped.

"Got any badges to give away, mate?" he asked.

The Bushman promptly took a "rising sun" from his tunic.

"You can have that," he said, "if you'll get me a feed of some sort. Scraps will do."

"Might find you something," the sailor replied. "We don't get too much ourselves."

He led the way to the messroom, and the Bushman waited outside the door. Presently the sailor came back carrying a tin dish. The scrapings of a curry saucepan were piled at one end, and a big junk of duff at the other. Some potatoes and haricot beans were heaped between. The Bushman squatted where he was, and long before he'd finished wolfing the whole dishful he felt a different man. He returned to the top deck with more in his stomach than he'd put there in any one session for thirteen weeks. He paid for it dearly that afternoon, but he didn't care.

While he had been below, another ship had drawn alongside, and someone told him that five hundred of his fellow derelicts had been put on board it. The Bushman wondered if he had missed something. No one knew where either boat would go, but the new outfit had a proper Red Cross on its side, and he could see nurses on board.

There didn't seem to be any congestion on its decks—that meant wards and bunks, perhaps clean clothes, and, possibly, decent food. If the new boat could take five hundred it could take five hundred and one. He waited for a favourable opportunity and climbed on board. Before long he was down below in a bed, the first he had slept in since leaving Australia.

He was put in a dysentery ward, and he very soon realised that he was lucky to be alive at all. He calculated the time since his first attack by the disease in Rest Gully. Ten weeks! This was the eighteenth day of August, and the men around him had landed at Suvla on the eighth, Ten days! and some of them were dying. What right had *he* to growl?

The bed next to his was occupied by an English boy; he could almost have touched him, by putting out his hand. Ten days previously the boy had been fresh and fit; now he was sent for. His face was drawn and shrunken, his eyes lost in their sockets. His head was like a human skull encased in gelatine instead of skin, his hands were almost transparent. At times he cried in pain.

During the night the Bushman slept little, even when the boat put to sea. He could not forget the sight of that wasted face or the sound of those despairing cries. In the morning the bed was covered.

Room was found in Malta for the Gallipoli overflow. The Bushman ended up in a hospital camp at Sliema, an acre of marquee tents with plenty of orderlies, a few nurses, and fewer doctors. The tucker at the camp did not differ much from that of Shrapnel Gully, but grapes and tomatoes were cheap, and the Bushman took a chance with them in spite of his still disordered stomach. Everything else on the island was dirt cheap too—according to the detailed account of a Tommy orderly you could have a complete night out for the sum of one shilling. The difficulty was to get the shilling.

There were enough Australian uniforms scattered about

Malta to make the Military Governor uneasy, and he took no chances. No repetition in Valetta of the outrageous behaviour in Cairo, if he could help it. You never knew what games the men in felt hats might get up to, so he decided to draw their teeth by cutting down their ridiculous rate of pay. Two shillings a week was the maximum draw allowed, and in any cables all references to money were blotted out. The Governor's caution was quite unnecessary—the representatives of the A.I.F. in Malta had left most of their kick in Gallipoli. Even with full pockets they could not have revived the joyous abandon of early days in Cairo.

After a week at Sliema camp the Bushman went on his first leave to Valetta. He was a sorry looking object. He had asked the hospital for a new outfit, and got an indulgent smile, so he brushed and scraped some of the grease from his tunic and battered hat, and borrowed a pair of khaki shorts and reasonably clean puttees. As he boarded the halfpenny ferry at Sliema he noticed with relief that the majority of the leave men on the boat were equally disreputable. He had drawn his two shillings that morning, and it brought the sum total of his wealth to six and sixpence. He had left the Peninsula with a solitary pound— the one issue, of pay, he'd had; but on board the *Ascania* it had gone the way of his badges. He meant to spend the six and sixpence on a decent piece of lace to send home, and a feed which knew nothing of army rations or hospital camp cookhouses.

After wandering for awhile about the narrow streets of Valetta he decided that he had enough for a milk shake as well and he went into a side street cafe. The Maltese waiter was sorry, but the morning: milk supply hadn't yet come, but if the signor didn't mind waiting a moment he would soon be obliged. He went to the door and shouted loudly to a goat-herd who was milking his flock of goats from door to door. A minute later a boy came into the cafe dragging an old nanny by the horns. He bailed her up against the counter and the Bushman watched his refreshment drawn from its source.

There were plenty of lace shops in the main streets, and the exhibits in their windows looked the goods, but experience with native traders in Cairo had made the Bushman wary. As he priced some collars in one shop, a nurse dressed in the British grey and scarlet walked in. He turned to her for advice and found at once that for the first time for many months he was talking to a fellow countrywoman, an Australian girl who had enlisted in the British Nursing Service.

The Sister helped him to choose a piece of lace. It was a beautiful bit of work and the price was four and six-pence. She assured him it was well worth it. The Bushman paid up, and as he jingled the few coins left in his pocket he openly wished he could send home a few more pieces like it. "But," he added ruefully, "eighteen pence is all I'm standing behind for a full week. Good-bye, Sister, and many thanks."

A few moments later in the crowded street he felt someone touch his shoulder and turned round. The Australian girl stood there with outstretched hand. As he took it she said in a low voice: "My brother is buried on Gallipoli. He might have been here ragged, after months of service, and hungry for decent food. Do go and have a good dinner—for me. Good-bye, Soldier, and bless you." Then she disappeared quickly into the crowd, leaving the Bushman staring bewilderedly at the half-crown in his hand. He started to follow her, but stopped at once as he realised the full meaning of her action—and words. They were not merely a gesture from an Australian woman to an Australian man in a foreign land; they were a tiny link in the chain of their common service, forged in the name of the brother she had lost, and with that knowledge the despondency which had haunted the Bushman since his evacuation from Gallipoli vanished- To be fit once more, to rejoin the men who were carrying on, to give all the service he could—while he could—to that his acceptance of his country-woman's gesture pledged him.

Two weeks later nearly everyone was boarded for England. The Bushman was keen enough to see the country, and he felt that perhaps in London he might rid himself of the last remnants of his disease. A few in his ward were passed as fit to return to duty; the remainder were shipped to Southampton by the *Brasile*, and they included an Enzed who protested strongly.

"But I'm perfectly fit, Sir," he assured a scandalised M.O. "I don't want to go to England; I want to get back to the Peninsula. Things are in a hell of a mess there."

"And you think you'll make all the difference, eh?" retorted the M.O. "Don't be a fool. You'll go to England."

But he didn't. The M.O. had never heard of "regiment fever," and the Enzed had it badly—so badly that, although he answered his name at the roll call before the London contingent embarked, someone else did so thereafter. He worked a simple swap with another man not quite so keen to renew acquaintance with Jacko, and left hospitals, base records and pay offices to settle the discrepancy as best they could.

The *Brasile* very nearly didn't get to England at all, since she attempted to go into Southampton by the wrong side of the Isle of Wight, and was rescued just in time on the edge of a minefield. That night the Bushman slept in King George Hospital, Waterloo. After Malta its organised efficiency was a revelation. He could only find one cause for complaint: the authorities hadn't discovered that in Australia at any rate, he-men usually slept in pyjamas.

Chapter Eleven
London - September 1915

The hospital, as such, was undoubtedly a model, but in one respect it resembled a gaol. If you were let out for exercise you were well guarded and carefully returned. When the authorities were satisfied that the Bushman had been there long enough, he walked out a free man for two weeks, subject to certain supervision by military policemen and some unwritten laws. He broke one of the latter before he had been loose an hour, for he went into the swankiest hotel he could see and asked to be shown to the dining-room. It had never been considered necessary to put this hotel out of bounds; its tariff and yards of red tabs and gold braid did that automatically. The Bushman in his innocence had butted into a holy of holies of the regular army. He took his time over a huge lunch, and it was nearly three o'clock before he ordered a liqueur and cigar. He felt that after a few more similar feeds he might begin to draw level.

A little later he stood on the street corner feeling quite pleased with the luck that had brought him to London, and wondering what to do next. At that time the Australian uniform was still a novelty and troops were turning up from limbs of the Empire of which the heart had never heard. A stout old citizen in a bowler hat accosted him.

"Pardon me, my lad," he said politely, "but would you mind telling me what that fur band round your hat stands for?"

The Bushman rose to the occasion. He put his chest out, "That, Sir," he said, "is the hatband of a famous Australian Regiment. It took part in the Landing—at Farm Cove, and it has won lasting glory in battles round Wooloomooloo."

The old gentleman was impressed. He insisted on shaking hands.

"And now," he said, "it has come ten thousand miles to win

fresh laurels on the battlefields of Europe for the cause of the British Empire. Thank you, my lad. Thank you."

An old lady came next, but she knew an Australian uniform when she saw one. She said: "Well, Anzac, what are you doing with yourself this afternoon? Would you like to come to a party at Lady Hill-Mountain's? I'm collecting men for her, and she told me to be sure to catch some Australians."

The Bushman accepted the invitation gratefully, and the old lady hustled him across the street to where a fellow huntress was shepherding some earlier captures. He watched her darting to and fro after men in uniform, and when the party reached its required strength it boarded a tram and eventually was conducted through the grounds of Lady Hill-Mountain's mansion to the billiard-room. There a conjurer was doing his tricks before a large audience; in the drawing-room a pianist and singers amused some more, and a dancer performed in a reception room for others. The Bushman had scarcely settled down to enjoy himself before someone came along with the announcement: "Tea is ready. I'm sure you boys must be starving. Come along, please. This way."

It was a bare half-hour since the Bushman had finished the feed of a lifetime topped up with a big bottle of beer. He hadn't room for a crumb, but he had to make a pretence of eating something, and he eyed the table in acute misery. It was laden with the chicken, the hams, and the fruit for which he would many a time that year have swapped his soul. It was impossible to say no to such waitresses, and they merely put his diffidence down to politeness. He would have gladly given away all his new badges to have been let off this feed, and by the time he got away from Lady Hill-Mountain's he was prepared to admit that all arrears had been overtaken at last; there might even be a credit balance.

Some days later he discovered Trafalgar Square and a typical recruiting meeting. The speakers were red-hot, and the audience stone-cold. The lions were draped with Union Jacks, flaring posters half-way up to Nelson told Great Truths about King and Country, and orators at the table pleaded and cajoled, volleyed and thundered, but all to no purpose. The Bushman looked critically at the crowd. There was nothing wrong with the bulk of them, physically, and they couldn't all be married men. What was the matter? One of the speakers enlightened him.

He was short and fat. As he warmed to his subject his face changed colour from red to purple. He soon exhausted his patience and dropped persuasion for invective. In the end he frothed at the mouth, but his hearers had thick hides.

"Conscription's coming soon," he shouted. "It's you who are going to fasten that disgrace on Britain for the first time, and you'll carry the brand of it all your lives, you cold-footed, chicken-hearted slackers. The aristocrat of this country is doing his bit; he won't need conscripting; nor will the horny-handed toiler; he's there now in his tens of thousands. It's you we're after—you middle-class, you afternoon tea Johnnies with the cigarettes; you Gerties and Gussies in the straw hats, and we'll get you yet, never fear. There's a wounded Australian down there"—he had spotted the Bushman's hat—"come across the world to fight for a mob too cowardly to fight for themselves. Come here, lad," he thundered, "and tell them what you think of them."

The Bushman promptly pushed his way to the platform. Snow had always told him that he had more hide than a hawker's dog, but the chance of trying out his voice under Nelson's shadow was too good to be missed. He got a flattering reception and talked for ten minutes without stopping, but he got no recruits. When he gave up trying, the orator shook his hand, men patted his back, and women kissed him. A Canadian followed him on the platform with no better luck, and as he left the meeting the little orator looked like having an apoplectic fit at any moment.

"Who's that old sportsman?" he asked a Tommy.

"Wot! Don't yer know 'em?" was the surprised reply. "'E ain't 'arf canin' 'em up, is 'e? That's 'Oratio Bottomley!"

The Bushman spent one week of his leave in London, most of the time in a Regent Street Service Club reading old

Australian papers, since the weather was far from favourable. He had no better luck when he went to Scotland, where he soon found that people talked of a lovely day even when it was raining. He decided to come back some day and explore the British Isles thoroughly—when army "Out of Bounds" notices were a thing of the past. The only real kick he got out of his two weeks' leave came during its last night in London. There was a Zeppelin raid.

Leave was strictly limited to the two weeks, but the Bushman was quite satisfied when he reported to Horseferry Road. He was feeling perfectly fit again. Not one word of any kind had he heard from the Regiment, but occasional casualty lists reassured him. They were only odds and ends, so apparently the campaign had settled down to a stalemate. Until he could find out for himself what was happening, the doings of the Regiment would be shrouded in mystery. On his way to Weymouth Camp the Bushman spent a lot of his time wondering how soon he could get out of it.

Chapter Twelve
At Sea - October 1915

Montevideo Camp lay a couple of miles from Weymouth and it held representatives of nearly every unit in the Australian and New Zealand forces. No one there took things very seriously except the Major-General in command, and no one took him seriously except himself. He wore a double row of ribbons, mostly the reward of stout service at Kings' coronations and Indian durbars, and his long suit was taking the salute of a march-past.

There were three classes in the camp: permanently unfit, temporarily unfit, and fit. The Bushman was given an overhaul on arrival, and with a little persuasion the M.O. passed him as fit to return to duty. On the morning after he got there he fell in in the front line of his temporary platoon, wondering how long he would have to endure Montevideo Camp. From the look of things it promised to be as bad as Liverpool. A warrant-officer came on parade, glanced up and down the line, and bawled: "Any volunteers for the Anzac draft—two paces step forward—march!"

The Bushman jumped several paces and "proved" right under the warrant-officer's nose. Three men had been fired out of the Anzac draft for getting drunk, and once more the Bushman blessed the Army's quaint ideas of punishment. He was given one of the vacancies and joined the "Wild Hundred," the weirdest assortment that ever came together in the history of the A.I.F. Besides infantry, light horse and artillery, it included odds and ends from units unknown to, anyone bur the keepers of Base Records. The few Enzeds in the draft contained one Maori who helped to make history later on. Practically every man had been wounded in the early days of the Landing, but their hides were now whole again and they were ready to jump out of them.

The draft spent some of its time pretending to drill, and wasting ammunition on the rifle range, but it was mostly occupied route-marching along the pleasant lanes of Dorset. There were a number of large camps around Weymouth, and the town was always infested by hordes of second-lieutenants. The prejudice against saluting—always more or less active—grew full-sized and led to endless rows. The leaders of the "Wild Hundred" decided on reprisals. It marched always as an armed party with a spare two-star in front and a warrant-officer at the rear. Their job was to catch those by the wayside who failed to pay the required compliments to an armed party, and all one-pips came in for special attention. The sport made marching through Weymouth popular, but the Bushman wasn't sorry when, after a last hilarious night, the draft entrained for embarkation at Plymouth. It was the last body to return from England to Gallipoli.

On the *Andania* the draft was swallowed by two thousand Tommies, but there were actually spare berths. The food was transport fare at its worst, but by the judicious expenditure of thirty shillings the Bushman got one decent feed a day——from the officers' mess. The draft kept to its own quarters so rigidly that the four officers responsible for its behaviour began to have a less anxious time. They never knew, until afterwards, what happened while the *Andania* lay off Valetta.

It was so close—that was what made the situation exasperating. There were the bright lights of a civilised town, the last that many men expected to see, for the next stop was Anzac. They had better chances of Heaven than of leave passes ashore, but surely Heaven itself arranged for a dinghy in a convenient position on the end of a short heavy rope. Half a-dozen of the wildest spirits manned it and pulled ashore, but after a few drinks one of the party became decidedly merry, and finally suspicious questions were asked. They put over the story that they were an unofficial picquet sent ashore to retrieve a deserter, and then it occurred to them that the *Andania* might sail, leaving them all genuine deserters, with a ship's boat pirated into the bargain. They decided to return while the going was good, and they got round the difficulty of their drunk member in a way that helped to prove their bona-fides. They "arrested" their prisoner in a side street and marched him openly through Valetta. While pulling back they sobered him with good Mediterranean sufficiently to enable him to climb the rope, and the escapade ended safely. However, a few days before the *Andania* reached Lemnos, all points scored by the draft for good behaviour vanished overnight.

It all happened over a harmless game of Nap—at least the draft thought it harmless as long as it kept to its own quarters. Two-up had been cut out as a concession to Authority, and the draft was amazed at its self-denial, but it sternly refused to play a childish game like Housie, the only one legalised on board. The Nap school was in full swing One morning when an uninvited guest appeared in the shape of a Tommy Redcap lance-corporal. He'd made a steady living during the voyage by confiscating all the visible loose cash of his compatriots caught playing- an illegal game. Certainly he always invited them to apply for it at the orderly-room, but the bluff worked; they were satisfied to make their first loss the last. In an unlucky moment the Redcap decided to discipline the "Wild Hundred." Reports of fabulous piles of notes and silver were too much for his caution—and anyway, wasn't he a lance-corporal? He stood for awhile watching the "kitty" grow, and after one glance the players ignored him.

"How much in it now, boys?" he asked. He leant over and picked up the pile of silver, pretending to count the coins. Even then the gamblers took no notice of him until he turned and began to climb the stairway.

Then they woke up to the game. The Redcap turned at the top of the stairs and faced several angry men.

"There's seventeen shillings here," he said. "If you want to claim them, go to the orderly-room."

There would certainly have been a boom in courts-martial

if an Anzac sergeant hadn't appeared. He accepted the corporal's invitation to the orderly-room and soon came back with the silver. But the blood of the "Wild Hundred" had been well stirred. Not even a Tommy lance-jack could be allowed to put over such an insult with impunity.

Somewhere amidship a canteen was open every evening, and the congestion around it was so acute that a queue was obliged to form and file past the window. The Redcap had the job of regulating the traffic. He stood with his back to the flow and his face to the stairway, and he saw nothing of four figures moving up quietly behind him with averted heads. When he was suddenly grabbed and frogmarched up the stairway, the multitude looked on with mouths agape. Surely there would be a firing party after this? And him a lance-corporal an' all!

The Redcap struggled fiercely, but his captors had him in a practised grip. As they reached the deck, excited voices from the rear filled him with a new fear; "Put him right over, Choom, while you've got him." The answer seemed to seal his fate. "Don't worry, Choom, he'll steal no more of your silver!"

He pleaded fervently.

"For God's sake don't throw me overboard, boys, I've got a wife and kids at home."

The replies were meant to be consoling.

"All the better for them if they never see you again."

"You'll only die on Gallipoli—you might as well die here; it's cleaner."

"Now, then, over with him. One-two-three!"

The night was pitch dark and a high wind howled. The transport was rolling. For a second or two after he hit the water the Redcap did think he was battling for life in the Aegean Sea. By the time he climbed out of the big canvas swimming bath, the whole of the "Wild Hundred" was apparently sleeping soundly in its bunks. When, half-an-hour later, the ship's adjutant walked down the gangway, the snoring was too unanimous to be convincing. He called loudly for the N.C.O.'s of the Anzac draft, and at last, several of them appeared rubbing their eyes. They were informed that the whole draft would parade on the boat deck at ten-thirty the following morning. If it thought it could get away with such mutinous behaviour it would soon find its mistake. The adjutant was counted out—in Arabic—as he retired.

The draft's officers had a bad time in the mess that night. They prayed hard that the four ringleaders, if they were identified, would have provided themselves with water tight alibis. If they had known that the four included the solitary Maori on board they would have given up the case as lost, but the draft was equal to the occasion.

Next morning, when it paraded in two ranks, an observant spectator might have noticed that the rear rank was unusually close to the front one, and put it down to the draft's natural ignorance of drill movements; but it was part of a carefully worked out plan. A reconnaissance of the ground showed that almost for a certainty the inspection would begin at the end nearest the ladder, and the ring leaders fell in in the rear rank and covered off the first four positions in front. It worked out according to plan. The inspection did begin near the ladder, and as the Redcap, closely followed by an orderly, the ship's adjutant and the draft's C.O., reached the farther end, there was a rapid and noiseless shuffle from rear rank to front of the first four files, while the remainder of the draft stood to rigid attention. The Redcap identified four innocents apparently without difficulty, but later on in the orderly-room they were able to prove a perfectly truthful alibi. They had been drinking cocoa in the privacy of their cabins while the outrage was being perpetrated. Very reluctantly the case against them was dismissed, and the verdict was loudly cheered from one end of the Andama to the other. For the rest of the voyage—mercifully brief—the officers of the draft found life not worth living.

At Lemnos the "Wild Hundred" dissolved. A few whose units were still at Anzac put off on a minesweeper, and as it drew near the familiar parts of the coastline the Bushman began to feel nervous. He had been away for twelve weeks, and during that time not one word from the Regiment had reached him. He did not even know if it still held the old position on the right flank.

As the minesweeper approached Anzac it might have been a ferry-boat crossing Sydney Harbour, for all the notice the Turkish batteries took of it. The usual parties were at work on the beach, and everything looked the same, but little or no firing of any kind could be heard. There was not a solitary shot to welcome the little contingent which stepped ashore early in the afternoon, but its officer took it to a sheltered spot from force of habit.

"I'm damned if I know what I'm supposed to do with you fellows," he said. "I've had no orders. I expect you remember where you saw your units last. You'd better clear out and find them."

The Bushman didn't wait to say good-bye, but once when he looked back he saw the remnant of the "Wild Hundred" scattering in all directions. He followed the beach until he came to Victoria Gully, and then he took the old familiar pad over the first ridge. Twelve weeks before he had staggered painfully over those hills; now, even with a pack and full gear up, he could have climbed them at the double. As he neared Shell Green he felt like a school- boy getting back after the holidays, but he could not check a shiver of apprehension as he passed one familiar landmark after another. Snow might be there, safe and sound, or—

When the Bushman got to the track behind the back terraces he broke into a run.

Chapter Thirteen
Gallipoli - November 1915

The two men standing near the signallers' dugout wondered who the new arrival was and why be was in such a hurry. Beachy Bill hadn't dropped anything on Shell Green for a week. When the Bushman held out his hand they had to look a second time before they recognised him. The only thing Australian about his rigout was his hat. The rest was Tommy tunic and breeches, puttees and infantry equipment. He was three stone heavier and clean shaven.

"Well, I'll go hopping to hell if it isn't old Blood! Where've you been to all this time?"

They shook hands warmly and in his agitation the Bushman could scarcely get out his question.

"How're all the mob? Snow?"

"Snow's all right. He only came back last week."

"But what happened to him? I've not had a word since" I left."

They laughed.

"He's been knocked twice—first time he didn't have to go away. Second time a bomb splinter got him in the leg—nothing to skite about. By Gawd, you've been on good country, anyway. Remember him when he went away. Tom? Where'd you get to?"

"Oh, Malta first, then England."

"England! You lucky old cow! What sort of a time did you—"

The Bushman left him talking and made for the tunnel. Everything was exactly the same, except that the sap across the valley was deeper, and- a hill of loose dirt showed that tunnelling was going on somewhere. At the entrance to the supports he met men from his squadron. They greeted him with excited cheers. "Old Blood is back. Pass it on!" Snow heard the uproar and came running to meet him.

They sat in their old dugout and yarned for a full hour. Snow wanted to know what the hell the Bushman meant by swinging it away for three solid months and then coming back in a Tommy tunic. The Bushman had a look at the scar on his leg and laughed at the idea of that being worth a gold stripe! If it was, his record as a Diarrhoea King was worth half-a-dozen.

Snow had been sent to a hospital in Alexandria, and although he did not know it at the time, he had been posted in Egypt as a deserter, thanks to his habit of arranging his own passages. After leaving hospital he had spent some weeks in a convalescent home, but the heads there were very tight with leave.

"We had to help ourselves to passes at last," chuckled Snow. "Jimmy was there. We only had to get hold of the forms."

"How did you wangle 'em?" asked the Bushman. "It was easy in Ma'adi—Jimmy had a pal in the orderly room."

"It was Jimmy's brain-wave. I'd never have thought of it. The orderly-room was a little E.P. tent right on the stone wall alongside the water. Jimmy stood just inside the door talking to the Tommy sergeant, and somehow I stumbled over the ropes and fell in—wallop!—and yelled for help. 'Course the sergeant rushed out to lend a hand, and while he was out Jimmy pocketed a few forms—he knew where they were. He'll do time for forgery yet."

"Didn't you have to go back to Ma'adi?"

Snow grinned.

"I was *supposed* to go, but the day I came out there was a boat leaving for here. It was dead easy this time, Blood. Things were in such a mess they didn't know who was on board, and they didn't care either."

"What! You stowed away again?"

"Why not? Think I was going back to clean up horse-lines with a lot of War Babies? I say, you'd better go and report. We've got a new Major, thank Gawd."

A few days later the Regiment exchanged positions with another unit. The new home was the pick of the whole flank, but men were scarce. With a third ally the Bushman and Snow went on what turned out to be permanent night post. It lasted for five weeks, until the Last Night of all. The post was at the top of the Beach Line, and night observation was easy, even when the little destroyer didn't throw its inquisitive light on Jacko's doings. They dug three palatial sleeping possies in the walls close to the post, and, excluding broomstick bombs and fatigues, both of which fell thickly at times, they asked for nothing better while the war lasted. Flies had gone and "chats" seemed to have lost their energy. There was a squadron leader who took an interest in his job, and even a cook who sliced up bully beef in an effort to improve it. They fitted up the post with a sandbag seat, removing it carefully with the first gleams of day, until one unlucky morning when Snow forgot.

They were resting in peace in their respective dugouts with oil-sheets pinned over the openings to keep out the light. They heard approaching footsteps and strange voices; from the conversation it was evident that a Brass Hat was paying an unexpected visit. It was too late to hop out and pull away the tell-tale sandbags; they could only lie low and hope that the Big Noise, whoever he was might be thick in the head or soft-hearted; but he was neither.

"So *this* is the way your men do their observation, is it?" he asked the unlucky subaltern who was showing him round. "Too tired to stand up at their post! You'll see that they do in future. I've heard a lot about the disciplinary slackness of this regiment—evidently I haven't been misinformed. I shall make a special note of this particular post—Number Four."

Either of the guilty observers could have touched the Brass Hat by putting out a hand. They lay quaking in silence until they heard the last of footsteps; then Snow put his head out and cursed himself for his carelessness. He had got the subaltern—a decent sort—into a row. That was the worst of it.

"Who was it, Snow?" asked the Bushman.

"Dunno who it was," Snow replied. "But I'd like to make

the old bastard stand there looking through that loophole till he had more humps on his back than a cow camel."

"I know who it was," said the third. "I heard a rumour he was making an inspection. He's the Big Noise in the Enzeds—you know, the bloke they call 'Make-'em-double-Alex'."

Then the weather changed, and heat and thirst became almost pleasant memories. All through the afternoon and early night rain fell in torrents, turning the sloping trench bottoms into swirling streams, and flatter sections into pools of mud. There were no shelters in the front line, and men on post stood in soaked boots and sodden overcoats. A few raincoats were issued out to each troop, but there were not enough of them to keep even the observers dry.

The Bushman's shifts that night were first and fourth, and as he scrambled up the slippery steps to the post at one o'clock, an icy wind chased the scudding clouds. His feet had been wet all day—during his time off he had tried to rub some warmth into them, but without dry socks the effort was useless. Now he stubbed his toes repeatedly against the wall to keep them from freezing. He could hear low tapping sounds further along the line—others were trying the same dodge. He wondered if Jacko opposite was any better off; he couldn't be any worse.

The observation post was shallow and fronted a deep valley. The loophole was long and fairly wide, and it looked downwards. No bullet from the opposite trenches could find its way through, but observers had to stand in a crouching position. Since the Brass Hat's visit they had not been game to replace the seat. The Bushman stood there with bent body and numbed limbs, praying for the appearance of the searchlight. While it rested on Jacko's trenches it was safe to relax and straighten one's back. At last his prayer was granted. He saw the yellow beam flash across the black water and rest for a moment on the cliffs of Gabatepe. Then it crept slowly along the coastline until it reached a point opposite where he stood. He closed his eyes for a moment and stood erect. How Jacko must have cursed that light! It made his trenches as bright as day.

The wind lulled and the sleety rain stopped suddenly. Something else began to float downwards—something white and powdery, and the Bushman, despite his discomfort, looked at the snowflakes on his sleeve with interest. It was the first time he had seen any. Before long the low scrub in the hollow gleamed and sparkled, as again and again the destroyer threw its yellow light across the water. The sandbagged parapet was soon coated and the mud on the trench floor turned again to liquid. The Bushman heard steps shuffling towards the post, and the flash of a torch showed a welcome sight—the sergeant carrying a rum jar and the squadron-leader following closely behind him. Every man was served with a double ration extra that night, but no rum issue could do more than bring warmth momentarily. It could not dry saturated clothing, and daylight found the Bushman awake and shaking. The bottom of his overcoat carried icicles.

By midday the worst of the blizzard had passed, but there was cold comfort from the cookhouse. The water pipes at the reservoir in Clark's Gully had burst, and everyone went on voluntary "snow fatigue." The best drifts were over the parapet and the Bushman tried fishing with his quart-pot hanging on the end of a broomstick bomb handle. Then he remembered having seen a pool of water lying on one of the back terraces, but when he went to investigate he found nothing but frozen mud. He probed with his bayonet and discovered quite a little glacier underneath. The colour of the ice didn't matter; he took a dixie-full to the cookhouse and returned to his dugout with enough for a quart of tea. Snow was sitting there, nursing his swollen feet.

"Where's the wood?" he asked, for fuel was scarcer than ever. The Bushman, for answer, raked in the back of his sleeping possy and pulled out what looked like a bundle of broom-handles. They had been provided by Jacko—as the tail of a bomb he was specialising in at the time. With their bayonets they splintered them up and lit a fire on the floor of the post; but the wood was poor quality, and by the time it had burnt down the quart hadn't quite boiled. Jacko, however, was considerate.

"Look out!" yelled Snow, grabbing up the precious quart as they dived for their dugout's. Something thudded on the parados. It was a dud, and the additional handle was just enough to bring the quart to a boil. They drank Jacko's health gratefully.

Chapter Fourteen
Gallipoli - December 1915

The Bushman shouldered a kitbag and climbed down the terraces to Shell Green. He was bound for the beach, and he knew it was probably the last time he would go there. The sky was clear and the sun shining, but an icy wind blew from the ocean. If bad weather came up again in the next two days it might mean Constantinople—for most of them.

Two days to go! At first everyone had laughed at the rumour of evacuation. They refused to believe that blood and sweat had been squandered in vain; that thousands had endured misery, torture, semi-starvation and death—for nothing. Throughout those seven months they had comforted themselves with the hope, the belief, that in the end it would all have been worthwhile. Failure was bad enough, but it was bitter to think that it was due to a combination of incompetence and neglect. It came home forcibly to the Bushman as he passed a tiny cemetery. Some of his closest pals lay there—in a few days the crosses above their graves would be chopped up by the Turks for firewood.

Anyway, could they get away with it? Had Jacko been taken in by the "silent stunts" and the furious fusilades that had followed them? Or the sham fatigues? A few days previously a hundred men carrying empty cans and boxes had marched solemnly in a circle, showing themselves momentarily for the benefit of Turkish observers as they entered a sap leading up to the firing line. They might think that supplies were being stored up for the long winter months, when bad weather would make the landing of stuff difficult. Or again they mightn't.

The exodus had been under way for some days. As soon as darkness came, parties of men and loads of baggage left the line at regular intervals. On the final night a handful of men would hold Anzac. The last party to leave the position held by the Regiment would number fifteen, all told. Fifteen to hold ground which usually needed some hundreds! They couldn't hold it, of course, against even a raid, let alone a serious attack. They could only pray for luck.

The Bushman had been picked for the last party. There had been some growling when the selection was made—men who had been there the whole seven months thought that the job should have been theirs automatically, and one enthusiast offered a fiver for a place in the team. Snow's frost-bitten feet barred him from consideration, and be had already gone, cursing his bad luck.

As the Bushman came on to Shell Green he saw a small party working at the old latrine near Headquarters, and he wondered what it was up to, for the pit had been out of action for some time. He put down his load and went over to find out. The pit had been dug on the floor of a short terrace made specially for the purpose, and several men were covering it carefully. First they wove a close lattice work of thin boards over the narrow opening. Then they placed sheets of newspaper over the boards and a layer of fresh soil over the paper. At the approach, and on the firm ground behind the covered pit, they scattered more soil. The Bushman, as an experienced dingo trapper, recognised the touch of a master hand and looked on admiringly, but he wondered what decoy they were going to use. How did they propose to get Jacko on to the trap?

"This way," replied one. "Ten to one he'll be hungry." He threw a few tins of Fray Bentos on to the solid ground behind the hidden pit. To banish suspicion still further, he took off a boot and made a few footmarks with it on the loose soil. It was hard to believe that someone hadn't walked across. "A light shower of rain now," he went on, "and it'd be set. I'd give a quid to be planted somewhere where I could watch some Abdul go in." He paused, and then another bright thought occurred to him. "And I'd give another quid to be well on the windward side of him when he climbs out!"

The Bushman continued his journey to the beach.

Everything was amazingly quiet, except for an occasional shot away to the north behind Suvla. That morning, the last parties had been taken over the final track they would travel, and shown the jetty where they would embark. The nights were still freezing, and the C.3 fifteen had been warned that they could carry away no overcoats. They had already been sent away with the baggage that morning. The Bushman had found a discarded coat in the Post, and he turned down the hill to the jetty to see if he could work out a little scheme which had occurred to him.

The beach there was only a strip of a few yards in width, and the engineers had dug some funkholes in the sandy cliff fronting it. The Bushman stuffed the spare coat into a sandbag and threw it into the back of the closest dugout. It was just possible that he might have time to retrieve it before he embarked, and during the rest of the night on a minesweeper it would be a godsend. Otherwise Jacko was welcome to it.

He followed along the beach, and as he passed Victoria Gully he saw another party of men at work near the Ambulance, but his sense of smell told him that, if another trap was being set there for Jacko, a vastly different bait was being used. The smell was so unfamiliar to Gallipoli that he doubted first his nose and then his eyes. From a dump near the tents men were carrying cases to a deep pit. An officer stood by watching them break the cases open and smash each bottle with a trenching tool before throwing it in. The smell of wine was enough to make a man drunk. The Bushman supposed that it had been meant for the use of field hospital cases, but he couldn't remember hearing of anyone who had had a taste of it. He wondered what they were doing with the surplus rum, and as he rounded Hell's Corner, he staggered back from a smell which must surely have carried across the Narrows into Asia Minor.

The beach was littered with broken jars, and the cobble stones below them were stained a luscious brown. Two men wandered disconsolately amongst the wreckage—prospecting. They agreed, gloomily, that it was a bloody shame and that the Heads were madder than ever. It was a dead put-away. Jacko wasn't a fool. He must be able to smell it, and he'd know that if they smashed rum-jars they must be going to do a bunk. Here and there they unearthed a broken jar bottom holding a few drops—once a yell of delight announced at least a spoonful. They licked the earthenware in turns.

The Bushman at last got to the end of his journey and handed over the baggage. Then for the first time for many days Beachy Bill became active. He plastered the narrow strip of cobblestones thoroughly and drove everyone to cover. Not satisfied with that, he began dropping shells at regular intervals along the tracks leading to the right flank. After sitting in shelter for an hour, the Bushman got sick ,of it. He followed a sap to Hell's Comer, and found one of his squadron there wondering if it were safe to run the gauntlet along the beach. There were funkholes there at regular intervals, and a few hundred yards would see them to reasonable safety. They ran for it.

They had several narrow escapes, but at last they got out of the danger zone and parted company. The shelling dwindled and the Bushman preferred to risk shrapnel on the hills to snipers' bullets along the beach. He reached the safe side of. Shell Green before he heard a report that sounded dangerous. He dropped into a handy dugout and turned to watch a solitary figure doubling for safety. A deep gully led downwards to the sea, and the first dugout on its side was neatly covered with a ground-sheet. As the shell burst, the fugitive dived sideways, and disappeared head first. In a second or two he was out again, followed by someone whose afternoon nap he had rudely broken. The Bushman saw fists flying.

Chapter Fifteen
Gallipoli - December 1915

From the Post above the Beach Line a tunnel followed the crown of the ridge outwards, and it came to an end at the Outlook—a small crescent-shaped redoubt. Turkish sappers had tried hard to get possession of the territory it commanded; they could then have enfiladed the back areas of the post across the valley to the left. The activities of both sides finally ended with posts within eight yards of each other. After a few bombing duels the occupants left each other alone and gave their attention to areas further back.

Soon after dark twelve men groped their way along the tunnel to the Outlook and took it over in silence. Those they relieved had done their last job on Gallipoli, and there was some quiet hand-shaking before they disappeared, They were marching out, and it seemed unlikely that they would see again those who stayed behind.

The twelve "diehards" divided into pairs. They took what shelter they could from possible bombing and sat closely together for support and warmth. They could do no observing, for the redoubt had been dug hurriedly and much of the soil thrown out on the wrong side. There was no way of finding out what might be happening eight yards away, and nothing at all might happen if Jacko were left severely alone. The Job was to listen, to remain noiseless and, if possible, motionless for nine hours. From the back areas and the Beach Line they heard occasional shots and the crunch of a bomb, but they knew that they were not being aimed at Jacko.

Those twelve men had to back their luck heavily that night. They might possibly hold up a casual raid on their post, but if a business attack came, the tunnel would be cut off long before they could get back to the thin support in their rear. A false alarm would throw the programme into confusion. They had been told that they had been picked for this job in the Outlook because they had cool heads. Before they had been there long there was no doubt about their feet. To make footsteps even more noiseless they had wound strips of blanket round their boots, but they gave no warmth. The moonlight was bright and the night still. No sound could be heard from the Turkish post and the tension was nerve-breaking. Frost settled on their tunics.

The Bushman felt a touch of cramp and he had to move and ease his leg muscles. He took a couple of slow, careful steps and looked at his watch before he crouched again beside his mate. It was half-past ten, and five of the nine hours had gone. At that moment another batch of men would be stealing away, and the number left would be down to fifty. As he crept back to his seat a bullet thudded into the sandbags above the tunnel, but he realised thankfully that it had been fired from a distance. A sniper, planted somewhere across the gully to the left, imagined that he had found a loophole and became industrious. For nearly an hour he put a shot a minute into the same place.

At first the change from complete silence was welcome, then the trickle of sand from the burst bag after every shot became just as monotonous. The Bushman took to counting them to pass the time, and his mate whispered that the bastard fired every time a different louse bit him.

At midnight a humming sound drifted faintly across with the mainland breeze. The bodies of the listening men stiffened—momentarily they held their breaths. It was a Turkish aeroplane flying low. They caught a distant glimpse of it as it passed from the direction of Gabatepe along the beach. Was it possible that, with the bodies of men moving behind the lines, the activity of the embarkation points and the minesweepers lying close at anchor, the Turkish observer would see nothing? The sound of the engine had scarcely died away when three shells in quick succession screamed overhead. Was that the signal for the Turkish charge? So convinced of it were the diehards that they stood back against the rear wall with fingers to triggers and bayonet points upwards. After a few moments of suspense they crept back to their seats. Silence fell once more.

When the Bushman looked at his watch again it was two o'clock, and he heard sounds in the tunnel—the curious swish of muffled feet. It was the sergeant.

"I want you two to go back now," he whispered. "C.2 party is just pulling out. You'll be the only ones there. One of you take from the tunnel to the left, and the other towards the Beach Line. Watch the saps closely."

The Bushman and his mate got back without delay. After eight hours' listening the relief of movement was heaven sent, and an occasional look-over heartened them in the belief that, after all, they were going to get away with it. There was neither sound nor sign of movement over the parapet. Here and there rifles had been tied to positions on the firesteps. They pointed upwards and tin-cans hung to their triggers. Above them, from other cans, water dripped slowly into the lower ones. They were timed to fire at intervals for an hour after the last party had gone. In places slowly burning fuses led to bombs lying over the parapets.

Slowly—more slowly than ever—the minutes of the last half-hour ticked away. The two men patrolled their sections continuously and met every few minutes at the tunnel entrance. At last they heard the swishing sound. There was no delay—they took their places on the end of the retreating file and passed silently up the candle-lit gallery leading out on to the back areas. At Brigade Headquarters they were joined by the diehards from their fellow units, and their numbers were quickly checked. Dismay spread when one party was found to be a man short, and a few precious moments passed before he was retrieved. Overlooked somehow in the final muster, he was at last discovered calmly observing through a loophole. For a little while he had a brigade's position to himself.

With steady steps the diehards crossed Shell Green and climbed over Gun Ridge. There were covering parties lying there, the men who had marched out half-an-hour before. They gathered as the little column passed through, and followed closely to the rendezvous at B. Depot. There, beside the plank and sandbag pier, lay a string of rowboats. They were manned without delay, but before he filed on, the Bushman dived into the dugout and grabbed the overcoat he had hidden there. He dropped down in the stern of a boat, and as the signal was given to go ahead, a solitary shell passed overhead on its way to Anzac Cove. It was Beachy Bill's good-bye.

The coastline quickly slipped from sight, but the ridges behind held their sinister shape until the row-boats were nearing the minesweeper. The Bushman watched the fatal hills until all trace of them disappeared. He wondered if anyone would be called to account for the tragic waste they had witnessed. The flower of his country's First Division had been sacrificed, but it lived to fight again, and, reinforced and rebuilt, it would yet win a great battle. Those seven lurid months had justified Australia's faith and belief in itself.

Suddenly, at different points from Anzac to Suvla, the coastline caught fire as shells from destroyers found the targets of abandoned material prepared for them. A mighty explosion inland was the signal for a general bombardment, and a crackle of Turkish rifle fire replied—at empty trenches. The row-boats had long since passed out of range, but the men on them, for once, were not in the mood to see jokes. They climbed on board the minesweeper, cold, hungry and downcast, but daylight brought the honest reflection that none of the blame for the ghastly tragedy of Gallipoli was theirs. A few hours later the minesweeper drew alongside a transport in Mudros Bay and the Bushman soon caught sight of Snow searching the little groups of men with anxious eyes. Few on board that transport had ever expected to see the diehards again.

Chapter Sixteen
Egypt - December 1915

On Christmas morning the transport lay easily at anchor off Alexandria and the brigade lay uneasily about its decks. Men wondered when they would get off—if ever—and what they would get for dinner—if anything. Rations had been scant enough during the five days on board, and the cooks had evidently been scavenging to find enough for the morning's breakfast. The times when such little discomforts would have been considered a contribution towards winning the war had gone. There was considerable growling, for everyone knew that it was a case of negligence, if not straightout robbery. Still—Christmas? Perhaps, after all, a pleasant midday surprise might be bidden in the cookhouse. There was nothing like optimism.

The morning passed without any signs of a move, midday also, without any of a feed—except for saloon passengers. It would have been a tactful act to have drawn the blinds round that dining-room. If in answer to prayers some of the diners did choke—they remained on duty.

Snow was missing for a time about midday, and when he reappeared he beckoned the Bushman to one side, wiped his mouth, patted his belly, and produced three stripes from his pocket.

"Put these on, Blood," he said, "and get down to the mess. If I can pass for a sergeant, you can. There's only scraps left, but they're better than nothing."

The Bushman needn't have bothered about the stripes. Nearly half the men on board had promoted themselves to sergeant's rank by the simple process of making three indelible pencil marks on their hats and sleeves—the hallmark of a Gallipoli N.C.O. They were cleaning out the dishes when the Bushman arrived, and he threatened to call down the R.S.M. if something wasn't forthcoming. The bluff worked, and he scored a feed—of a sort.

At half-past two, a welcome order was passed round, and by three o'clock the brigade was sitting on its swag ready for disembarkation; but it remained seated until nine that night. Then the gangways were lowered and men spat back choice curses and pious prayers for the speedy torpedoing of the *Bettana*, as they once more set foot in Egypt. Not long before daylight a troop train decanted them at Zeitoun, and they were shepherded into a camp, but few stayed there. Every steak-and-eggs joint within miles of Heliopolis sold out long before sunrise, and the breakfast provided later by King and Country was greeted with derisive cheers. It was Fray Bentos and biscuits!

An advance guard left for Ma'adi early next morning, and it included the Bushman and Snow, The Bushman's rigout, although unorthodox, was reasonably clean, but Snow's tunic was tattered and his breeches held together by nails and string. At Bab el-Louk they saw a dazzling sight—real soldiers! A guard of honour was on its way to officiate at the wedding of an Australian girl who was marrying a Lord, and, judging from its badges and colours, it evidently came from Ma'adi.

"Looks as if we'll have to put up a fight to get into that camp." remarked Snow. "They reckon there's five hundred war babies in our tents and mess-huts. I'm going back into my old possy; I don't care who's in it."

He seemed right about the five hundred, for the streets of Ma'adi were swarming with reinforcements. They made way for the new and weather-stained arrivals with appropriate respect—or so it appeared. When the Bushman and Snow reached their old tent they found it had several occupants who looked doubtfully at them, and even more so at their swags. Snow solved the problem very simply. He sat down by the doorway and pulled off his shirt.

"You watch these Kiwi Napoleons 'imshi,' Blood," he whispered as he began to drop imaginary chats on the sand. Until the remainder of the Regiment turned up that afternoon they had the tent to themselves.

That night beer flowed fast, and when the canteen closed several "corpses" had to be rolled into horse-blankets and carried back to the lines. Others, able to stagger home, took a supply with them for the morning. At reveille all efforts to straighten them up failed, and the squadron paraded with uneasy feelings. It seemed a bit hard that men, who for seven months had shirked neither danger nor hardship, should be crimed the day after they got back to a peace camp. After all, they were only sticking to a time-honoured custom. They had knocked up a cheque on a seven-months job, and they were going to knock it down before they signed on for another, and to hell with the whole Army Act.

Somehow that morning the sergeant's roll seemed at fault, for several names weren't called; nor were they for nearly a week. The squadron had a leader who, to recognise service, was prepared to jump on discipline hard, and he probably never knew the prestige he gained by his tactful action. He crowned it by getting a dead-house put up alongside the canteen, and the defaulters played up to him by keeping well out of sight inside it. Snow peeped into the tent when they came off the afternoon parade and called to the Bushman.

"Hey! For Gawd's sake come and get an eyeful of old Trooper!"

The Bushman looked in. Three "corpses" surrounded by a barrage of bottles lay huddled on the sand, sleeping it off. "Trooper" sat beside them, doing his best to revive them in turns with spoonfuls of "medicine" from a half-empty dixie. Four days later they came on parade, sick and sorry, but ready for another war.

After a few evenings in Cairo it soon became apparent that the place had slipped badly. Certainly most of the cafes were as good as ever, but a number of favoured haunts were out of bounds. The new A.P.M. was hot stuff; even the unit which had once owned him joined with others in wanting to know why he had ever been allowed to leave the Peninsula alive. The Bushman's regiment concurred cordially.

There were strict orders out about catching the last train to camp. Anyone who missed it would be treated as A.W.L. and given a night's lodging in the cobblestoned yard at Bab-el-Hadid unless he dodged the Jacks and spent precious piastres on a taxi home. The Bushman and Snow were late out of the Kursaal one night and their gharri got to Bab-el-Louk as the bell rang and the grille began to lower. One or two scrambled under in time, and others began to climb over, but it seemed that this time honoured custom was no longer in order. The A.P.M. was on the platform surrounded by a formidable bodyguard of his satellites, and the climbers were sternly warned back. The Bushman and Snow were about to dash for the nearest taxi rank when they heard the uproar on the platform. The train was full of men, and the men were full of beer, and the telling off of the A.P.M. was something too good to miss,

"That's what you would do!" they yelled. Every window held the head and shoulders of a raging man. They leant out and shook their fists under the nose of the A.P.M. His easy smile was fresh fuel. "You crawled for your pips, and as soon as you got them you faded off the Peninsula, you cold-footed, malingering, lead-swinging bastard!"

The train began to move, and the A.P.M. patted his shoulder calmly.

"Yes, but they're there, they're there. And I know you and you"—he pointed to foaming individuals—"and I'll get you one of these days—yes, *you* and *you*."

The Bushman and Snow decided that they'd heard enough, but a last shout reached them above the rumbling of the train,

"How much did 'thirty-three Boulac' have to pay you before you'd leave it in bounds?"

Chapter Seventeen
The Desert - March 1916

The optimists who thought the Regiment was due for something like an extended holiday at Ma'adi were soon disillusioned. Training began again almost at once—training which most men reckoned they knew backwards and which many didn't care if they never knew at all.

Those who had been longest on Gallipoli took it hardest. It was no use pointing out, gently, that drill, range practice and mounted tactical work was merely a refresher course designed to make them once more familiar with a soldier's job, in which ragged shorts, bare legs and bearded faces had no place. And in any case the "Deep Thinkers" and "War Babies" had to be licked into shape. The Regiment consequently heard with relief that its days in Cairo were numbered, and that it was to move camp to a spot called Serapeum, on the Canal. That, said the know-alls, was handy to the embarkation point whence, horses and all, they would board ships for France.

Khamsins and a regimental cookhouse made life a little hell at Serapeum, but the waters of the Canal turned it into a good imitation of heaven at Toussomn. Next came the mobilisation of all mounted units at Salhia. It seemed likely that, after all, they were to follow the infantry divisions to France, and perhaps they might have if Jacko hadn't bobbed up again—in Sinai. He had given a Yeomanry brigade a rough handling at a place called Romani, and the Horsemen got half a day's notice to saddle up.

They welcomed the prospect of meeting Jacko again. He had won on points in the first round, but messages had been left for him at Anzac warning him to watch his step in the second.

"Romani!" The name carried a touch of the romance of ancient history, and anyone who knew anything of desert campaigns got an easy hearing. It seemed that Napoleon had fought a battle there with someone, and so had various others right back to the Crusaders. Before them, the Saracen, the Roman, the Assyrian and the Persian had left their tracks in the sand and their bones beneath it. Now it was to become the playground of the latest army from the farthest off continent.

It was nearing midnight when the Regiment clanked its way across the pontoon bridge at Kantara and halted on the business side of the Canal. The day had been hot, and both men and horses felt the weight of full marching order. They had made their first real move as mounted troops, and even mounted action was possible, for rumour said that Jacko had cavalry. The Long Patrol had begun, and its end lay two and a half years ahead on the mountains of Transjordan. The path before it lay through trackless desert and windswept, waterless waste, by scented orange orchards and almond groves, over rocky denies and mountain passes and through a Dead World. It was to be tested by the extremes of heat and cold, of hunger and thirst, of disease and death. And it was to be finally welded by success and the meaning of mateship—of manhood.

The Bushman tied his horse to the picquet line and went with the rest of the troop to fill his bottle at the big canvas cistern near the railhead. There was an armed guard over it, for water was scarce. When he returned to the lines his horse was pawing the ground uneasily. He imagined that it could smell the water in his bottle, and he felt like a criminal. He vowed he would get it a drink somehow, if only a couple of quarts. It would be hard if he couldn't bluff the Tommy guard. He led the horse by a circuitous route to the rear of the dump near the cistern.

He made the first attack on the guard as himself—filled his bottle again without argument, and emptied it into the canvas bucket he had left hidden behind the dump. On his second trip he went without his tunic; on the third without his hat. Then he began all over again, and at last the gallon bucket was full. His horse nearly gave him away when he held it to its head. When he got back to the lines he remembered that his bottle was still empty, and he hurried to the cistern, to find it was empty too. But Snow didn't let him go altogether thirsty.

The Regiment moved slowly over the plain. It carried small patches of stunted scrub struggling to live, but the only signs of animal life were the burrows of the desert rat. In the distance sharp peaks stood up above the plain, and at times the wind came in burning gusts. Then a light dust cloud appeared ahead, and soon afterwards a column rode by, making in the direction of the Canal. It answered no questions, but its dejected air spoke volumes. A fine brigade had been out-manoeuvred, but the fault did not lie with the men who rode in downcast silence.

There was water at Romani, and men and horses drank their fill, brackish though it was. The Regiment made its camp beside palms growing in a hollow beneath a giant dune. The position was bounded by a semi-circle of steep hills, and in two places there were "gateways" leading to the undulating plains eastward. It was a stiff climb through ankle-deep sand to the outpost line, but at least the job was no longer play. Just over the fringe of hills lay the bodies of a horse and a man. There was action ahead, and the spirits of the Regiment rose. It had an additional reason for satisfaction: the cookhouse had been left behind.

The Bushman—now wearing a stripe—drew the rations for his section and spread out the spoil on a horse blanket. At first his mates refused to believe it was all issue stuff. They counted the slices of bacon—at least one a man more than could have been coaxed from a cookhouse dixie. The supply of potatoes suggested a market garden in some oasis; there were even a few-scraggy onions! And, best of all, the tea and sugar—saved from the grease of a cookhouse! Even the inevitable Fray Bentos seemed different.

"That'll tell you." remarked Snow. "A man can get ahead of it now if he isn't too greedy. Here y'are. Blood, you're cook."

He threw him a couple of tins of beef.

"What about some rissoles for tea?"

"This won't suit some of the war babies, all the same," replied the Bushman as he began peeling the onions. "They can't forget about their sheep stations, but they'll soon come at it."

"The Major wants you, Blood," said the troop sergeant.

"He's up at the head of the lines."

The Bushman found a special job waiting for him—to guide a party from another regiment to Oghritina, where his own had been the previous day. He packed his haversack, drew his horse ration from the feed heap, and reported to the neighbouring Headquarters. A burial party was going out, and from what he had already seen of Oghritina, the Bushman was glad that his job was merely to guide it there.

The little column crossed the hollow and slid down the steep pass between the dunes. It passed through some scattered palms, and then faced a steady rise eastwards. The sand was ribbed where other horsemen had passed over it, and once beyond the first rise the desert was dotted by bare peaks. Soon, part of the column branched off to the right—it was bound for Katia on a similar errand. High in the air above the palms the Bushman could see greyish specks circling.

Three hours' riding brought the column to Oghritina. From the south and west the hill sloped gently, and its top was flat and crescent shaped. Its other sides were nearly a sheer drop, and palms clustered thickly at their bases, Several dead Turks lay at the foot of the hill in the path of the burial party, and the site of the garrison's Headquarters stood in a small circular dip half-way up the slope. There were bodies there, stripped and unrecognisable, and around the hilltop lay those who had fought to the end.

The Bushman tried to reconstruct the action. The attack had evidently come from three sides, and it would have needed an entrenched battalion to hold the position against four thousand Turks, let alone a squadron. Most of the bodies lay in a little hollow right on the hilltop. All of them had been stripped and some partially buried. It was well-nigh impossible to tell Yeoman from Turk, for identity discs had gone to make a Bedouin necklace. At the site of what had been Headquarters, papers were scattered about. They were mostly army forms, but the Bushman examined some packets of letters on the chance of finding something of value to the relatives of those killed or captured. A glance at one letter made him whistle. In the hands of a blackmailer the bundle would have been worth a fortune. He made a bonfire of some of the rubbish and watched the incriminating letters go up in cinders. He hoped, for the sake of Bedouin morals, that there weren't any more of them blowing about the desert.

All day the burial party toiled at its gruesome job, and in the afternoon the Bushman found them a small addition to it. From the hilltop he thought he saw something move in a hollow, and he rode over to investigate. As he approached, vultures, disturbed from a banquet, flapped heavily upwards. They had been finishing the work of the Bedouins. They had stripped the body of its clothing, the vultures were fast cleaning its bones. The Bushman swore to do in the first person he heard thereafter singing the "Bedouin Love Song."

The two mounted brigades which took over the job of outposting the Canal avoided the mistake of whittling down their strength by splitting up into small or isolated camps—a mistake which had cost their predecessors so dearly. No matter how far patrols penetrated, or how long they were out, they came back to the shelter of the regimental camps.

The Turk, satisfied with the success of his surprise attacks on Oghritina and Katia, retired behind the waterless screen of desert stretching from Bir-el-Abd to Mazar, and the two brigades began the job of seeing that it was not crossed again in strength, unchallenged. In their turns the regiments patrolled by day and night, and reconnaissances in force repeatedly pushed into the heart of Turkish territory.

When summer heat swept over Sinai in all its pitiless

strength, the Horsemen found desert campaigning no child's play, but at its worst it was a welcome change from the shackling cramp of Gallipoli. They were doing the job they came across the world to do—work that mattered—and their spirits were never higher.

Chapter Eighteen
The Desert - June 1916

"When ther sa-ands of ther desert grow co-old," sang Snow. "I wish the bloke that wrote that was here now. Don't you. Blood?"

The Regiment was saddling up, and sweat dripped from both horses and men. There had been warnings about the forthcoming stunt being a particularly dry one, but it looked like having one redeeming feature. Most of the riding would be done by night, and then the blessed sand did cool down a little. The return journey—usually in the forenoon—was always the worst, since the ordinary craving for sleep was turned into special torture by the heat, and water was always scarce, except the brackish variety. The horses, compelled by necessity, had taken to it, but men could not, except in the shape of tea, and tea was scarce, too. A few had been drilling themselves to go without, even when fresh water was plentiful, in the hopes that they would feel the pinch less in the real perish which everyone expected sooner or later. Their abstinence didn't help them, for, as it happened, the dash on Bayoud put most of the experimenters in hospital,

The main sport, in the desert was trying to catch a Jacko outpost, but Jacko was too wary. He always seemed to know when a dash was coming, and he usually pulled back a mile or two to some spot whence he could comfortably watch a thirsty column turn tail and make for home. Still, it was what D.H.Q. called "getting in touch with the enemy," and, fortunately for the health of the Horsemen, Jacko was watching his step carefully in the second round.

As a result of his caution he missed some glorious openings along the old Roman road. There were places where one machine-gun from comparative safety could have put a whole regiment out of the war. No advance or flank guards could have saved it in a narrow track with half-a-mile of sheer sandhills on either side.

At the old Katia well men ate and drank and filled their bottles. There would be no more water for the horses and probably none for themselves until they got back there next day. The heat did not slacken with night, and on the outpost at Sagia they sat through it hatless and coatless in sweltering discomfort. Before daylight the column moved on, but few men dared to put a bottle to their lips as they rode slowly over the sand mountains towards Bayoud. There was no escaping some of them; they struggled up on foot leading their horses, and slithered down through deep drifts on the other side. The morning air was foetid and stagnant—there was no breeze to break the power of the pitiless sun. At ten o'clock, when the Bushman's squadron was a mile from Bayoud, the order was given to halt and dismount.

Then the wind came—at first gently—and the Bushman, sitting in his horse's shadow, watched the dunes getting ready to move once more. They had been doing that from the Beginning. A shimmering veil of fine sand began to creep slowly up their sides, their pointed peaks to hide in yellow haze.

Suddenly the wind rose fiercely and swept desolation before it with the blast of a furnace. It lifted the loose sand on high in lemon-coloured clouds and goaded the peaks into violent action. Spiral columns whirled upwards from their points and crests of drift poured over their flanks in waves, there to lie until another wind claimed its day of sport.

The Bushman's horse moved restlessly and he shifted into the new patch of shade. He took the cork out of his bottle, but on second thoughts he put it back again. Better to wait, he thought, for the chance of making it. into tea—not that it would need much boiling. He knew that if he drank the lot as it was he would be just as dry again in a few minutes. The wells at Bayoud had been partly destroyed by Jacko, but in any case the water in them was unfit for use. And there was no chance of putting salt on Jacko's tail that trip.

The order came to mount and the column wheeled to begin its journey back. The Bushman's heart sank a bit when he realised that there would be little chance of water before they reached Katia. He could stand up to it, so could most of the others, but what of the horses? He could feel his own floundering every time it ploughed through a deeper patch of drift. He was riding on the right flank guard, and he caught a glimpse of distant palm trees through the haze. The leading troop turned in its direction and the flank guards were signalled to come in to the column. When the Bushman rode into the Hod, men and horses were scattered about in the scanty shade, and some, nearly thirst-mad, were cleaning out a soakage. The water stank, and those who sipped it vomited. He lit a fire and boiled the water left in his bottle. Shared with his section it gave each man a few mouthfuls of tea, and he felt new life as he swallowed his, scalding hot. Some men were done. He saw several collapse and carried to better shade. There were ambulances, even water-carts, somewhere.

The well at Sagia held a scanty supply and the column was straggling by the time it got there. To get enough water for the men alone would have taken hours. The smell drove the hordes nearly frantic, and it needed the colonel's firmness to control some of the riders. A queue was formed, but many men held back. The Bushman went to Snow.

"The captain says that anyone who thinks he can get to Katia can try," he said. "What about it?"

Snow nodded. They spurred their horses away from the smell of water and moved slowly off. Some others had already started. In straggling groups they crossed the plain and climbed the first sandhill on the track to Katia—six miles away. The Bushman's spirits revived and he began to rally Snow, who was suffering torment. His fair skin had become purple and he made choking attempts to clear the congestion in his throat. Once or twice he swayed, and the Bushman caught at him in a panic, fearing sun- stroke or collapse. One horse could never carry two of them. But Snow fought doggedly and they urged their jaded horses onwards. The wind still shrieked across their blistered faces, and the haze played tricks with the dark and distant horizon,

An hour passed—an hour of silent struggle—and the Bushman calculated that they had covered a little more than half-way. He remembered one or two landmarks, and even at their slow pace he reckoned that they were moving faster than a bullock team. Then, suddenly, the horses began to step out. They knew; it was only a matter now of hanging to the saddle. At last the outline of distant palm trees broke through the haze and the horses made a pitiful attempt to whinny. Both men were riding in a semi-stupor, and they wondered if they were seeing a mirage—if the well were still miles away and the horses mistaken.

At last it stood out quite clearly. They could see men already there lowering buckets over the stone coping, the ropes running in grooves cut by centuries of wear. The ride was over. With fumbling hands they undid their neck-ropes and reins and made fast their buckets. The water came up sweet and cool. Nine times the Bushman drew a gallon for his horse, and from each bucketful he took a pint for himself.

They led their horses across to the shade and unsaddled. They got more water from a shallow soakage in the Hod and drenched their sweating bodies. By the time the Bushman had had a drink of tea and a smoke, he felt equal even to Fray Bentos and biscuits. He wondered what the shade temperature had been that day, and later on he went across to where the Field Ambulance was stationed. He almost thought it had been worthwhile when he discovered that under a palm thatch the thermometer had registered a hundred and twenty-two degrees.

Chapter Nineteen
Camp - June 1916

There was leave to be had to Port Said, but no one was very enthusiastic about it. There wasn't a decent pub in the place in bounds, and nearly everyone was broke. Further, leave to Port Said often meant a nine days wonder afterwards. The Bushman refused it when it came to his turn, but Snow accepted, provisionally. His roll wasn't quite big enough to finance a decent week, so on the night of pay-day he took it to the school.

His luck was out. He was a consistent head backer and he made his share of the furious uproar round the ring when a "grey" was discovered amongst the pennies. No one, of course, knew how long it had been there, but Snow was quite sure that the two-tailed coin had cost him his leave. For several successive nights nothing would break right for him, and he came back at last with a miserable hundred piastres in his pocket to see him through to next pay. He dropped down in the bivvy and poured out a tale of woe.

The Bushman gave him no sympathy. He left two-up severely alone, and he told Snow that, providing other fellows with cash for beer and "bints" was as big a mug's game as putting silk dresses on publicans' daughters at home. It was notorious that by the fourth night after pay a few of the two-up kings had most of it. His theory was that more "greys" and "nobs" found their way on and off the "kip" than the players had any idea of.

"Don't you believe it," retorted Snow. "It's too risky. They'd get kicked to death if they were caught. Those fellows win because they've most money to start with; they can stand a bad run. I could go there and win a hundred notes any time, if I had a hundred to start with."

The Bushman's next question showed how little he knew of the technique of the game.

"How would it be," he asked, "to start with a small bet, and double up whenever you lost? You must win that way, sooner or later."

Snow laughed at his ignorance.

"Who do you think is going to keep on doubling up every bet? You must think they're all 'magnoon.' Why, you can only double once even when you're betting against the centre. He always draws his stake on the third spin."

"Then—" The Bushman stopped and began to work out a scheme that had occurred to him. He could see himself going down to posterity as the man who invented an infallible system for winning at two-up. He turned out his pockets and mustered two hundred and twenty piastres.

Then he did a few pencil calculations.

"Anyone been heading 'em more than five times tonight?" he asked.

"Five times! They've been lucky if they've saved their stakes."

"Who's keeping the ring?"

"Frank."

"That'll do. He's a pal of mine. Give us that hundred, Snow. I'll give you two when I come back. I've worked out a scheme to rob them."

After some protest Snow handed over the note.

"I might as well kiss it good-bye," he said. "They'll rob you, that's what'll happen. Mind, if you come back broke, I'll kick you to death myself."

The Bushman found the school tucked discreetly away behind a little sandhill. A small ring of men stood round several blankets pegged securely to the ground, and a lantern flickered sufficient light at each corner. The school was on its last legs, for the two-up kings had cleaned it up and departed. Bets were seldom more than a modest twenty piastres, but that suited the Bushman's scheme, and the amount of his capital admirably. On a big night he would have been laughed out of the ring.

He looked on for awhile. A spinner was being repeatedly barred. "And I'll bar 'em all night," warned one. "while you butterfly 'em. Ah, that's better. Tails, some money! Twenty piastres tails."

The butterfly artist handed over the "kip." The next spinner was content to speculate a miserable ten piastres only, and the ringkeeper's "Set. and well set. Fair go! was loudly interrupted by a voice from the far side of the ring.

"I'm not set yet. Hundred piastres a skull! Hundred a skull. What sort of a school's this, where a man can't get a decent bet. Hundred a skull!"

The ring-keeper sat back on his haunches in disgust. "Can't someone set this war baby and shut him up?" he asked. "He didn't know there was a war on till the Indian hawker told him. All set then. They're up—and—two tails."

By then the Bushman had taken up the position he wanted on his knees beside the ringkeeper.

"Next spinner? Right. Twenty wanted in the centre."

"Here's five of it, Frank." The Bushman dropped his coin on the blanket. Usually the spinner was set in one bet, but the state of the School was such that the ring- keeper didn't mind splitting it. The rest of the stake soon came in.

"Get your side bets on. Fair go, and—they're—two heads!"

The Bushman threw down ten piastres at once. The second bet was always doubled, but few who bet against the spinner cared to follow him much further. This one proved to be in form. He drew his stake at his third attempt, but when a fourth and a fifth spin showed heads, the Bushman began to look down his nose.

Having taken only a quarter of the original stake, there was sufficient margin to allow him to double up each time, but at the sixth spin he had the last of his cash on the blanket. If heads showed once more he would have to face Snow's jeers piastreless. "They're up and they're down, and—two outs!"

The Bushman heaved a sigh of relief and collected three hundred and twenty piastres, all of which except five was his own. He had won his original bet, but it had been too close to be pleasant. He could stand up to heads five times, but a trot past that would break him. He needed a lot more capital to be safe even with five piastre bets. After that the spinning went more evenly. There was a run of tails and he collected steadily at the rate of five piastres a time. Soon his pockets were bulging with silver, and when the school closed down for the night he had five hundred-piastre notes in his wallet, and some loose coins which he gave to the ringkeeper. He found Snow on picquet when he got back to the lines and handed over two of the notes in triumph. Then he outlined his scheme in detail, quite convinced that it was possible to make a small but steady living, unless—

"Yes, unless you try to follow some bloke who goes mad and heads 'em half the night," interrupted Snow. "They'll rob you then. You'll see."

Before many nights passed the Bushman did, see. Flushed with continuous winning, he was lured out of his caution and began to punt. Unluckily for him, the first time he departed from his system he struck a lunatic who headed 'em ten times, and he did in every piastre he possessed—in cold blood. He decided then to give two-up best, but Snow's luck changed. He did a record "trot," and he woke the Bushman that night by using his chest as a table on which to count his winnings. After that he was seldom without a hundred pounds in the bank in Cairo.

Chapter Twenty
Romani - August 1916

In darkness and silence men tied their horses on to the lines at Et Maler and few of them troubled to take off their gear as they lay down on the sand to snatch what rest they could. It was nearing midnight—the night of the third of August, and they felt, and hoped, that the strain of the two previous weeks would end with daybreak. The unexpected had happened, and a Turkish army was within striking distance of the camp.

There was no denying that Jacko had put over a smart bit of work. He had brought an army—including heavy artillery—across the desert, marching by night and hiding from aerial observation by day. He had actually reached Oghritina before his move was discovered, and a timely aeroplane warning saved the advance guard of a brigade making an ordinary reconnaissance from surprise and probable disaster. Gradually the invaders closed in towards the Canal, and they would have welcomed an attack, but this time the choice of battleground lay with the defenders. For once they had the pleasure of sitting back and watching Jacko come on.

There were only two mounted brigades to bar the way to the Canal, and their camps were at Romani and Et Maler. Certainly there was an infantry battalion entrenched near the railhead, but Jacko had no need to attack it. If he could dispose of the Horsemen, he could walk round the position and deal with it afterwards at his leisure.

For two weeks the mounted brigades took turns at twenty-four hours in camp and twenty-four out of it. Just before midnight a brigade saddled up and moved to the "Booby Hatch"—the gateway to the Romani-Et-Maler positions where the incoming brigade passed it. At daylight the outgoing column began a daily round of worrying Jacko as much as possible and finding out what games he had been up to during the night. Each day the advance guard was held up a mile or two closer to Romani. There was no water between Katia and Romani, and once past Katia the invaders would have to strike quickly, for midsummer heat still raged. No attack on the Canal could succeed without command of the water areas at Romani. Around them the decisive battle would be fought—and won.

On its last day out, the Regiment had been held up a little more than half-way to Katia. It could not water either there or at Hamisah, and its bottle supply had to suffice. Outposts sat in the grilling heat with few chances of firing a shot, for Jacko prepared his positions during the night, and he knew enough to find and conceal the best places. Soon after dark the Regiment placed its night posts and began its ride back to camp, but not even dry throats could keep the singing troopers silent once the enemy was well in the rear. There was nothing forced about those songs. Their message to the desert was from men who would not, could not, be beaten. A favourite anthem was "Alexander's Ragtime Band!"

There had been some small outpost clashes around Katia while Jacko was pushing his way in, and in one of them Snow got his third issue—a bullet in the back. For anyone else it would have meant Australia and a discharge. The Bushman's luck still stuck to him, and as he lay down beside his bivvy and tried to get some sleep before "stand-to" came, he wondered what would happen that night to the posts left on the plain between Romani and Katia. Already, some nights previously, an officer had been shot dead by a sniper at close range, and his post had only escaped being cut off by hard riding and good luck. The posts were placed a considerable distance apart, and the horses held a little way behind them. The occasional hoof-stamp, the unavoid- able champing and jingling of bit or stirrup, enabled the Turkish patrol to locate the position of the men in front with fair accuracy. The objective of this outpost line was to report any mass movement of enemy troops, but its value was negligible, and proof of that was given when the post reached Romani on the morning of the battle several hours after it began.

It seemed to the Bushman that he had scarcely closed his eyes before he heard the sound of distant shots. They meant that the other brigade was in action somewhere near the Booby Hatch and that the decisive day had come. He anticipated the stand-to order by a minute or two, and carried his saddle to his tired horse. It had had a good drink on returning to camp, and it was as well. Two thirsty days lay ahead.

The Regiment did not go to the support of the other brigade at once. Instead, men moved into formation and sat dozing at their horses' heads until day broke. Then, for once, they went into action at the gallop. In less than a mile from Et-Maler troops swung together and horses were handed over. Under cover of hollows and sandy outcrops the Regiment advanced on foot to the assistance of the other brigade, which had gallantly and resolutely fought a delaying action since midnight.

They might be delaying Jacko's direct advance on Romani, but he seemed to be having things mostly his own way all the same. So thought the Bushman as he lay behind a little sand hummock and sighted carefully at the advancing Turkish line. He could see bodies of troops moving round the right flank and out of range—apparently their object was to get astride of the railway line and put the defenders of Romani well up in the air. At the moment the air was monopolised by Jacko. His planes were having the time of their lives. They bombed the dumps at the railhead to iheir hearts' content, and artillery seconded them vigorously.

Then the original defending brigade drew out and retired through the supports to its horses. Once it reached them, its retreat out of range must have looked very like rout—to the Turkish observers. Soon it was followed in much the same manner by the remaining brigade, and the way to Romani was apparently left open. As the squadrons in turn galloped away from the pursuing shrapnel, and wheeled behind the dunes skirting the railway line, it did look as if Jacko was scoring a bit of a win—for once.

All that afternoon the Regiment lay flattened on the top of a steep sandhill and watched bodies of Turkish infantry moving to the shelter of palms at the bottom of a hollow surrounded by giant dunes. The heat streamed down pitilessly on to their recumbent bodies, and those who had squandered a precious water ration suffered badly. But the endurance of the Turkish infantry was tested to a far greater degree, and exhaustion beat them. No troops could have made good the hilltops surroundings the trap of the hollow where they had concentrated, and few could even have fought their way to where they did in the face of such adverse conditions. Their retreat was cut off by resolute shrapnel fire, and their flanks were threatened by a Scottish battalion which had marched from the Canal. They made a few half-hearted attempts to force the hilltop where the Regiment lay, but it needed no more than an ordinary barrage of rifle fire to drive them back to cover.

The Bushman became aware of a commotion behind him on the steep slope, but at first all he could see was a cloud of dust. A horseman wearing a helmet and brandishing a stick came galloping towards them, and from one of his legs the end of a blood-stained bandage streamed in the wind. The steeper the rise, the faster he seemed to gallop. It was the new Brigadier.

The feelings of the Regiment had been mixed when, a few months previously, it had been told that a new man was taking-over the brigade—temporarily. Some of the South African veterans who knew him remarked that while he might make manure of the brigade, he certainly wouldn't let it go to sleep. He had paraded each unit in turn and introduced himself. When he told them what gallant fellows they were, they promptly put him down as one more "bulsh" artist, but they pricked up their ears when he assured them that he wasn't particularly concerned with spit and polish. He was a Field Man and he would deliver the goods there and want full measure in return. He had begun by stirring up the outposts in person that same night.

The Bushman didn't know exactly what the technique of a

brigadier's job was, according to the book, but he had seen pictures of a general pinning little flags on a map and surrounded by immaculately dressed staff officers. If that was the proper way of doing things, this galloping fiend must have been all wrong. He seemed to have been everywhere that morning, and on a different horse every time anyone saw him. As fast as his staff found him it lost him again. His camp boast had been no idle one—he was a field man, and fortune could not but favour a leader of field men even to the provision of spectacular moments for his appearance amongst them.

As he urged his tired horse through the line of men lying in shallow sandholes, the firing in the hollow below ceased suddenly and a white flag was hoisted. For a brief moment the Leader watched it in silence. It signalled the surrender of a thousand men, the winning of a battle, the defeat of an army. He turned exultantly and waved his stick to the crouching men as he shouted: "Well done! Well done! You've made history today, lads; you've made history!" Then he galloped on, and the ringing cheers which followed him came from men whose throats were parched but whose hearts knew the thrill of victory. Not one was there amongst them who would cease to treasure that moment while life lasted.

Chapter Twenty-One
Katia - August 1916

At daylight the Horsemen moved off on the tracks of a retreating army, and soon came to the battleground of the previous day. Their rifle fire during the delaying action had not been wasted; they found many dead on the plain behind Wellington ridge, and numbers of abandoned wounded showed the haste of the Turkish retreat. Small bodies of an exhausted and demoralised rearguard surrendered without firing a shot. "Moya, moya!" they called hoarsely as they threw down their rifles; but there was no water to give them. The bottles, full when the battle of Romani began, were empty. It was soon to be the Horsemen's turn to fight with empty stomachs and a raging thirst—at Katia.

The Bushman had been lucky. With a few others he had found his way into a Hod where there was a tiny soakage. The water was brackish and stinking, but he was too thirsty to care. He filled his bottle and a Turkish spare one that he had picked up that morning but before very long both were empty again. When the Regiment halted behind some straggling ridges a few miles from Katia he gave the last few mouthfuls to a boy who had joined the troop a few days before. He could scarcely speak.

The order to dismount was welcome. The sun was nearly overhead, and most men crawled into the patch of shade under their horses. They could no longer fight the craving for sleep; at the risk of being trampled on they huddled on the hot sand and covered their faces. The restless horses would not stand motionless long, and the sleepers woke to find the blinding sun streaming down on them and drawing rivers of sweat from their bodies.

During that long heart-breaking wait tempers snapped

under the strain, for in every mind lay the suspicion that, once more, someone's blunder was being paid for. Two mates quarrelled violently, each accusing the other's horse of disturbing his own and robbing him of a shadow. They agreed to settle the dispute with their fists after accounts had been squared with Jacko.

By midday they had been there for an hour and some men attempted to eat, but without water it was better to go hungry. Away on the right flank they could hear occasional firing and a. few shrapnel bursts showed that the Turkish artillery had been withdrawn well behind Katia. There was now no chance of outflanking the retreating enemy. The sandhills beyond Hamisah were impassable for horses even if they had not been made impregnable by redoubts where a few riflemen could hold up a regiment. And what would be the fate of a frontal attack on Katia on foot?

Another hour passed, and another, and most of the vitality left in the minds and bodies of the men crouching in the sand went with them. It was rumoured that they were waiting for the arrival of another brigade. Then, said the ranker strategists, five mounted brigades were to be launched at Jacko at the extended gallop. The first would keep going until it passed Bir-el-Abd; on the way it would ride over Jacko's artillery and machine-guns and tell him to keep his surrender for those coming behind. Once in possession of the wells of Bir-el-Abd it would wheel and take him in the rear. The other brigades would follow at decent intervals and mop up Katia and Oghritina in their stride. Lastly, all drovers would be called out to muster what was left of Jacko and drive him into the Canal. Not one of him would get away if only—if only enough of the Heads would drop dead to put the Galloping Leader in full command. It would be the greatest mounted charge in history! Seven thousand horsemen thundering across the battleground of all the ages, to complete Victory? The strategists were wrong. Instead they were sent to face the machine-guns in Katia on foot, with thirsty throats and exhausted bodies.

At long last the order came to mount. The Turk was

watching closely, for shrapnel came with the crossing of the first skyline. In extended order the Regiment moved forward at a steady gallop towards Katia, and it reached a low fringe of sandhills not far from the scalded plain before the order was given to close in on the horse-holders.

A few minutes later the line of men doubled from cover to cover, and the Bushman wondered why more of them weren't going down, so accurate was the range of the Turkish artillery. The advance reminded him of the old game of rounders; for the second line had to wait until the first left its base. As they neared the scalded plain the cover became scantier, and from a safe spot behind a hummock the Bushman turned to watch the fortunes of the second line as it approached the position the first had just left.

One man kept going. At first it looked as though he had been crowded off his base, then that he was going for a rounder to put his side in again; but it was only Possum, who seldom stayed with his troop unless it was right in front. The gunners who could hit him had not been left in Katia that day. He had the whole of their fire to himself as he ran, but he flopped down amongst the front line unscathed.

Again the line went forward. The scalded plain was several hundred yards in width, and less than half-way across it an irregular line of sand humps gave the only remaining cover whence a charge could be made on the hidden machine-guns. The ground was hard, and the pace of the men increased, but the shooting did not waver. Flecks of dirt spattered about the Bushman's feet. The man next to him pitched suddenly forward, and, glancing along the line as he ran, he could see others lying still, or attempting to crawl back to the cover they had left. The sand hummocks in front were broken and shallow, and to find shelter men had to draw together and lie flat. The Bushman wondered how many of them could reach the next cover—the palms at Katia? None, unless the Turkish gunners lost their nerve. As the second line closed up in readiness to take part in the final rush, a sergeant fell when a few yards would have seen him to safety. The Bushman joined several others, and between them they dragged him under cover.

They gave him what first aid they could—lying almost flat on the ground, so shallow was the outcrop behind which they had sheltered. They expected that at any moment the order might come for the final charge. Until nearly sundown they lay there, and then the order came—to retire.

The wounded man was suffering badly. Three bullets had passed through his body; he could not even crawl. There were no stretchers, and to carry him to the first line of sandhills in the rear meant crossing a hundred yards of coverless ground. It would need several men to do it, and it could only be done by the grace of the Turkish gunners.

Six men took off their tunics and wrapped them tightly round their rifles. They pushed them under the body of the wounded man, and as they lifted him to a crouching- position one supported his head and another his legs. They knew that. no matter how carefully they stepped, every movement meant agony to the silent figure they carried—not quite silent, for, as they left the cover of the sand hummock the wounded man spoke huskily: "You fellows are Britons to stick to me like this..."

Crouching, swaying, walking almost on each other's spurs, they staggered on. Every moment they expected a burst of fire that would send them down. The Bushman could hear the breath of the man in front of him coming in laboured gasps; he was one of the older men, already grey-haired and worn by life, but he kept doggedly on.

Ahead of them others were retiring, some carrying wounded men pick-a-back, some running from cover to cover, some too exhausted to do other than walk slowly. The setting sun blurred them as a target, and they were widely scattered, but poor visibility could not hide six men moving in a bunch and at a snail's pace. They crossed the dry swamp unscathed, for the Turkish army, too, held its sportsmen.

Only once, as they reached the first small skyline, did a sharp burst of fire scatter sand about them. Then the wounded man spoke again.

"Put me down behind the sandhill and wait for dark.

What's the use of six of you taking chances? You've been good mates."

They moved slowly on in the fast fading light. They soon lost sight of others moving ahead, and could only keep going in the direction of the horses, praying that a sand-cart, had been sent to meet them. No one had breath to spare for speech. At last, in semi-darkness, they came to the horses.

There was no sand-cart there, and no one knew where the Ambulance was. For the third time the wounded man spoke.

"I can hang on if you put me in the saddle."

There was nothing else to do. Slowly, carefully, they lifted him on to his horse's back—the horse he had brought with him from an Australian farm—and he began his last ride. One man rode beside him, another took the reins.

As they disappeared into the darkness the Bushman prayed that when his turn came he might meet it with the same quiet courage.

Chapter Twenty-Two
Leave - September 1916

As a camp, Hill 70 was unpopular, but this time it meant beer, football and leave, so the Regiment welcomed it gladly after spending several weeks hunting Jacko back to where he came from. He hit back once or twice, notably at Bir-el-Abd, but although he had lost on points, the golden chance of a knockout at Katia had been allowed to slip, and he lived to fight again. The second round ended at Mazar.

Leave! And to Alexandria! It was a new city to explore and loot, a relief after Port Said and an improvement even on Cairo. There were more Europeans and fewer Arabs, and one decent pub was actually left in bounds. The Hotel Windsor was well patronised. It was a useful place in more ways than one,

The leave camp was at Sidi Bishr. It lay on the beach beyond Ramleh, and restrictions were light. Leave lasted a week, and a hundred men from each regiment got away together. Snow was still in hospital, so the Bushman mostly hunted by himself.

One day in the Rue Rosette he was hailed by several fellows from his own squadron. They were standing at the doorway of a quite respectable building and trying to arrive at the meaning of a name on a brass plate. The Bushman was invited to translate. The inscription read–"Madame Latour, Sage Femme."

"Fam's woman, any fool knows that," insisted one of the group, "but what's sage? You ought to know. Blood, you're a French scholar."

Somehow the Bushman had acquired the reputation of being one. He certainly remembered more of his school French than most of his troop, but that was little enough. He studied the plate with an air of profound knowledge.

"Sage means wise," he pronounced. "Madame Latour, Wise Woman."

"I thought that was it; she's a fortune-teller," exclaimed another. "Come on, let's go up and get our fortunes told. She might know when the war's going to end. I'll shout for the crowd and Blood'll have to interpret if she can't speak English."

They needed no persuasion. They swarmed up the stairs and knocked boldly at Madame Latour's door. An elderly and stout woman opened it and looked at her visitors suspiciously. She enquired their business in French, of which no one understood a word. From her general appearance the Bushman decided that the meaning of "Sage Femme" wasn't fortune teller whatever else it was, so he dropped to the background and left the dumb crambo to his mates. They made heavy going of it.

"You savvy madame," explained one. He pointed out the lines on his hand and pulled another man's hat off and rubbed what he thought were bumps. "Tell our fortunes; how soon will the blanky war end; and will a bloke get knocked."

Madame came to the conclusion that they had mistaken the Rue Rosette for the "Rabbit Warren"; if they weren't lunatics. Her voice rose ominously. She gesticulated and pointed to the stairway. The Bushman caught a reference to gendarmes and thought that it was time that he took a hand in the comedy. He had remembered at last what "Sage Femme" did mean.

"Mais voyez Madame," he began laboriously. "This mot— 'Sage'? Ces hommes pensent que vous direz les nouvelles—la fortune—quand le guerre finish, and all that. You comprends?"

Madame did—at last. She began to laugh hysterically and called several women from an inner room to enjoy the joke. One of them knew enough English to be able to explain to the puzzled fortune-hunters.

"Madame say," she said as connectedly as her shaking sides would allow, "zat generalement she only attend ze ladies, but zis time if ze case urgent, she make ze exception. Which soldat—?"

A yell of laughter interrupted her. They understood now and turned the joke on to their interpreter. They grabbed the grinning Bushman and pushed him into Madame's arms.

"*This* is the one, Madame," they howled. "Tres malade. Nine months since he go to Cairo on leave. You savvy Marcelle—the ex-Continental? Tres malade—Madame—etwin. You make him pay double."

They rushed downstairs and spent some minutes recovering on the pavement, but it was a long time before the squadron stopped making kind enquiries about the date of the Bushman's party. At last they decided to see what the Rue Rosette dancing palace was made of. They had heard glowing accounts of it, but so they bad of a certain Number Six, which proved on investigation to be the Mahomet Ali Club!

"It's somewhere about here," said one. "Perhaps the fams' there mightn't be quite so 'sage.' We can get a beer, anyhow."

They found it at last, and went in expecting to find dancing provided as a show, but it seemed that you did your own, and if you didn't bring a partner there were plenty to be picked up on the premises. Several couples had the floor, and from a corner another draft from the squadron shouted an invitation to join their party.

"Plenty of room boys," said one. "Here—ya Wallad—five more 'beeras'—igri."

"Aren't you going to introduce the girls, Joe?" asked the Bushman as he sat down.

"Sorry. Yes, of course. This is 'Bluey'—talks every language but English; especially 'feloos'. And this is—er—'Gunboat Smith'! And of course you all know Fluffy, the wife of the regiment. If you don't—soon—it'll be your own fault. She heard the regiment was on leave and came up to hold a reunion. Everyone's invited. Special taxis to the Windsor—afterwards."

"Bluey" was dressed in blue—hence her nickname. She might have had Greek ancestors. "Gunboat Smith" might have been anything, but she looked torpedo-proof. Fluffy claimed to be "dinkum Parisiennne." She took an interest in the Bushman at once, he being about the only member of the party whose acquaintance she hadn't already made in Cairo. She insisted that Joe should take a snap of the whole group, and as the shutter clicked the Bushman, who was squatting on the floor, found a shapely Parisienne leg dangling over his shoulder.

Joe still has the negative, holding it as evidence against a decently unmarried man.

Chapter Twenty-Three
Sinai - December 1916

For the rest of the autumn the Regiment wandered from camp to camp in Sinai, and in December it split up into squadrons and took over positions on the flank facing the desolate regions leading towards Akaba, where barren ranges could not even accumulate sand. Jacko had fallen back on to the fringes of the Promised Land, but although he was a hundred miles away, outposts and patrols were done just as religiously as if he had been across the road.

The Bushman's squadron finally pulled up at Mageibra. There were a few tents available, but far from sufficient to accommodate all hands, so bivvies had to be manufactured from hessian and ground-sheets—excellent substitutes in summer, but of little use when the sands of the desert did at last grow cold. Occasionally a few clouds drifted across the sky, but the weather prophets laughed at the idea of rain. It never rained in Sinai. So argued Snow as he sat with the Bushman outside their bivvy watching the sky actually become overcast. The Bushman wasn't so sure. He reckoned he had bought sheep at home on the strength of far less likely looking clouds, and advised Snow to wire for the firm offer of all the goats for sale in Sinai.

Then it began to rain. The Bushman ran with his quartpot to the nearest sand-hummock and embedded it firmly. He knew that there couldn't be more than one fail in Sinai, and he was curious to find out what the annual rainfall was. As he stood watching his gauge, he heard wild shouts in the hollow below the camp, and looked round to see Snow doubling for the horse-line? The novelty of water from the sky was too much for the discipline of the horses. Four rows of them were bucking, rearing and squealing with excitement. The anchors and built-up ropes, ample for the needs of everyday, couldn't stand the strain. They gave way in a dozen places at once, and whole troops of horses came to earth in the weirdest tangles. A few made a complete get-away and circled the camp triumphantly with up lifted heads and tails and defiant strides. By the time they were recaptured and new lines put down, the lone storm was over. The Bushman measured the contents of his gauge carefully. Allowing ten per cent. loss through splash, he estimated that the annual rainfall at Mageibra was 47 points!

Christmas came and its feast more than made up for the famine of 1915 on the Beltana. Seven-pound tins of plum pudding were placed on issue, and after awhile they went begging. Parcels poured in from home—it was impossible to get ahead of the "mungeree" on hand, and experience had shown how useless it was to hoard up anything but tea and sugar. There was panic in the camp when rumours of an early move ran round and everyone doubled up at every feed until the supply was lightened to a carrying weight. Once this point was reached, men breathed thankfully, if less freely. At least they would not be compelled to leave good "mungeree" for the Bedouins.

When not doing outposts or patrols the squadron passed its time at two-up and poker—and football. Orders came out that everyone was to play, and for once orders were popular. Each troop ran two seven-a-side teams, and fifteen-minute spells in ankle-deep sand were enough to provide exercise and fitness. Squadrons, and finally regiments, played matches in the centrally situated ground at Hassaniya.

Snow had joined up again at Mageibra, and this time his return was quite in order. He neither stowed away nor deserted, but how he managed to persuade a medical board to pass him as fit for duty remained a mystery. When the Bushman had a look at his back he swore that the members of that board must have been blind drunk. There were holes in the still contracted muscles, which made Snow move, for once, with the stiff precision of a Guardsman. He couldn't bend at all, but he insisted on playing football. The Bushman—now senior corporal in the troop, forbade such lunacy sternly, and threatened to parade him if he persisted; but Snow only laughed at him and reminded him of the time when he had been a worse fool on the Peninsula. Eventually the stiffness in his back wore off, but not before he had invented a new way of going down on the ball. He sat on it.

The football ground at Mageibra had a natural grandstand—a steep sandhill rising from one side-line. One afternoon it was packed and the camp over the hill absolutely deserted. Not even a picquet stayed with the horses, and Jacko, if he had been about, could have helped himself to the whole outfit. A. and B. were playing C. and D. That in itself wouldn't have been a special draw, but someone, somehow, had kidded the major into playing. The chance of laying profane and violent hands on a senior officer without the certainty of facing a firing squad afterwards was one that seldom came along and twenty-nine men lined up fully determined to make the major eat a full issue of sand for once. The referee, too, was thoroughly with them. The squadron, packed on the hillside, waited with mouths open ready to cheer.

It wasn't easy, all the same. The major had taken care to insist on a place in the three-quarter line, and he showed surprising speed. He took no chances of being caught with the ball. In vain his own side fed him at likely moments and the opposition left tempting gaps and chances of a score. At last a forward, loafing offside, found an opportunity and the referee's blind eye. He not only dumped the major, but he seemed unable to let him go. In twos and threes both sides packed sacks on the mill and churned up a small sandstorm in the process. Snow, who was playing full-back, sprinted in desperate fear of being too late, and so did his opposite number from the other end of the field. With mighty bounds in the air they dived and collided on top of at least twenty-seven other joyful souls.

Chapter Twenty-Four
Palestine - March 1917

News came through of Magdaba and Rafa and of further exploits of the Galloping Leader—now in command of another brigade. The Regiment grew restless; it had had more than enough of playing at the job with the business end of the front a hundred miles away, and it hailed with satisfaction the day when the scattered squadrons came together again at Hassaniya. Soon afterwards the brigade began the long and leisurely ride which took it out of Sinai for ever.

Once beyond Salmana, the desert slowly faded out, and with every mile came a fresh promise of something different ahead. There was more life in the stunted scrub, and rough grasses grew in the hollows; there were even occasional fig trees and flocks of goats shepherded by ancient Bedouins. Springtime poppies by the wayside made men whistle and sing and jump off to grab a buttonhole.

The Regiment camped for a few days at Masaid—the first of the seaside resorts which did so much to lighten the third year of the war. There was an inspection, but it was an easy one. A famous cavalry general wanted to get an informal close-up of the units, which acted like soldiers even if they never looked the part. When the Regiment's turn came, it stood to attention in front of its horses while the general, accompanied by their colonel and a few lesser lights, rode slowly along the lines. The Bushman—now a sergeant—stood at the end of his troop, and it happened that he was the shortest of the half-dozen men on either side of him. Big Bill, the farrier, stood six foot three and weighed fifteen stone. When the general saw Bill he shook his head sorrowfully and remarked to the colonel:

"You know, Colonel, it's not fair to ask horses to carry such men. They're too big. If these are Light Horsemen, I'd be curious to see your country's idea of a Heavy Dragoon. My own opinion is that a cavalryman's weight should be limited to nine stone four!" After a moment's pause he went on: "I've often watched your fellows drilling; they can stick on all right, but, my dear Colonel, they can't *ride*."

The colonel swallowed the first part of the indictment in silence, but the second was too much for him. It must have taxed his self-restraint severely, but he managed to keep certain customary nouns and adjectives out of his reply.

"Well Sir," he retorted, "I've often watched your fellows drilling. They may be able to ride, but they can't stick on!"

Nine stone four! That, thought the Bushman, would rule out everyone above Jockey-weight. The general's theory seemed to be that a heavy man necessarily rode heavy. He wished he could have shown him the nuggety little brown horse standing on the lines behind Big Bill. It had carried him right through the desert, and when Bill included an emergency kit of tools in his full marching order, he rode over twenty stone. But he was a horseman. The Bushman had to go through a few Schools of Instruction before he learnt that most cavalrymen, even generals, had been taught to "ride," which, was probably why so many of them couldn't "stick on,"

Masaid had already been a camping ground for several other brigades, and firewood was desperately scarce. Everything which wasn't green or wet, or thoroughly nailed down, had been burnt, and the resource of the Horsemen was put to severe tests. One sergeant was placed under arrest for allowing his troop to bring home a load of telegraph poles, and only his record saved his stripes. Snow turned up one night with a "single seater" on his back. He had souvenired it from B.H.Q., and he called on his troop to help him convert it into matchwood before necessity made some Staff Bird discover its disappearance.

That single-seater was nailed, bolted and rivetted together in a way that did credit to its builders. In vain the troop dashed it on the ground and jumped on it. It defied them. Then, with bayonets, they tried to split some of the boards, but cast-iron had a straighter grain. The lid and a few splinters—about enough to boil a quart—were all that they could salvage, and, with ingratitude as rank as the single-seater, they told Snow to take the stinking thing back to where he got it. Snow had no intention of risking a court-martial on a charge of destroying Government property. He dumped the scarred corpse of the single-seater near the officers' mess, and a few days later routine orders contained an acrimonious paragraph. The brigade was told that "such practices must cease."

From another camp beyond El Arish the regiment saddled up for its last ride in Sinai. At dark, men were still riding over loose sand and through stunted scrub, but they knew that some time during the night they would cross into another Continent—the third in which they would campaign. It started a heated geographical discussion—whether Sinai was in Africa or Asia- Wasn't the Canal the real boundary? In the course of the argument Snow forgot two things: that "no smoking" had been passed back, and that the colonel of another regiment was riding a few yards behind him. He lit a cigarette, and after exactly two draws his name was taken. They ultimately cost him seventeen and sixpence each, and "Onslow" cigarettes were thenceforth voted the most expensive brand on the market.

The change from sand to soil came very gradually, but not long before daylight the Bushman could feel the difference in his horse's stride. It was firm, with spring in it; the rolling gait was gone. He could no longer see scrub by the roadside, but he had to lean over from the saddle to convince himself that he was riding through grass—something he had not seen since leaving Australia. The swish of it was music; he looked forward to the daylight halt when he would be able to unbit and let his horse enjoy real food. He wondered if he would see any grasses he knew, and the thought of Queensland and waist-high Mitchell grass gave him a catch in the throat.

Daylight came, and to men who had sometimes despaired of ever seeing the end of the sands of Sinai, it was like the dawn of paradise. The country was undulating; it was green, and horses tugged impatiently at their bits in their eagerness to taste grass once more. Around the patches of young crops poppies showed in splashes of scarlet, and the Horsemen passed a mud hut with melon vines and tomato plants thriving inside the sod-wall enclosure. There were orchards of apricot trees laden with young fruit. Skylarks rose from beside the road and fluttered upwards, singing. At sunrise the order came to dismount, and the Bushman solemnly rolled in the green grass. He had done that before, after the break of an old-man drought in Australia.

The Regiment's first camp in Palestine was at Sheikh Zowaid, and a two-mile strip along the ocean was still Sinai—in character. There were places where you could stand with one foot on raw sand and the other on grassed soil. Had the sand ever been soil, or the soil sand? The water on the beach provided an even more baffling problem. The soakage m a trench dug a few feet from the ocean's edge was fresh, and horses drank with their hind feet in the Mediterranean.

There were patrols to do, and reconnaissances. New names and new places became familiar. Occasionally there were villages to explore, and in Khan Yunus there was even a shopping centre. Beyond Sheikh Nuran the regiment discovered Jacko's famous "pepper pots." Being short of barbed wire, he had gone to the trouble of digging miles of holes in the ground; they were five feet in depth and three in diameter, and they lay in diagonal lines— too wide for a horse to jump over and too close together to allow a track across. The soil had been spread flat on either side, giving no warning of the trap to horsemen moving at the gallop; but Jacko never had the pleasure of seeing a regiment floundering in it. He was threatened from a flank and forced to abandon the positions it protected without firing a shot.

His front line now followed the hills linking Gaza and Beer-Sheba, and No-man's Land lay in the stretch of country between the Ghuzze and the Imleh.

Chapter Twenty-Five
Gaza - March 1917

The Regiment soon moved to Shunnar, but wherever it patrolled it stubbed its toes on other units, for there were camps along the beach from Sheikh Zowaid to Belah, and troops for miles. Then it was rumoured that an infantry division was on its way from the Canal, and that seemed to show that the Horsemen weren't going to be asked to do all the work any longer.

"Just as well, too," remarked Snow. The squadron was returning from a patrol which had enabled it to get a good look at the country between the Wadi and Gaza, and it dismounted beside the road as the infantry marched by. For miles across the Wadi the country sloped gently up to Jacko's redoubts, and the ground was littered with small stones, just big enough to make a bullet ricochet nicely. "But, I say, Blood! Who are these coves. They sound like a lot of galahs in a dead tree over a dry waterhole."

The Bushman made a shot at it. "They're not Chinamen, so they must be Welsh. Soon find out. Hey! 'Sieeda,' Taffy!"

Some of them replied at once. They were a likely looking lot, young, fresh and eager, but it was their last march as a Division. There are five thousand graves in the cemetery at Gaza and Welshmen fill most of them.

At two o'clock the Horsemen were astir, and an hour later they rode out into thick fog. Men could see those next to them and the rumps of the horses immediately in front. They moved slowly across the wide and broken approaches to the Wadi, and halted many times until the column was safely on the farther side. Silence was broken only by the click of horseshoes on the metal lying loosely on the scaly hillsides. There was no delay, no losing touch; the leader of the column that day knew his Job, and the fog must have tested him severely. Instead of clearing soon after daylight it persisted until well into the forenoon. It helped the men on horseback, but it was fatal to those on foot, for it robbed them of several precious hours. No attack could be launched until it lifted.

Before the first shots were fired the Horsemen had put a cordon round Gaza. They met no opposition, for Jacko simply didn't think it could be done. Long before midday a ring of strong posts held all the high ground commanding the approaches behind Gaza, and probably the most surprised man in Palestine that day was the Turkish general, who was quietly arrested by a section while driving along the beach road towards the town. The corporal scored a D.C.M., and his men a case of oranges from the back of the general's gharri.

The Bushman sat with his troop on a ridge from which he could see the outskirts of Gaza. The frontal redoubts were hidden from sight, but continuous rifle and shell fire soon proclaimed that the Welshmen were in action. If their attack succeeded, the mounted troops were to pour into the town from the rear, although their main job was to hold off any possible reinforcements. None threatened any of the positions the Regiment held, so its part in the first battle of Gaza didn't cost it a single casualty.

There was one distant redoubt which the Bushman could see plainly through his glasses. It commanded the left flank of the Turkish line and for some time it seemed to be out of things. Then, shell after shell burst over it; but they could have been saved, for Jacko knew how to dig shrapnel-proof redoubts as well as the next man. Nothing but high explosive would have been of any help to the gallant Welshmen who tried to storm that position.

The Bushman watched them advancing. They moved slowly in extended order up the slope towards the redoubt, and he calculated that they had a good mile to go before they could begin to put up an argument. For awhile Jacko ignored them;

he was lying low and probably praying to Allah to send a few more. To the distant onlooker the trap was obvious. When the Welshmen had half-a-mile or more of coverless ground behind them, Jacko would open out.

Suddenly he did. From carefully-hidden positions machine-guns swept the advancing line, the gunners laughing at the shrapnel which still broke vainly over their heads. The Welshmen came on at the double. They took what they hoped was cover, but none of them got within hundreds of yards of the redoubt. In a few minutes it was over. The Turkish gunners could see no living thing to fire at.

Darkness came before the sounds of battle dwindled to an occasional shell burst, but still the Regiment remained where it had been posted. It was obvious that the attack on Gaza had failed, and rumours spread that time was precious if the Horsemen wanted to see the safe side of the Wadi again. They wondered at the delay, not knowing that a troop was temporarily missing and that the brigadier refused to move until every man in his command was accounted for.

It was midnight before the Regiment mounted. Until then the Bushman had kept his sense of direction, but he soon lost it, and so did most others except those close to the front of the column. Its leader followed a cable laid on the outward journey, but, steadily as he moved, the broken ground made it impossible for the column to do the same. Slowing down over a gully meant increasing Speed once across in an attempt to regain touch, and often it was a case of hang on, trust your horse and back your luck. Of all the night rides the Regiment ever made, the one from behind Gaza was the wildest and weirdest.

In the dust and darkness any sort of order was scarcely possible. Men often only knew they were in touch only when their horses pulled up with a jerk on the rumps of those in front of them. The column passed through stretches of country pitted with Bedouin grain cisterns, empty and uncovered, and only one horse came to grief.

The Bushman and Snow managed to keep together somehow, with the latter outside. Suddenly Snow's horse swerved violently inwards from the edge of a cistern, but someone pressing closely behind was not so lucky. The horse propped too late. In its attempt to jump the cavern it could only succeed in planting its front feet on the farther side, and slid down rump first, carrying its rider unhurt to the bottom.

Without help from overhead the man was safely trapped. Even when standing on the saddle he was unable to reach the stone coping of the cistern's edge. He couldn't have climbed the wall in daylight. His horse would have become a choice prize for some Arab and his disappearance a mystery until reported a prisoner-of-war. But someone thought he saw a horse disappear in the dust, and pulled up to investigate. His resounding shout stopped others.

They made a rope of bridle reins and soon drew the man to safety, but it would have needed hours of work with pick and shovel to rescue the horse. The only thing that could be done for it, they did. A rifle shot made sure that it would never endure the misery of being owned by an Arab.

Just before the second attempt on Gaza, the Horsemen heard stories of a new engine of war about to be let loose on Jacko. It seemed too good to be true. Snow settled ail doubts by bribing his way into a closely-guarded Tommy camp hidden in the thickest of palm groves. He came back to the lines like a child who had been shown a delightful new toy but not allowed to play with it.

"They'll do the trick this time," he assured his troop. "There's three of 'em. They'll amble into Gaza before Jacko gets over the shock. Hope I'll be where I can see 'em in action."

But he wasn't. The Regiment spent a couple of days before the attack in "demonstrating" near Hareira. There was no gaily riding round Gaza this time. When the attack was finally launched, the Regiment was in reserve, and it waited by its horses ready to go into action if called on. It waited most of the day in boredom until three Jacko planes discovered the scattered groups of horses and men. Then, for awhile the Regiment had a small war all to itself. Every available rifle lent a hand to keep those planes at a respectful height, and all Jacko had to show for his bombs was one wounded horse. His aim was atrociously bad.

Withdrawal took place at sundown and once more the Regiment was spared its issue of resultless slaughter; but as it rode away in line of troop column, Jacko's artillery woke up. With his first shot he got a direct hit which made splinters of an ambulance waggon and its men and horses.

There was no need to call for stretcher-bearers, for four men were already racing the second shell to the wreckage. One made it a head-heat and the squadron muttered "Good-bye, John!" as the H.E. lifted horse and rider in a cloud of dust and smoke. The horse crumpled, but a second later the bearer was seen dragging a wounded man clear of the smashed cart. Not even a splinter had found him.

The Regiment got back to camp tired and dispirited. The second round at Gaza had failed as dismally as the first. Someone asked Snow how the tanks had fared. Snow laughed.

"One never got into action at all, and the others are scrap-iron on the ridge where Samson's ghost walks. They'll do him to hang on his watch chain."

Chapter Twenty-Six
Palestine - May 1917

A few weeks spent in camps along the Wadi made the Horsemen wish that they had never left the desert. By the end of May the face of the country had been pulverised into fine dust, and whichever way a column rode, the wind seemed to chase it. Only officers and N.C.O.'s privileged to ride outside the line could dodge a twice-daily issue.

Snow rode in from watering parade with four bottles round his neck and a bucket on either foot. His face was grey, and he spat out part of Palestine. Presently the Bushman joined him. He, too, had been on the watering parade, but his face was clean.

Snow's little peculiarities had made him one of the squadron-leader's outlaws, and he was regularly passed over when promotions were going. He was quite happy as a trooper until "Nat Goulds" began to come out in routine orders as lance-jacks, and then his stripeless sleeve chafed.

"Stripes are handy sometimes, Blood, aren't they?" he said. "Next time I go to a war I'll be a good soldier. I won't stowaway, or desert either."

"And don't go telling a sergeant that he isn't fit to hold one stripe, let alone three. That's not the way to make your marble good."

The advice was injudicious.

"Your marble isn't too good just now, anyway," retorted Snow. "You'll do your stripes if you go 'magnoon' again— like you did at Fara."

The Bushman shut up. It was a sore point, for he had gone "magnoon" and he knew it. He had been given a simple job to do with a section, and had gone miles too far, blundering right into the teeth of a troop of Jacko's cavalry and necessitating the despatch of half a squadron to salvage him. He had been spared the orderly-room, but had been well ticked off by his troop-officer and squadron-leader. He changed the subject tactfully.

"Well, let's hope we'll stay here for a bit, anyway. Anything's better than fourteen camps in thirteen nights, like we've had lately."

Snow soon recovered his good humour.

"Remember the night we changed camp twice? When we pulled off our saddles the second time B. was next to us and the major was just about done in. He picked a place for his doss, but while he was away for something the captain's batman lit a fire on it, and when the major came back he made it worse by offering him a drink of tea. 'Take it away,' he says. 'Take it away. Your batman's lit the fire just where I was going to sleep. Take the tea away.' Then I heard one of the fellows praying to Gawd to come down and lead them, and I offered to swap squadron-leaders. 'No, by Gawd' he says. 'You can keep yours.'"

What sort of a squadron-leader would you like?" asked the Bushman.

"One with as much fight in him as this cove," answered Snow. He went to the corner of the dugout and gazed fondly into the depths of a biscuit tin. "He must be getting hungry, Blood. I'll have to get something to exercise him."

The biscuit tin imprisoned an outsize in spiders—unlike any spider seen outside Palestine. It had a cigar-shaped body a couple of inches in length and covered with fine grey fluff. Its legs were short and its jaws had serrated teeth. Someone—no war history records whom—discovered that if two of the breed were placed together in close confinement they would fight to a finish. They were specially plentiful at Sha-uth, and every unit had its grand champion which held the title by the right of its annihilation of all pretenders. The Regiment's representative was owned by "Possum," and that morning it had cleaned up its opposite number in a neighbouring brigade before an audience which included brigadiers and colonels. Possum came back with a pocketful of notes and had challenged the whole spider world of Palestine on behalf of his champion.

Snow came back with a jam-tin and a disconsolate air.

"Couldn't find any," he said; "but he can exercise himself on these."

He emptied the jam-tin on to the ground and recaptured a cricket before it scuttled away. The spider was waiting with open jaws as he dropped it into the tin. The result was a speedily disembowelled cricket.

"Savage, isn't he?" said the delighted Snow. A couple of scarab beetles went the way of the cricket, and he cleaned the corpses from the tin to clear the ring for the big event. "Now, you old tiger, see what you can make of this fellow."

He dropped in a monster scorpion. It had claws and shell like those of a lobster, and an evil-looking tail and sting. Snow felt some anxiety—it was the first time. he had matched his champion with a scorpion.

He needn't have worried. The spider was as scientific as he was savage. He ducked and side-stepped, and put the scorpion out of action at once by chopping off its sting with one snap. Then he proceeded to make mincemeat of everything but the shell, and prowled round the tin looking for fresh victims. Snow was starting out to find some more, but the Bushman stopped him.

"Don't overwork him," he said. "He might strain a muscle. He'll be worth a few hundred piastres to us if we take him steady."

He was right. Perhaps the Grand Champion hadn't properly recovered from the strain of his brigade contest, but Snow's candidate made short work of him.

From Sha-uth the Regiment moved to Marakeb. There was nothing to do there except look after the horses, and the beach lay only a few yards from the bivvies. No one wore a shirt even at rifle inspection, and for three precious weeks the Regiment enjoyed a real loaf.

For the first time since the days of Romani the sergeants ran to a mess, and even a canteen. The Bushman built himself a luxurious bivvy, and lying there half-naked one afternoon, after a morning in the Mediterranean, he came to the conclusion that this was the best of all wars. The mess was a particularly happy family, from "Sherry" the sar-major downwards. A new recruit in a temporary farrier-sergeant had just come up from the squadron. He was to be initiated that evening.

"You know, Joe," Sherry told him, "you've got to shout for everyone who comes into the mess at least once the first night. It cost me five hundred piastres when I put up three stripes. With the mob that's here you'll be lucky if you get off under a thousand."

Joe took fright. "Not me," he said. "I'll shout for the squadron fellows, but that's all. I've only got fifty piastres, anyway."

"That don't matter, Joe," a chorus of voices reassured him. "We square up every week-end, and we get paid on Saturday."

Joe was obstinate. "I'll shout for the squadron fellows," he repeated, "but no one else."

"Now look here, Joe." Sherry's voice was reproachful. "Surely you're not going to get the regiment a bad name? What's a few hundred piastres to a man who likes beer? Why, you told us that you ratted the kid's money-box at home to buy a bottle."

After tea that night Joe was initiated with much ceremony, but some hours later he had to be helped to his bivvy and put to bed. If his heart was hard, his head was soft, but he turned up for breakfast next morning. Sherry shook his hand warmly.

"Congratulations, Joe," he said. "Never seen a new hand stand up to it better. Every mess on the front's talkin' about the way you poured it down their necks. I knew you would."

At that moment the canteen sergeant took his place at the table. He had some slips of paper in his hand.

"Sorry to have to bite you chaps before pay-day," he said, "but last night Just about cleaned the mess out, and I've got to send away an order this morning. Got to send the 'feloos' with it too. Here's your accounts to date. I want to collect on 'em before stables."

Everyone pretended to pull a long face, but turned away at the sight of Joe's. There was no pretence about his.

"'Ere! What's this?" he stuttered. "Eleven hundred and twenty piastres! I never——"

"Oh yes, you did, Joe," interrupted Sherry; "but you was too shot to remember. All the fellows from the Fifth came along, and then the Seventh, and then the Enzeds. You shouted three or four times for the whole crowd. Don't you remember Jock tried to stop you? He said it was all right to wet your stripes, but you told him yours was as good as his and you'd drown 'em if you wanted to."

By this time everyone had himself well in hand, and after a glance at the serious faces round the table Joe pushed away his plate and got up.

"All right," he said in a shaking voice. "If that's the way you rob coves in this mess. I'm goin' back to the lines. An'——an' you can parade me to the major before I'll pay it."

There was a rest camp near Marakeb, established for those on the border-line of a sick parade. Each sergeant got instructions to send his worst cases there, but the Bushman had no need to study his troop roll. He had one man who gave him a continuous headache. How this old nuisance had ever been passed into the army was a mystery. What hair he had was nearly white, and he owned up to a grandson fighting in France. He wouldn't take on a soft job of any kind; he was there as a trooper in the line, and no sergeant was going to shift him. The difficulty was to fit him into a section, for he had the natural crankiness of old age when it came to living and working with youngsters. At last, in desperation the Bushman put him leading a packhorse, but on the ride back from Khalasa the old chap knocked up. When the move to Marakeb came, the Bushman ordered him to the Rest Camp without delay. After two days of it he came back.

"You sent me there to get rid of me," he snapped. "Next thing they'll send me to hospital, and after that they'll send me home. Well, I'm stopping here, and you can put me in the orderly-room if you like."

The Bushman gave him best.

There were stadiums, Y.M.C.A.'s and two-up schools at Marakeb, but the announcement of a lecture by the old padre from D.H.Q. was enough to thin the attendance at all three places of amusement. His lectures usually dealt with local geographical or historical features, and when it became known that he was to deal with Samson and Delilah, the ring-keeper at the school had to roll up the blankets.

There was scarcely a shirt to be seen on one back as the crowd sat down on the sand round the hummock where the padre stood. The ocean breeze was soft and warm, and it seldom changed temperatures until after midnight. The padre began with a picture of what that part of Palestine looked like when the Wade Ghuzze was a mighty flowing river, and offered an explanation why it had died. According to him, the Philistines were a much maligned tribe. Their activities were mainly those of the old Scottish raiders and the ancient fortresses of Jemmi and Fara were proof that they had kept the Pharaohs of the day busy. He dealt at length with the legends surrounding Samson, and gave Delilah a severe handling. When question time came he was asked to settle a bet. Was it not a fact that Delilah was, in private life, a noted Cairo prostitute? The crowd waited eagerly for the answer, but the padre had one ready.

"Well," he said, "history is silent on that point, so you'll have to call the bet off. But," he added, "there is quite satisfactory proof that there are ninety thousand Delilahs in Cairo to-day, so next time you go on leave you had better be careful. I know it's no use telling you to be good!"

A favourite pastime at Marakeb was catching the spy, or trying to. The rumour ran that one of Jacko's secret service aces was working in the neighbourhood disguised alternately as a

Bedouin "bint" and a Tommy staff captain. and that a D.C.M. awaited the man who grabbed him. No one succeeded in landing either the spy or the decoration, but Sergeant "Magnoon" made a praiseworthy attempt.

He was returning to camp with a section when he saw someone approaching who answered the description perfectly—a Tommy captain wearing red tabs. The officer was rather surprised at getting a salute; he was astounded when he found his path barred by four troopers. Sergeant "Magnoon" requested him courteously to disclose his identity and state the business that brought him into that particular area.

From bewilderment the staff captain waxed sarcastic, and then furious, but Sergeant "Magnoon" held firmly to the attitude of a good soldier determined to carry out a painful duty. He was sure that the captain, if he was a British staff officer, would be the first to admit that he, Sergeant "Magnoon," was bound by his oath of allegiance to King George the Fifth to let slip no chance of arresting the notorious spy whose devilish work was costing His Majesty the lives of so many of his devoted soldiers. Once more he must request the captain to accompany him quietly to the orderly room. Most sincerely he hoped that he would not be compelled to use force.

No one knew what happened in the orderly-room, but some hours later that staff captain left the officers' mess convinced that if that regiment kept mad sergeants it also kept a good brand of whisky. The colonel's groom saw him home, partly to make sure that he wasn't molested by other lunatics, but mostly to see that he didn't fall off his horse.

Chapter Twenty-Seven
Palestine - July 1917

Urgani came next. As camps went, It was an improvement on most of them, if only for the reason that it was within easy distance of the reservoir at Shellal, and water was plentiful. But the daily job lay beyond the Wadi, and there was no escape from the dust blanket of its broken gullies. Once on the other side the country changed; it was firmer and littered with loose stone. Ridges rose in gradually increasing height all the way to the Imleh, and those fronting it were steep. No-man's Land ended there, and Jacko's snipers hidden in the broken ground across the dry bed were active and accurate by day. By night, however, they seemed to go to sleep, and that may have been why one squadron of the regiment went exploring on foot right to the gates of Hareira and got back safely.

The Bushman's troop had the job of maintaining some sort of contact between the explorers and the horses, left in the Wadi bed. For awhile the troop brought up the rear; then it halted and divided, the officer taking charge of one half and the Bushman the other. If Jacko had had any sort of listening post within half-a-mile of the route the squadron took, he must have heard it, for a step-dancer could scarcely have picked his way over the loose stones in the dark without kicking some of them.

Eventually the Bushman stationed his half-troop on the side of a sharp rise. Below, a hundred yards away, a well-worn road passed beween the post and the Imleh, leading towards Beersheba. The men lay side by side facing the road, and their orders were to remain silent and motionless. Before half-an-hour had passed they heard a camel train coming from the direction of Gaza, and its drivers were making all the confident noise of a column well behind the line. It passed within a stone's throw of the motionless troopers in happy ignorance; but the Bushman didn't feel at all happy. A specially observant Jacko might have noticed something arranged about what looked like a row of boulders, and he waited for a safe chance to pull his line a bit further back.

He waited in vain. The tail of the column had scarcely passed before he heard another coming not far behind, and an almost continuous procession lasted for over an hour. At last all sounds of road traffic died away, and the Bushman was about to rearrange his post when another and far more ominous noise came distinctly from half-left. There was no mistaking the contact of iron and metal. The horsemen abroad could only be Turkish, and the line of their movement was directly on to his flank. Unless the patrol wheeled it would pass within a few yards of the post.

The Bushman had strict orders; no firing unless actually attacked. He passed a whispered order to keep still, and crawled quickly to where the Hotchkiss section lay. He had time to move the gunner to face the approaching patrol and the rest of his men to a half-left position before a troop of cavalry crossed the opposite crest.

The road below curved slightly, and just across it stood a small stone hut, evidently a point of rendezvous, for the patrol halted there and waited until it was joined by a couple of sections which had made a detour. They were so close that in the starlight greys could be picked out from chestnuts. One good burst from the Hotchkiss could have put that troop of cavalry out of action, and only that it would have imperilled the squadron further out, the Bushman might have wished that Jacko had better eyesight. As it was, all he asked was that the patrol would quietly ride in the opposite direction.

Jacko, however, was in no hurry, and when two men dismounted and walked across the road, it looked as if the game was up. They crossed in front of the silent line, stopped, sat down, lit cigarettes and began to yarn. There must have been a joke in it somewhere, for one Jacko laughed heartily, unaware that he was covered by half-a-dozen rifles less than fifty yards away. At length they threw away their cigarettes and walked leisurely back to their horses.

The Bushman heard an order given, and felt mightily relieved when the patrol wheeled well to the left. Just as welcome was the appearance soon afterwards of a messenger with an order to rejoin the rest of the troop at once. When at last they got back to the horses he felt much as he had on the night of the Evacuation.

Perhaps Jacko saw traces of the expedition by next day's light; at any rate something stung him into showing that two could play at that game. He brought a light battery overnight within range of the Wadi, and gave several camps an unaccustomed shock. Every regiment within coo-ee went out after that battery, but Jacko was good at the game of tip and run. The battery was safely back behind the Imleh before most of the regiments had crossed the Wadi. and all they could do was to provide it with more target practice. After awhile they retired, somewhat disgruntled, and the Regiment, which brought up the rear, came in for the last few shells. The shooting was poor, but the Horsemen felt anything but comfortable. Snow pointed to the troop in front of him at the moment when something was shrieking directly overhead.

"Makes you feel it's going to get you fair between the shoulder blades, doesn't it, Blood? Look at those blokes."

Everyone was apparently thinking the same. With each swish there was a slight sway forward, and the timing was perfect. No physical jerks instructor could have asked for anything more unanimous.

Patrolling between the Wadis became the old game of going as far as Jacko's outposts would allow and then sitting down and exchanging shots which fell a few hundred yards short. It was different on the ridges fronting the Imleh, and the Bushman's troop spent one disastrous day there. Hill 630 was the most dangerous spot to outpost along the line. It overlooked the Imleh and its top was flat and coverless, but there was even more risk on the steep and apparently safe slope behind. Snipers could "howitzer" it from top to bottom.

The first section for duty climbed safely to the top from a flank and flattened itself on the bare ground behind a small rocky outcrop. It was safe there as long as it lay very low. There was nothing to be seen in the broken gullies opposite, for the snipers were well hidden. They didn't waste shots at the hilltop; instead they concentrated on the reverse slope. Their bullets skimmed the skyline and dropped with deadly accuracy to the gully in the rear.

The troop-leader had a soldier's fault of over-conscientiousness, and it cost him his life that day. The first section had been relieved, but it had scarcely rejoined the troop before continuous bursts of firing sounded from across the Wadi- They made the officer uneasy about the position of the post. He climbed the hill from the flank and crawled safely to where the men lay, remaining with them for half-an-hour. Everything by then was quiet.

The Bushman, left in charge of the troop, watched the hilltop through his glasses, and at last he made out the officer crawling slowly away from the post. Instead of coming back by the flank, he continued straight ahead, and when half-way down the slope he stood. Almost at once the firing began again.

The Bushman saw him fall. He shouted an order for the M.O. and a sand-cart, and galloped with a section to a sheltered spot on the flank. They crawled to where the officer lay; they found him alive, but his face was drawn in pain.

"Keep down, you men," he gasped as they dragged him behind the cover of some boulders. "It was my own fault, Sergeant. Look after the troop."

The troop lost more than its officer—it lost a friend, a soldier who played the game to the last.

Chapter Twenty-Eight
Palestine - October 1917

"My Gawd!" remarked Snow. "To think that a man's balmy enough to fight for this country. Get an eyeful of it. Blood."

The Bushman's eyes had quite enough of it already; he'd just come back from an all-day patrol into a region more forbidding than the worst of Sinai. There was water of a sort in the desert, and dates, but here even the rats and the lizards made no attempt to live. Still, some lunatics had built a railway there and had meant to take it right through to Akaba.

The Regiment had just finished five days' hard at Asluj. Jacko had blown up the wells there and fatigues had been working night and day on the dangerous and exhausting task of quarrying out slabs of stone from the bottoms of the shafts. Even when cleaned out the supplies in those wells weren't sufficient to keep the horses going, and a number had to be watered every day at Khalasa. But the job was finished and a move was to be made that night; where no one knew and few cared as long as it took them away from Asluj.

"How's the back now?" asked the Bushman. Ordinarily Snow's pitted back had stopped troubling him, but the heavy work underground had found some weak spots, for he never spared himself.

"Not too good," Snow admitted, "but I'll be all right again when we get into the old saddle. There's some news, anyway. Bob's got his pips."

"Good man." said the Bushman, "He's earned them. Wonder if he knew they were coming?"

"Dunno," replied Snow; "he's been away at Khalasa all day, but 'A' troop's getting ready to christen him. Come over and see what they've done."

They found 'A' troop putting the finishing touches to the

144

full insignia of a second-lieutenant, a hoop-iron Sam Browne complete to the last rivet, and two big stars hacked out of the lid of a biscuit tin. When the sergeant arrived he was invested with mock ceremony. Thus did a troop of men farewell its most popular N.C.O., its regret tempered with genuine pleasure at his promotion.

It was dark that night when the Regiment moved off, and by daylight it had ridden thirty miles. Once more the Horsemen had done what neither Turk nor German had thought possible, and an army by midday held the Beersheba-Hebron road. The Enzeds came in for a sharp skirmish early in the morning, but most of the day was spent in reconnaissance and looking for water. Luckily, a few days earlier a storm had burst over the foothills, and some gullies still held surface water. A few Bedouin reservoirs and a deep well were also discovered, but it was a long job bucketting up enough to water even a squadron of thirsty horses.

For four days the Regiment pushed its way gradually along the road which led to Hebron and thence to Jerusalem. Ridges became ranges, and ranges mountains, and a few snipers hidden along the narrow track leading upwards could, and did, hold up an army. The terraced slopes gave them cover which could only have been destroyed by heavy artillery, and attempts to locate those snipers cost the Regiment dearly.

The Bushman sat in his rough bivvy brooding. Nothing in his years of service had stirred him like the news of that afternoon. He had seen many men go with regret, but not with feelings of resentment, until now. *This* was how his country treated men who, in its cause, faced years of risk and hardship! He looked at the pictures and headlines in a Sydney paper which someone had sent him, and he cursed his country for a land of dirty scabs, as Snow parted the bivvy flaps and squatted down beside him.

"That's the way I'm feeling too," he said. "Blood, what's the strong of this yarn that he showed himself on purpose? D'you think it's true?"

The Bushman nodded.

"True all right. He was having trouble at home; that's why he put in for leave. Well, he's gone, and the squadron'll never be the same again—never."

"Why wouldn't they give him leave? The colonel could get it!"

The Bushman replied bitterly: "The colonel isn't a station hand, that's why. You don't get leave unless you've got pull."

"And don't they take any notice of a man's record? He was on the Peninsula the whole seven months, and never off duty for one day. What about the years since and his M.M.? There's not a man in the whole war who stuck to it better."

"Oh, yes, they know all that; they made a hell of a song about it when they turned him down. But, you see, they're short of recruits at home. Look at this!" He grabbed the paper. "Even the 'Sufferers' won't enlist now unless they insure their bloody lives first, and they're putting on a new stunt they call the 'March to Freedom.' Here's a picture of 'em. And look at the women leading round horses with empty saddles! Didn't I tell you how it would be when they turned down conscription? It's a land of scabs, and a good one to be out of."

Snow looked at the paper in silence. Then he stamped it into the dust.

"Christ! What a country to be fighting for! All the same, I hope Jacko lets me get back there, if it's only for the chance of getting a shot at an 'anti.' Too loud to fight, Blood, that's what's wrong with it."

Beersheba fell before horsemen at the gallop and the infantry smashed through at Sheria and Hareira, the strongest points in the Turkish line. The Regiment withdrew from the Dhaheriyeh hills to take part in the go-as-you-please from Gaza to Jaffa, but as it was moving back to Beersheba, the

Bushman, as orderly-sergeant, fell out to collect the squadron's mail. The job delayed him nearly an hour, and by the time he reached the arranged camping ground the Regiment had had fresh orders and was on the point of starting for Sheria. Jacko was on the run and had to be kept moving. The Bushman had to go on to Beersheba to water his horse and to drop out of the chase temporarily. He was instructed to camp there that night, collect a few other stragglers, and follow on next morning with a troop which had remained posted out towards Dhaheriyeh.

Next morning there was no sign of the troop, and when afternoon came, he decided that he had waited long enough. With twenty-four hours' start the Regiment would take some catching, especially since his only clue to its movements was the direction he had seen it take over the hills. At three o'clock, with a couple of mates he started in pursuit. He still had a feed for his horse in its nosebag, but his haversack was empty, and, to make matters worse, not one of the party had a solitary cigarette.

For awhile they followed a track which skirted the bases of the hills leading in the direction of Sheria. More than one unit had passed over it, and while daylight lasted the party made good progress, trusting to luck that it was on the track of the brigade. When darkness came it was a different matter, for by then they had passed through the first chain of hills, and, judging by the dust on the flatter ground, columns seemed to have been moving in all directions. Since it was probable that the jumping-off place in the chase after Jacko would be Sheria, the Bushman kept bearing to the left, And later in the night be blundered into a camp of Tommy infantry. He located the officers' mess and asked if his brigade had passed that way. He was told that brigades had been passing continuously, but that D.H.Q, was at Sheria and that a couple of hours' riding would get him there.

"Cross the Wadi here and stick to the right bank," said his informant, who wore three stars. "You can't get slewed —a crow could fly there backwards."

The Bushman stared. This didn't sound like a Tommy

captain, and the next remark, "Think you can keep one down, Sergeant," made him wonder where he'd got to. While he swallowed several gratefully he discovered that his benefactor was an Englishman who'd been jackerooing in Queensland. When he, at last, returned to his party, it refused to believe that he'd actually been shouted for in a Tommy officers' mess until he breathed on it and handed round a packet of cigarettes.

It was still starlight when they saw the outlines of an E.P. tent encampment overlooking a deep Wadi. The Bushman made sure that it was D.H.Q., fastened his horse on the lines, cadged a tin of tobacco, and rolled himself in his blanket in quick time. The Regiment was only a few miles ahead, and its limbers were due at a dump close handy during the forenoon.

He took his time next morning. He was now right behind the positions of the Gaza-Beersheba line which had long been looked on as impregnable. The feigned attack on the Hebron-Jerusalem road had drawn defenders there in a hurry, and drawn them, as the general had calculated from the strongest points of the line. One resolute thrust there took the infantry through, leaving both Gaza and Beersheba in the air. The success of the third battle of Gaza was as complete as the failure of the first two.

The Bushman soon found proofs that Jacko had got out in a hurry. He felt sorely tempted to do some souvenir-hunting amongst piles of baggage, but there might have been time to set a few booby traps as at Beersheba. He contented himself with a couple of new ground-sheets until he came to what had obviously been the cookhouse of a Turkish Headquarters. Something lying beside a wild jumble of utensils caught his eye. It was a plucked fowl! He picked it up gingerly and tested it carefully with his nose before he stowed it away in his haversack. It might have been poisoned, but for the sake of grilled chicken the chance was worth taking. He could imagine the light in Snow's eyes when he produced that bird!

Snow, however, got none of it. When the Bushman did finally overhaul the Regiment he found that his troop was on a detached job, and he didn't get a chance to rejoin it for several days. For once he didn't mind being away from it. The adjutant attached him to Headquarters as generally useful, and he got a chance of doing some of the galloping which kept Jacko moving all the way to Jaffa.

Jacko did his best, but for once his rearguard failed to save him. This time there was no repetition of Katia— the Horsemen kept on their horses. Flanking tactics, alternately to right and left, and at full gallop, forced the abandonment of positions almost as soon as they were occupied. The speed of the extended horsemen gave them safety, and on the big day at Beit Affe the casualties in the Regiment were only four wounded.

The drive lasted until darkness came, and by then Jacko had been driven out of the hills, and forced to look for refuge in the Wadi Ghuet. It proved a trap from which there was no escape, and by morning the nominal roll of the Turkish army was minus another thousand. Small bags of prisoners had been taken during the day, and even Headquarters could claim a few. It was a case of fast horses and slow Jackos, but the Bushman always claimed that those prisoners were the result of his bad shooting.

Headquarters moved in the centre of the drive, and on several occasions caught sight of a few more or less exhausted stragglers. The Bushman, as a spare part, had attached himself to the colonel as an extra galloper, and his seemed to be the only rifle in his party when three Jackos broke from the shelter of a small stone building and made a dash across some open ground towards a deep Wadi. Musketry Regs. said to aim well in front of a running man, and the Bushman did. He put up such a dust barrage in front of those Jackos that they threw their rifles down and their hands up. A little later they were smoking Headquarters cigarettes.

By the time the great Beersheba drive came to an end, the Horsemen had reached the land of oranges.

Chapter Twenty-Nine
Palestine - November 1917

Snow's section was sitting inside a ring of orange-peel and praying that Jacko would refuse to be driven any further, for a month at least. The troop was on pumping fatigue, and it had withdrawn to the shade of some olive trees ostensibly to eat bully beef and biscuits. Somewhere about Askalon the familiar figures of "Wallads" with bags or "oringees" had appeared, and their tactics, and prices, were familiar too. Snow paid five piastres for his first five oranges, but he swore he would eat the next ninety-five for nothing. And he did.

There were points about the country, apart from its oranges. The soil was good, and a few villages were something better than collections of mud huts. Just as the desert had graduated into the partial civilisation of the Gaza front, it in turn had become more promising as the advance developed. If the improvement continued, another few hundred miles might bring the Horsemen to a White Man's country. The map of the Palestine coast carried magic names like Beyrout and that, surely, would be the next objective.

"Don't you believe it" asserted the troop strategist. "It'll take a flank move to empty Jacko out of here. That's where we go next."

He pointed to the mountains lying a few miles inland. The troop laughed at the idea of forcing the road leading to Jerusalem.

"They won't," replied the strategist. "They'll come at it from the Hebron side. Jacko—"

"Never mind about Jacko," interrupted Snow. "Any 'oring-ees' left?"

Someone threw him an empty sandbag.

"Haven't you had enough yet, guts?"

"I want a dozen more to make the hundred," replied Snow. "I'll be set then. Anyone got a tin of bully? I can see a Wallad coming."

No one had.

"Well, give us an empty tin," persisted Snow. "I'll make him wish Fray Bentos had never been born—like we do."

He took the empty tin and flattened its jagged edges carefully. Then he filled it with dirt and wrapped it up again in its florid label. Fray himself might have thought it had just left the factory.

"You won't catch him with that," said one. "These Wallads are pretty fly to it since the Enzeds worked off some Ideal milk labels for fifty-piastre notes."

"We'll see," said Snow confidently. "Hey-ya, Wallad! Tala hinna!"

The Arab came up at a run- "Hulla-Hulla?" he asked eagerly. The craving in Palestine for tinned beef—outside the troops—would have doubled Fray's output if he could have started a factory there and taken payment in oranges.

"Aiwa," replied Snow affectionately. "Inta quice—Arabi Ingleesi soa-soa. Bulla-Bulla quice keteer! Oringees?"

He held out the tin and the Arab handed over a sandbag full of oranges, but before he had retreated far with his prize it came to pieces in his hands. He expostulated in classical Arabic.

"It's a new brand," Snow assured him. "We've been eating worse for years, What! You don't believe me? Imshi, then, you magnoon musquice yomaris kelp!"

A bombardment of peel helped the Arab out of range and Snow delivered judgement with a full mouth.

"If a man robbed, these thieving bastards for the rest of of his life he wouldn't get square with 'em. You'd have had lamb cutlets for tea to-night if it hadn't been for that soft-hearted old Blood- We went into a compound to try and buy one this morning. I grabbed a fine fat one and offered the kid a fifty note, but he howled and yowled so much that Blood reckoned it must have been a pet, and made me let it go."

"You'd have looked well if someone from D.H.Q. had been

riding by," said one of the troop. "Blood would have done his stripes."

"Well, he won't be wearing stripes much longer, anyway," replied Snow. "He's one of the next for a 'pip' whether he knows it or not. I got the oil from the orderly room."

At that moment the Bushman joined the group. He looked at the pile of orange peel.

"I wouldn't eat any more if I were you," he said.

"Why not?" asked several.

"They're on issue to-night, one a man, in lieu of something they robbed us of on the Peninsula. I just got it from the Q.M."

"Gawd's trooth!" murmured Snow. "Isn't it just what the silly bastards would do—issue oranges when a man can pinch more than he can eat! And one a man, too!"

They rode home by Ludd that evening and the Bushman dropped out to see if he could buy some green vegetables; for general distribution in the troop. He was joined by another man bent on the same errand, and after a short search they found The road leading to the central market place. Both men had seen, and smelt, the worst of Old Cairo, but it was a sanatorium compared with what they found in the heart of Ludd. The square was so small that sunlight seldom found its way in, and the cobblestones were littered with piles of refuse and human excreta which dated back to Genesis. Half the population seemed to be afflicted with a disease of some sort, and the two horsemen were about to turn and ride out when they saw the "Missing Link." Its progenitors had succeeded in making it human, but only just.

It was the figure of a man dwarfed to well under five feet, and naked except for a hessian girdle round its middle. Its skull was flattened on several sides, and its face dribbled continuously. It carried a short stick and hobbled from stall to stall—its skinny claw stretched out for baksheesh but it got more kicks and curses than piastres. The small boys of Ludd ran true to type: they sneaked up behind the "Link" and pulled at the ragged ends of its hessian girdle, darting aside with shrieks of glee when their butt turned on them with gibbering curses.

Joe unslung his camera at once. The difficulty was to catch the Link in one of the few patches of sunlight. He beckoned to a policeman and explained what he wanted with the help of a few coins. The policeman promptly grabbed the Link and dragged it into a sunny spot; but in the grip of the Law the Link grovelled and cried profusely. Joe wanted a happy picture, and there was only one way to get it. The Bushman held up a piastre. At once a watery smile of comprehension replaced a tearful, scowl, and the camera clicked as the coin dropped into the Link's eagerly outstretched claw. Then the two horsemen fled with all possible speed, hoping that they had not been smitten with a palsy or the leprosy of Naaman while in the market place of Ludd. They were barked out of it by some lineal descendants of the dogs that licked Lazarus.

Chapter Thirty
Palestine - December 1917

"I think I've made everything clear," said the squadron-leader to a little group of officers and sergeants. "I'll leave you to explain the job to your troops."

For a couple of weeks the Regiment had been holding positions not far from Jaffa, and one or two minor raids proved that Jacko had found his second wind. He still had plenty of kick left. The Bushman's troop had no officer, so he was temporarily in charge of it.

"We're for it tonight," he told the expectant men. "A raid on Jacko's possy in the big almond orchard behind One-Tree Hill. A hundred of the squadron."

He outlined the job. Jacko was digging in in the orchard in a way that looked as if he meant to stay there. A listening post wasn't objected to, but a permanent redoubt would make it unpleasant for whoever was holding One-Tree Hill, and the idea had to be nipped in the bud. The squadron had been given the job, and ten minutes to do it in.

"We sneak out from One Tree Hill and lie down as close to Jacko as we can safely get. After we're in position, a battery opens on 'em and keeps going for ten minutes. As soon as it lifts, we rush the post, and in another ten minutes it drops on to it again. That's to stop any chance of a counter-attack, and by then we're supposed to be back behind One-Tree Hill. Anyway, we'll have ten minutes to scupper, whatever the battery leaves of Jacko, and find out just what he's been up to. I've got to bodyguard the officer making the inspection with eight men, and we form the rearguard coming back."

"Who's going with you?" someone asked. The Bushman replied: "I want Snow, Jack, Bert, Vic, Hughie, Nick, the 'Dancing Duck,' and—oh, yes, the 'Stiff Trooper.' He's swung it back to the squadron just in time."

He had. The Bushman had greeted him with "Picquet to-night" the previous evening, as soon as he hit the lines and three days later the Stiff Trooper was in the 14th A.G.H. with a useful part of his anatomy perforated in two extra places. He got no sympathy from the Sisters. They told him it served him right for being greedy.

The raiding party assembled in the hollow behind One-Tree Hill and moved quietly out amongst the closely growing: almond trees. Then it turned to face the Turkish post and lay down. The night was dark, and the stars gave scant light through the thick branches overhead. As the first shot from the battery sounded, the Bushman looked at his watch. The first three shells burst well in front of them, but the fourth fell dangerously close.

"By Christ, Blood, I don't like the look of that," whispered Snow, who lay close beside him.

In a few seconds the raiders knew that one gun was firing-short. The branches above them were blasted into splinters by the low-bursting shrapnel, and almost at once the call came for stretcher-bearers,

For ten minutes they were the only men who left the line. A boy near the Bushman groaned and rolled over clutching at himself in pain. He wondered how many of his chosen eight would be left him for the rearguard job. Snow was still beside him, but three of the others had already gone as a fourth gave a half-suppressed grunt. Through the din the Bushman heard a quaint argument.

"I'm hit! No I'm not! Yes I am. By Ch-h-rist—it stings!"

The barrage lifted and seventy-five of the hundred men were on their feet in an instant. They charged like madmen, and the few Turks standing in the shallow trenches were remorselessly bayoneted—hands up or down. All but four.

The Bushman had a job to keep in front of what was left of his little command, but he managed to beat all but Snow in the race to the trench. He got there in time to prevent four Jackos from going the way of their fellows. They stood crouching in a small sap, their rifles lying on the dirt in front of them. With a quick movement he kicked them to one side and grabbed an uplifted Turkish hand. The Jacko scrambled at once to level ground, followed by his dazed comrades, Snow helping up the last with a prod in the rear. The Bushman handed over the four of them to someone, and followed the officer who was quickly examining the redoubt. Then the remainder of the squadron, which had formed a momentary covering party beyond, began to fall back towards One Tree Hill and the Bushman extended his four men behind them.

The raiders retired slowly, for they had wounded to take back with them. The rearguard kept well behind, and during the short retreat it got one shock which tested what was left of its nerve. A cactus hedge lay on the flank, and with dramatic suddenness a figure jumped it and came racing after them. The Bushman had begun to press his trigger when he thought he saw a hat on the fugitive's head.

He shouted loudly: "Who are you? Quick!" and a rattled yell in reply saved a somewhat useless life. No one bothered to ask the badly scared runner how he came to be left behind, but his feet were warm by the time he overtook the squadron.

Behind One Tree Hill the Bushman checked up the troop. His brother sergeant, old Jock, lay amongst the wounded in a shallow ditch near the redoubt. The night's work had made a big gap in what were left of the squadron sergeants who had made merry in the mess at Marakeb, Two already lay in graves at Beersheba, and two others had gone up to commissioned rank. Now, three more had seen their last days of service.

The Bushman found Snow kneeling in the ditch beside old Jock. The wounded man was in pain, and Snow was rallying him with prospects of his discharge and a "fish and chips" joint in Sydney. One by one the wounded men were carried to a safer area, but not before Jacko's artillery had found the ditch. A shell burst high and the pellets hissed harmlessly to earth; but the Bushman heard the whiz of a nosecap, and a sickening "phut" of impact as the body of the man beside him fell across his own. It was one of the officers, and his reply to the Bushman's enquiry was an apology.

"No, I'm all right, Sergeant. Sorry I squeaked, though."

The Bushman knelt in front of his bivvy and made a movement to crawl in on to his blankets, but he had sense enough to draw back and sit upright. While he kept his head up he was able to remain conscious, more or less, but directly he lowered it the great big world seemed to double its revs. He was as nearly drunk as he ever had been.

Still, he had managed to find his way home, which was more than either of the others could do. Three of them had been summoned that night to the orderly-room and told that they were to proceed next day to the Cadet School in Cairo. Then the adjutant took them to the mess and shouted as a matter of course. The colonel came in, followed at intervals by three squadron leaders and numerous subalterns, all equally bent on welcoming the three recruits to commissioned rank. After the seventh round of drinks the Bushman lost count. He might have stood up to whisky, but they were on cognac brewed at Richon, probably only a few months previously—and it contained shrapnel as well as "fix'd baynits." Later he remembered seeing one of his fellow cadets staggering off in a wrong direction, and another collapsing on the horse-lines, to the great joy of the picquet. By a supreme effort he was able to get to his bivvy unaided, and he sat looking at it for an hour before he was game to crawl inside.

He had plenty of time to straighten up next morning, for a hitch occurred and the others left for Cairo without him. He thought he had slipped and would have to wear stripes a bit longer, but the matter was settled that day and he left by an evening train. He didn't know until some time later that he could thank the colonel's resolute action for his commission at that stage.

When Snow said good-bye he pushed something into the

Bushman's hand,

"You might be short of 'feloos' up there, Blood," he said. "No, take it, you old fool, and spend it. I've got a hundred notes in the bank in Cairo, and Gawd knows if I'll ever go on leave again."

The Bushman took it. It was a cheque for two thousand piastres.

Chapter Thirty-One
Officer School - March 1918

A small group of Australians and New Zealanders stood near the Zietoun lecture hut, and beside them lay a pile of new valises carefully branded with names and units, for numbers had become a thing of the past. So had issue uniforms. Each man was turned out in a way that would have brought tears of joy to the most exacting lover of spit and polish; tunics and breeches were of the latest cut, and the shine of belts and top-boots would have won half-a-dozen wars. The cadet school had broken up, and somewhere about two hundred N.C.O.'s had pulled off their stripes. They had qualified to wear Sam Brownes, and buy drinks at Shepheard's.

The Bushman had found the three months' course both interesting and amusing, and the hard physical training had left him exceptionally fit. Still, apart from map and compass work, he didn't believe that he was any better qualified to lead a mounted troop than he had been before, but he had been given a valuable insight into Regular Army methods, and he had acquired a mighty respect for the efficiency of its N.C.O.'s in particular. Under their tuition, infantry drill, of which he had known nothing, became a simple matter, and in his examination he put a company through a number of movements with fluent accuracy. A New Zealander had topped the school, and at a sports meeting the bulk of the prizes went to those of the forty Anzacs who competed. Their prestige stood high at the start, for every man had been applied for by his own colonel. The C.O. of the school treated them almost with deference.

He was a colonel of Dragoon Guards, that C.O., and an imposing figure. He had taken part in the retreat from Mons, on horseback. Since then he had been helping to win the war by turning out hundreds of "Temporary Gentlemen," but he might have been more popular if he could have realised that in 1918 Mons cut about as much ice as Balaclava. Still, his Guards of Honour were famous through half-a-dozen fronts, and off parade his manners were charming. As one irreverent cadet put it, they would have made his fortune as a commercial traveller.

The school orderly-room was close to where the group of newly-fledged officers stood, and when the C.O. and his adjutant appeared on the verandah, the Enzed "dux" had an idea.

"I say, you chaps," he said, "let's go down and say good-bye. After all, they've not been a bad pair of poor blighters. We'll, give 'em something to make 'em put their chests out."

He stood off the group, and in a voice that had made New Zealand famous yelled: "In two ranks—fall in!" In a few seconds he had his little platoon marching on the orderly-room in the way that only Australians and New Zealanders can march—when they want to. They wheeled and formed platoon in front of the verandah, and having stood them at ease, the Enzed leader approached the C.O.

His salute was the last word in saluting history.

"Australian and New Zealand officers about to rejoin their regiments, sir," he said. "Have we your permission to move off?"

The C.O. was flustered for once in his life, so great was his surprise and gratification.

"Yes, certainly—er—certainly," he replied: "but I would like to say good-bye to each man personally."

He approached the little parade, followed by his adjutant. It made a brave show—each man as fit as three months' severe training could make him, and wearing the uniform of the King's Commission as if born to it. Finally, when the C.O. shook hands with the Enzed leader, his voice trembled with emotion.

"Gad, sir, these officers are a credit to the school, and an ornament to the British Army. Aldershot has never turned out anything finer. I'm proud, gentlemen, to think that I've been responsible for your training."

The Bushman arrived at Moascar in fear and trembling-. Hitherto he had managed to dodge the place, but there was a distinct chance that he might be put on the strength of the *cadre* there, and do several months playing at teaching reinforcements how to slope arms. Several officers of his unit were due from Australian leave any day, and he would be crowded out if they beat him back to the Regiment. Moascar, with its fragments, its reinforcements, and especially its quota of lead-swingers and hospital kings, was something he dreaded. He had to wait there several days for his movement orders, but in the end he didn't regret them, for he was on parade when Sergeant "Magnoon" made his famous address to a body of reinforcements about to join the brigade for the first time.

Sergeant "Magnoon" was doing his turn on the *cadre*. At first he was put in charge of the sergeants' mess, which he fed on geese and turkeys to the point of liquidation. He was orderly sergeant on the morning in question, and he came on parade armed with a long typed list of names.

The Bushman thought that, after all, there must be something to be said for Moascar if it could transform Sergeant Magnoon into a strictly orthodox N.C.O. He "shunned" the parade and stood it at ease in a way that would have earned top marks even in the cadet school. But that was all. He began his address with:

"The following gentlemen have been selected to serve His Majesty King George the Fifth on the Palestine front." Then he reeled off a long list of names and some instructions as to when and how the reinforcements were to proceed to their units. After that, he paused for a few moments and regarded them sorrowfully.

"I think" he said, "that it would be unfair not to let you brave lads know something of what you will have to face before you die nobly for King and Country. Your bodies are clean now, but before long they will be lousy. Your bellies are full, but soon, very soon, they will be empty. You will know the extremities of hunger and thirst the torments of blistering heat and shrivelled tongues, of icy cold and quaking limbs. And one dark night"— he paused impressively—"you will crawl over the parapet and few, very few, of you will ever come back."

Kantara had changed from the days of its lone railway junction and its pontoon bridge across the Canal. When the Bushman crossed it on his way back to the Regiment its eastern side carried miles of encampments. There was a railway station where an express service started for Palestine, for the line which had followed the Horsemen across the desert now linked up with the old system ending near Gaza. But to many thousands of men the name Kantara will bring memories of one thing when all others attaching to it are dim—the canteen. No man serving had greater morale than the two Australian women whose high purpose and steady courage made that canteen possible. No soldier who crossed the Canal at Kantara will remember their names without reverence, affection and gratitude. Theirs was the spirit which wins battles.

By the time he was speeding across Sinai, the Bushman felt safe from Moascar. The comfortable day's journey contrasted vividly with the eighteen months of strenuous endeavour which had marked the horsemen's trail from Kantara to Jaffa. He left the train at Wadi Hanein and collected a couple of horses and instructions to report to D.H.Q. at Jerusalem. Next day he rode through in company with a number of officers returning home from leave, school or hospital. The front line was now the Jordan River. The Regiment was camped somewhere on the down grade, and the Bushman only stayed in Jerusalem long enough to find out where.

It seemed strange to be riding downhill for any distance, at last. For two years the blue line of the Judean ranges had been beckoning the Horsemen onwards. They had wondered what lay on the other side, and few had been optimistic enough to believe that the day would come when they would see for themselves.

The narrow road lay between barren stony hills, and as he followed its curves the Bushman caught glimpses of the Mount of Olives and Gethsemane. He passed by Bethany where hundreds of women and children were at work. They were carting small stones in baskets to the badly-worn roadway, and they were singing happily. The twin nightmares of Turkish rule and starvation had passed; they were being fed by the British Army.

For a few miles beyond Jerusalem the hillsides carried a faint green growth, but that soon disappeared as the road dipped downwards. The desert bad been red, but the wilderness was brown, and it became darker and more forbidding with every mile of descent The Bushman was quite prepared to find hell itself at the bottom, and from a height near Talaat-ed-Dumm he caught his first glimpse of what did become hell on earth a few months later.

At the foot of mountains higher than those he had just left lay a narrow expanse of flat ground, and traversing its centre he could see a dark line—the course of the Jordan River. To the south there was water—the sea where nothing could live. The valley itself showed patches of green on the farther plain, crops irrigated from the foothill streams. The season of springtime could not be denied, even by the Jordan Valley. It waited until it had the Horsemen in the grip of its midsummer before it came out in its true colours.

The Bushman found the Regiment at Talaat-ed-Dumm, and to his relref he was, posted to a troop as soon as he reported. The Regiment was on the point of moving on a Trans-Jordan job, and if he had delayed even half-a-day to see the sights of Jerusalem he would have missed it. As it was, he had barely time to get a few particulars of his new troop and find a groom before orders came to saddle up.

All that afternoon and for most of the night the Regiment rode downhill, and it made no extended halt until a few hours before daylight. Then the Bushman found time to visit his old troop. It seemed strange not to be squatting on his heels in the dust with the pals of three years service, and stranger still to be nervous about the way they might greet the new dignity of his belt and stars. He felt a thrill of happiness when he approached the leading section and heard it murmur; "Here's old Blood!"

He spent most of the hour yarning with Snow. The squadron had a new leader who had promptly put stripes on most of the outlaws of his predecessor—including Snow himself- He now bossed it as a section leader over a trio of youngsters still not entitled to a vote. He had also taken over the troop Hotchkiss. But for a bit of genuine bad luck he would have been qualifying for a pilot's wings at Heliopolis. At long last his daredevil pluck had received recognition, but his order to report to the Flying School had come through while he had been on a short leave to Cairo.

"A man's stiff all right," he told the Bushman. "They sent me a wire to report, but I never got it. And when I got back, the old Brig. told me I'd better see this stunt through and to go up as soon as it was over. Just as well these 'boy scouts' of mine are always getting lost. Here! Stand up—damn you! Can't you see you're talking to Lieutenant Old Blood!"

The order "Get mounted!" passed quietly along and the Bushman hurried back to his new troop. He never saw Snow again.

Chapter Thirty-Two
Jordan - March 1918

At daybreak the Horsemen crossed the Jordan. It had overflowed the banks during-the winter, and the approaches to the pontoon bridge were still soft with silt. The strong current put a curve in the swaying bridge, but the Regiment got over without mishap. Then, after a breakfast halt, it moved slowly over the narrow plain towards the Trans-Jordan mountains.

The Bushman had always thought that once a man acquired stars he got behind the scenes, but he soon found that he seldom knew more than his own groom, and never half as much as a Headquarters batman. It seemed that this stunt was a raid into the heart of Jacko's territory with a two fold objective—the blowing up of the Mecca railway and the stiffening of that rather mythical ally, the Arab. Until now the "Arab" had been represented by orange sellers and gharri-drivers in Cairo, Bedouins in the desert, and the riff-raff of the villages between Rafa and Jaffa, but they were not the real thing. On the top of the mountains lay Arabia itself, the home of the noble, brave, chivalrous and hospitable Sheikh, so beloved of fiction writers. The Bushman was curious to meet one—off the films or outside a novel—and he particularly wanted to get a close-up of a real Arab steed; but he refused to believe that any Arab would "fling back gold."

Near the Wadi Kefrein a small body of its new allies joined the column. They were picturesque enough in their flowing robes and hood like headgear, and their rifles were of the latest pattern. Their horses were small and pretty, but for speed or endurance any decently bred cattle-station camp horse could have put the best of them off the earth. The Arabs clamoured to be told where the general was, and when they were shown the little body carrying the red pennant, they galloped wildly round it several times in token of welcome and respect. The old Brig. replied with many salutes and assurances of "soa–soa."

There was only one real road up the mountains and Jacko held that securely against any frontal raid. He was quite satisfied to let the mounted columns try their luck with the goat-tracks, and so were the Horsemen. By daylight next morning they were on the tablelands of Gad.

The Bushman had been through some weird nights from the Evacuation onwards, but the one spent climbing those mountains held its own with any of them. Even the foot hills were far from easy, and a light drizzle of rain came with darkness. As the mountains looming above them faded out in the darkness of the overcast sky, many of the Horsemen wondered if the ascent were possible.

They came to places where there was a bare foothold for a man, let alone a horse, and in the darkness they could only follow and trust to luck. For several hours the column moved in single file, dismounted. There was small risk of losing touch, for most men held on to the tail of the horse in front, grateful for the power that pulled them over steep and slippery flagstones. During the brief halts they stood upright, shivering in the rain which fell more heavily as they gradually drew nearer to the mountain tops. When day broke an icy wind swept the tableland and torrential rain came with it. Except on rocky outcrops, the ground was saturated and movement was impossible. A precious day had to be wasted. That night the march continued, and by morning the Horsemen were within striking distance of Amman.

The squadron horses were picqueted close to the shelter of a low outcrop overlooking a narrow Wadi, and the Bushman, with a heavy heart, sat on a rock near his troop line. The attack on Amman had begun the previous day and his old squadron had suffered badly. He looked up to see one of Snow's "boy scouts" standing beside him.

"I thought you'd like to know what happened, Blood," he said in a low tone.

The Bushman nodded.

"You had your turn yesterday all right. Vic," he said. "Tell me everything he said, and did, right up to the end."

The boy's voice shook as he began his story.

"I believe he knew he was sent for, before we went in. We had to wait for a bit behind the hill while the M.G.'s were getting into their possies to give us covering fire, and he said to me: 'Young 'un. I don't like it to-day somehow!' I never knew Snow to say anything like that; did you, Blood?"

The Bushman shook his head. "Go on, Vic," he said. "Next moment we were off, and under fire as soon as we got over the skyline—shrapnel as well as machine-guns. It was worse than anything we've been in yet. There was no cover at all till we crossed the hollow, and at the end of the first rush we went down side by side. He was watching me all the time, Blood— just like a father; and when I pushed a few stones-together in front of my head, he seemed quite cheerful again, and he said: 'That's the way, young 'un; take all the cover you can.' In the second rush we got separated from Ted and Bert; they went to the right of a little knob and we kept to the left. When we got down again I was out in the open, but Snow crawled behind some rocks and yelled to me: 'They'll get you there, you bloody young fool; come here beside me.' He was safe there from the machine-guns, but there was no cover anywhere from shrapnel. I wriggled over beside him and—and he showed himself for a few seconds pushing some more stones up in front of me."

The Bushman broke a short silence. "You couldn't bring him in, Vic?"

"No; we had to leave him. All we could do was to put some stones round him. I got his papers. Then the order came to retire. I don't know how any of us ever got back."

The Bushman asked: "Was Bert badly hit?"

The boy nodded. "I'm afraid he's done, Blood. He got it somewhere in the back. There's only Ted and me left of the section, and there's more horseholders than anything else in the squadron."

The Bushman got up. He said: "Well, it's our turn to-day. We're going to attack the aerodrome. I must go and see what's doing. So long, Vic."

The squadron moved on the extreme left of the extended line. It was attached that day to another regiment and came under its colonel's orders. For some distance the advance took place over open and almost flat ground sparsely dotted with small boulders. Men walked slowly, several yards apart. They were within shrapnel range soon after they left the horses, but the Turkish gunners held their fire. They didn't wish to spoil the sport awaiting their machine-gunners further on.

The Bushman's troop numbered eighteen. He kept somewhere about its centre, and after awhile he noticed puffs of dust ahead; but Jacko was only range-finding. There was a little firing from the flanks, but it was mostly harmless. Then the line reached an area of hills and hollows flanked by long low spurs which ended in steep knobs overlooking the valley leading towards the aerodrome.

Once over the first ridge the frontal firing became more persistent. The Turk had riflemen waiting, and they fell back from hill to hill as the line drew closer to its objective. The Bushman saw his squadron-leader fall. His own troop was first on the flank of the other regiment, and several times he lost sight of the rest of his squadron as it passed between ridges.

The fire grew hotter, for the line was coming nearer to where the Turk wanted it. The centre of the advance followed a deep valley, and the order came to double. There could be no short rushes, for the ground was coverless. Running steadily the line reached the shelter of a high conical hill, and as it did the riflemen on its top retreated.

The Bushman and his troop found cover on the hillside leading up from the valley, and during a brief breather he checked his number. He had now sixteen men. They lay behind boulders, but above them the ground was bare. He could see nothing of the three troops on his left flank. They were somewhere on the, hilltop and exposed to the frontal fire of machine guns working boldly in the open behind iron shields. A sharp spur directly in front of him gave his own troop temporary shelter. Just below him in the hollow he could see the colonel commanding the attack, and with him were two of the senior officers of the other regiment. On the slope to the right men lay behind scanty cover, and on the top of the ridge a Hotchkiss vainly tried to silence some of the fire which seemed to pour in from every direction.

Then the order came to advance. The Bushman ran to his flank and shouted it, since he could see no connecting link with the troop on his left. He heard the order repeated, and almost at once an answer came back from the senior lieutenant. It was: "Further advance impossible."

Again the order to advance came from the valley, and again the reply was returned. Then the order changed to "Advance at all costs," and that sealed the fate of the three troops on the hilltop, for no one knew better what could or could not be done than the officer who had sent the reply. He could see the coverless ground and the shielded machine-guns, the stoutly built sangars where the riflemen secure from any covering fire given by the Hotchkiss on the pinnacle, and the colonel could not. He knew that nothing but disaster lay ahead, and he fell as he led his men over the hilltop. Of the three troops which followed the remaining officer, one man alone beat the Turkish machine-gunners in a desperate rush back to safety a few minutes later.

The fourth troop was the Bushman's, and the luck of its position saved it. When it advanced, it had cover amongst the hillside boulders until it reached the spur leading downwards. By then the line of men following the valley met the merciless frontal and cross fire which had wiped out the three troops advancing from the hilltop. It wheeled at once to the cover of the spur, leaving its quota of dead and wounded in the valley.

From where he lay the Bushman could see little of what was happening in front; he knew nothing of the fate of the squadron, but the Hotchkiss on the pinnacle to the right was making a gallant effort to check the beginning of a counter-attack. An officer whom the Bushman knew well by reputation ran in a leisurely fashion up the slope towards the post. Had he stopped he would never have moved from the hillside. It was a death trap.

The Bushman watched him with admiration and bated breath, for it seemed impossible for him to get through. The officer had a reputation as an uncompromising disciplinarian, and was probably the best-hated man in his regiment; but no one ever doubted his cool nerve. He got to the Hotchkiss post unscathed, and a few moments there were enough to satisfy him that the survivors of the attack would be lucky to get out of it. He came down the hill again at the same steady jog-trot, and again the Turkish gunners could not hit him. When he made his report to his colonel his voice was as steady as it would have been on parade.

The Bushman got his orders at once—to take his men to a little ridge in the rear, and to work with the Hotchkiss on the pinnacle while the wounded in the valley were being carried to safety, and to retire with it in turn unless the counter-attack developed dangerously. To reach the ridge he had to cross an exposed area, and before he began the dash he gave orders to his sergeant—his job was to see to any wounded, and the Hotchkiss was to reach the ridge whatever happened. It was as well that he did, for four men fell in the short rush, and when he reached the ridge top his troop had dwindled to himself and his three gunners.

In the few minutes' respite they had they worked with feverish speed building a small stone sangar. The Bushman took the ammunition himself and sent the carrier on. He was knocked up, and the fewer men behind the shelter the better. As the gunner steadied himself into position with his Number Two and the Bushman huddled close beside him, the first shots came from the slope they had just left. They spattered on the stones in front of the three men's faces.

For awhile the Bushman kept his gun quiet. There was little chance of replying to the fire with reasonable safety, and if Jacko came no further there was no sense in risking his rearguard for the sake of a chance shot. If the counter-attack persisted there was a wonderful field of fire in front of his sangar, and by lying low a few Jackos might try to cross it.

A few did. They made a sudden rush, but the Hotchkiss gunner quickly stopped it. The Bushman felt a glow of satisfaction as he counted the figures lying on the slope opposite. He nearly counted for the last time. A sharp fragment flew from the stone beside his face and drew blood as it grazed his cheek. Lead and nickel went the other way.

Then he saw the Hotchkiss on the pinnacle drawing back, and when it was safely established on a ridge to the rear, he judged that he had kept his gun where it was long enough, especially as he had seen the last of the wounded men in the valley carried away. He sent his Number Two first, with the carriers, and watched him duck and slither to safety. After a short interval Number One went with the gun, and the Bushman remained behind the sangar with a rifle. Finally he ran the gauntlet himself and made his way to the rear of the knob where he had sent the gun. In the hollow behind it he saw a few figures grouped round a wounded man, and he went to see if it were one of his own squadron.

It was a man from the other regiment. His leg was badly broken, and his carriers were resting him. As the Bushman was turning away, the major who had defied the machine-guns joined the group.

"Badly hurt?" he enquired.

The man on the ground replied gruffly: "Might be worse." Then his admiration got the better of his dislike. "Never thought I'd see you again, Major. Gawd! It's a pity a man like you has to be such a bastard in a peace camp."

During the withdrawal to the Jordan the horses had an easy time, for in the Regiment alone there were a hundred empty saddles. For two days after the disaster of Amman the Horsemen covered the retreat of transport and ambulance, and once more the Turk lacked the initiative to drive his advantage home. He dogged up the rearguards, but they could scarcely have held up a determined attack in spite of the support of their Arab allies. The Bushman saw them in action, once. He was outposting a position where it was just possible to see an occasional Jacko with a good pair of glasses, when a small body of Arabs rode up behind the hill, dismounted, and rushed up amongst his men. They demanded excitedly to be shown where Jacko was lurking, and the Bushman obliged them. He pointed. out a hill about four thousand yards away. The Sheikh in command gave an order which must have meant "Rapid fire." Jacko replied promptly. A shell shrieked overhead, and after ordering his men to cover, the Bushman turned to curse the lunatics who had drawn it. All he could see to curse was the dust of disappearing horses. One shell was enough for the gentlemen of Arabia.

The road from Es-Salt to the valley was open for the last stage of the retreat. It was steep and narrow, and the Horsemen followed it in half-sections. In many places it bridged the fast-flowing waters of the Nimrin, and it was congested by a long string of Armenian refugees. They were taking the Heaven-sent chance of escape. They carried their poor belongings on their backs or pushed them in carts, and some of the aged and footsore were given a lift in the limbers.

At one point where the road angled sharply a little group stood to one side to let the Horsemen pass. Many of them were leading the horses of a section, and they rode In gloomy silence, for with camp life ahead the loss of mates was emphasised with full force. Still, there were few who did not give a prolonged "Eyes left" as they turned that angle in the road, for the most beautiful "bint" in all Palestine stood there.

She had the figure of a Venus, the face of a Helen, and the air of a tragedy queen. It seemed a crime to think that ultimately she would become the prize of some greasy, pot-bellied old Effendim in Cairo. The Bushman felt sorry that he couldn't offer her a seat in front of his saddle. If he had been an Ober-Lieutenant of Uhlan Cavalry he might have done so and got away with it—and her too.

Chapter Thirty-Three
The Dead Sea - April 1918

A month later the Horsemen climbed the mountains again, but by a different road, for Jacko now guarded the southern passes and the main track leading to Es-Salt. The Number Seven route lay further north; it was difficult enough, but the rainy season was over. One squadron of the Regiment stayed behind in the valley to take part in an infantry attack on the foothills at El Haud; the others were included in a movement meant to occupy Jacko's time around Es-Salt and prevent reinforcements going down to resist the thrust from the valley.

The surprise part of the movement succeeded well. One brigade got to Es-Salt before Jacko could get out of it, and the main road to the valley was straddled by several squadrons early enough to give a German engineer the shock of his life. The horses were well hidden, and a troop commanded a sharp curve in the steep road. The men lay very low as sounds of a motor-cycle were heard coming downhill. It slowed as it neared the comer, and its rider only knew that the game was up when he turned the bend a few yards away from fixed bayonets and grinning faces. He jumped off his bike, and greeted his captors with the remark:

"Well, if you bloody Kangaroos aren't sick of the war, I am. How's good old Sydney these days?"

Over a cigarette he revealed the fact that he had once held a prominent position there in the Nord-Deutscher-Lloyd.

It was a five-day stunt and rations were issued accordingly for both horse and man at the beginning. That meant that by the fourth day everyone was as "miskeen" as any Bedouin praying for baksheesh, and no one had had any sleep worth mentioning since leaving the valley. If the attack on El Haud succeeded, the road would be open for a quiet ride home; if not, it would be hell for-leather back to the valley, by the Number Seven track, before Jacko cut it off.

On the morning of the fourth day the Regiment found itself several miles along the Amman road supporting another brigade. A sharp little action there had ended in the capture of three hundred Jackos and the marching of them over a skyline in full view of their compatriots. Soon after midday the Regiment took over part of the line. It was still far below strength and the Bushman's troop numbered twenty men when he proceeded to the post allotted to him.

It was a nasty spot, and Jacko had chosen it for the full force of his attack earlier in the morning; but since he had been roughly handled there, it was unlikely that he would try the same place during the night. A deep, and in places sheer, gorge ran almost to the roadway, and the post overlooked it. It was nearly dark when the troop took it over, and the squadron it relieved left in a hurry. Four sleepless nights had frayed its leaders' nerves rather badly. Beyond the gorge another regiment was supposed to be holding the flank.

Before darkness set in, the Bushman got into touch with the post on his right and estimated that he was responsible for roughly three hundred yards of the outpost line. To cover that he had twenty men, so he split them into six listening posts with instructions to retire to a little knob overlooking the road in case of a serious attack. It was the best he could think of in the face of his orders not to withdraw until he got definite word from Headquarters.

He hoped that the morning's lesson had taken some of the sting out of Jacko, but luckily he didn't know that his left flank was completely unprotected from nine o'clock onwards. The regiment posted there pulled out at that hour, and Jacko, if he had known, could have walked quietly round and down the road to the horses.

With his posts in position, the Bushman came back to the one he had stationed at the edge of the gorge. There was a narrow track leading downwards, and it ended on a broad ledge with a deep drop below. The corporal at the post told him that he could hear whispering on the ledge, so the Bushman crawled a few yards along the track and bowled a stone over. The reply was a startled oath in good Australian, and it was quickly followed by two undeniable Australian troopers. They got a shock when they found that their squadron had been gone for nearly an hour, and they told the world, including Jacko, out loud what they thought of its leader for leaving them. As they bolted down the hill towards the road the Bushman heard something that sounded like "windy bastard."

Midnight came with the outpost line left undisturbed. Then, at two o'clock, orders came to fall back on the horses. With scarcely a halt the Horsemen rode steadily until they reached the valley. They had very little time up their sleeves, and the brigade on the job of keeping the Number Seven road open, not quite enough.

In March there had been a few signs of life in the valley, but there were none by the end of June. The irrigated plots had long since been burnt off under the overpowering heat, the Jordan moved sluggishly, and the streams feeding it from the foothills had shrunk to trickles. The soil of the valley might return to life with winter rains, but its sea had been dead since the Beginning.

The Bushman took a day off from the regimental camp in the Aujah for the purpose of satisfying himself whether or not it was possible to sink in the Dead Sea. A deserted chemical factory stood not far from the mouth of the Jordan and fresh water was still obtainable there. He knew he would need some after his swim, and he tasted the sea before he walked into it. It was more bitter than salt. From the narrow shingle beach the water deepened gradually, but before he was waist deep he was quite satisfied about its buoyancy. He had to make a genuine effort to push his feet downwards. Then he swam some distance and floated on his stomach with head, arms and legs well above the water. There was no doubt about it—a man might drown in the Dead Sea, but he wouldn't sink.

When he came out he was glad to sluice his tingling skin with fresh water, and he wondered what the buoyancy would be like at the sea's distant end. A motor-boat patrolled there occasionally, and the current yarn was that to enable its screw to function someone had to get out and hang on to the stem.

On either side of the lifeless water rugged black mountains rose steeply. It was the world's dead end. For all he knew there might have been seventy times seven devils lurking in the neighbourhood, and he didn't want to risk taking any back with him. The Aujah had quite enough of its own. He got on his horse and rode away quickly.

Most of the camps between the sea and Jericho were near the river and the ground had not yet been completely pulverised. Some miles from Jericho the Bushman stopped and counted the dust clouds to the north. There were ten, and each one hid a moving line of men and horses. There had been little enough chance of dodging dust on the Gaza front—here there was even less. Only the blessed water from the foothill streams made existence bearable.

Still, the same streams provided Jacko with two stout allies—snakes and mosquitoes, until they were dealt with. In the rubbish along the Wadis and in the rough brush which grew between the hills a particularly deadly breed of viper lurked. A few vigorous fatigue parties soon cleaned up the Wadis, and, by building in their beds with stones, converted the sluggish streams into millraces where no mosquito could breed. Snake fatigues were popular. When some enterprising M.O. wanted live specimens to provide venom for experimental purposes, the task of capturing them was entrusted, appropriately enough, to Sergeant "Magnoon." The M.O. soon had more than he knew what to do with.

A section of camel transport was camped in a low gully not far from Jericho, and just before the Bushman passed it he noticed a mixed flock of sheep and goats slowly feeding their way towards the sea. They were scattered wide and their

Bedouin shepherd was far in the rear. They passed the gully and through the tents just as the Bushman pulled up on the bank. Beside a tent the Hindoo cook sat like a graven image until one unlucky goat came within reach of his lightning dive.

"Sekeena! Sekeena!" he shouted to a satellite as he dragged his prize into the tent. The goat had bleated its last long before the shepherd got within hearing, and he took his flock onward in blissful ignorance that it was one short. Long before he discovered his loss all outward signs of goal had vanished. The Bushman knew the officer in charge of that transport section, and he called in to say good-day, hoping. He was not sent away empty-pouched.

That night he and his groom and batman dined sumptuously on roast goat on toast.

Riding past Jericho, the powdered dust reached his horse's knees and the heat of midday became pitiless. The Bushman felt a depression—a weariness of mind and body which he had never known under the desert sun at its worst. It may have been because he was at the bottom of the earth's underworld where the very air was charged with disease and death. Or it may have been because the war was in its fourth year and seemed to have become unending. Every casualty list, too, had a bigger percentage of the Regiment's foundation members, and the luck of those remaining could not be expected to last for ever.

Chapter Thirty-Four
Aujah - July 1918

If life was trying on the ground floor of the valley, it was ten times worse in the basement. The camps on the Aujah were hidden in deep and narrow Wadis. Sometimes a running stream gave compensation, but the one in the Mellahah was salt, and no one was surprised at that. Fresh water would have been out of place in that corner of hell on earth.

Where the Mellahah junctioned on to the Aujah it was fairly wide, but it soon narrowed between cliffs of soil, in places quite sheer. At intervals smaller but equally deep Wadis joined up. Each had a dead end whence over ages of time soil had been slowly sliding downwards. Above them plains stretched away to Musallabeh on one side and the Jordan on the other. There were no signs of watercourses to account for such terrific erosions, and when the Horsemen had nothing better to argue about they put up theories to account for them. The most popular one was that the Original Bottomless Pit lay directly under the Mellahah, and that at one time the inhabitants had tried to dig themselves out. The soil had been sliding down into the pit ever since.

The head of the Mellahah was protected by small redoubts, and for awhile regiments occupied them in turns, leaving their horses at the Aujah junction. Then an infantry brigade took them over, and the plains of El Maskerah between the Mellahah and the western foothills became the Horsemen's playground. They patrolled them by day and outposted them by night. Jacko enlivened the day job by shelling even a single horseman, and malarial mosquitoes were equally active at night. There was, too, always the chance that after dark the sentries on the Mellahah's most forward post might see things. They belonged to a brigade whose motto in peace-time was "No advance without security," and it applied equally well in war.

The Bushman led his troop on to the flat ground above the Aujah a little before dark The Maskerah outpost was the job ahead, and the first stage of it was to report to the C.O. of the forward post on the Mellahah. The track, well worn by the nightly limber traffic, led for a good deal of the way through low timber, and by the time the patrol reached the open plain darkness hid it from artillery observers on Red Hill. It dismounted outside the barbed wire entanglements at the rear of the post, and the Bushman went in to report.

He felt a bit depressed when he came out. Things were obviously pretty bad when they were reduced to the necessity of putting such a hotch-potch into the front line. Until then it had been guarding railways and pipelines in Sinai. His sympathy went out fully to a Scotty subaltern who had been pitchforked into it on his way home from Mespotamia. The Jock had begun the war in the Black Watch and was finishing it in the "Jordan Highlanders"! He had come to the regimental mess one evening, related his troubles, got very drunk, and cried very bitterly.

The corporal of the picquet over the camp's back entrance could speak English and the Bushman felt relieved. He told him what the patrol's job was, and that a single horseman—probably himself—would return by the back road in several hours' time to report that the outpost line was in position. The corporal promised faithfully that, as he posted each sentry, he would warn him of the expected horseman's arrival.

The patrol rode off and travelled half-a-mile northward along the edge of the reed-beds, before it wheeled towards Musallabeh. There was a distance of about two miles to be covered, and the Bushman dropped a chain of cossack posts at quarter-mile intervals. There was plenty of room for a Jacko army to have slipped in between; but Jacko bad never had much liking for such stunts, particularly at night, and at the moment he was probably just as sick of the war as the German engineer captured on the Nimrin road—or the Horsemen themselves, for that matter.

By the time the Bushman reached Musallabeh it was bright moonlight. He took the balance of his men to a central spot half-a-mile behind the line of listening post and made his dispositions for the night. Then he left to report to the Mellahah; but he took good care to come at that post by the limber road in the rear.

He could see the sentry standing with fixed bayonet just outside the entrance into the wire several hundred yards before he got there, so bright was the moonlight, but he didn't know that the sentry was trying to nerve himself to the point of putting his rifle to his shoulder and pulling the trigger. He was riding past with complete unconcern when the sentry suddenly came on guard and made a wild lunge at his horse's neck. A quick swerve saved the horse, and a string of oaths from its startled rider woke the echoes, and the corporal.

The corporal swore that he had given the warning about the expected horseman, and the sentry swore with even more agitation that he hadn't. The Bushman believed the latter and he assured the corporal that he would be minus his stripes in the morning. He found his Black Watch friend alone in the mess and told him the story. The Jock told him that disrating a corporal in the "Jordan Highlanders" could make no possible difference to losing the war, so the Bushman decided to let the matter drop, but to ask increased security before he made any further advances on that post—even in daylight.

"You leave the troop in the timber," said the adjutant.

"No use taking it out to get shelled over a job for a half-section."

The Bushman nodded and gave the order, "Walk march." The day patrol on the Maskerah plain was a simple job—merely one of clearing the ground for a certain distance and dodging a possible pip-squeak in the process. Only a direct hit could do much damage, and the odds against one were long since Jacko had three horsemen to choose from, riding a hundred yards apart. The Bushman had gone on far more risky jobs without giving the danger a thought; he was inwardly disturbed to find that he was giving this one a good deal—for the first time.

He wasn't the only one. Few men, if they were honest with themselves, could claim to be the same in the fourth year as they had in the first, except the "Snows" and the "Possums." The original members of the Regiment had dwindled to a mere handful. Those who could stand it no longer were trickling away to jobs in Base Records, the Post Office—even the Police. Some had been sent to Moascar. The Bushman decided that it would be better to endure even that fate than run the risk of letting men down.

The patrol moved through the timber until it reached the edge of the plain. The Bushman left his troop under cover and moved out with a half-section. A hundred yards apart, the three men rode slowly towards a solitary tree about a mile away.

Someone did this job every day, but still Jacko refused gifts. A machine-gun safely planted in the reed marshes flanking the patrol's line of advance could have bagged all three men. If the supporting troop had come to their rescue it would have provided the artillery behind Red Hill with good shooting. Jacko's inactivity could only be put down to his incurable suspicion of a trap.

It was the desire of Brigade Headquarters that the ground should be cleared as far as the solitary tree, and for most of the way the three men rode unmolested. When the first shot sounded, the Bushman signalled the half-section to turn about. To camouflage his rank and so avoid the special attention of the gunners he carried a rifle and wore a bandolier, but on this occasion they seemed to want him and no one else.

The first four shells came in quick succession and passed well over his head. He expected the next issue to be aimed at one of the others, but they still came in his direction with an obvious pause between shots and a rapidly improving range. His men expected an order to gallop, but they didn't get it. Not one shell went their way, but Jacko wasted at least twenty on the Bushman before he reached the cover of the timber. His troop, watching the fun in safety and making bets on the result, may possibly have thought that he was the coolest thing on earth; actually he was about the windiest.

Chapter Thirty-Five
Trans-Jordan - August 1918

The summer months passed slowly by. Heat, dust, thirst and flies dogged the Horsemen by day, malarial mosquitoes by night. Once or twice Jacko livened the areas round the Aujah with a half-hearted bombardment, but otherwise the game looked like ending in stalemate. Still, life had one bright spot; the eternal problem of the cookhouse had been solved—after nearly four years.

The regimental institution had never been revived since the crossing of the Canal. No matter what rations had been poured into it, nowhere near the same quantity came out, and where the missing balance went to was a mystery. Some of it might have been accounted for by the tit-bits the cooks handed out to their mates, but most of it probably went up in smoke. The squadron cookhouse was only a moderate improvement, and sending cooks to "schools" mostly meant giving them three weeks' extra leave. From Gallipoli days onwards, with rare exceptions, the cook's job drew applicants who objected to work. The Willing Horse, who might have slaved on behalf of his own troop, persistently refused to, do it for a squadron.

Section cooking when it came was hailed with delight by all except those who were either lazy or dignified. At least everyone got his issue to the last ounce, and nearly every section held someone who could knock up a feed. The system worked well for years, but the gradual passing of the older hands made the spirit of self-help slacken, and, in the Mellahah, things were going from bad to worse when the great reform came. The reorganisation of the canteen system was largely responsible for it.

At first it was nearly impossible to get anything worthwhile from the canteen, for as soon as a supply came in, the brigade camped nearest bought up all the sausages and tinned fruit, leaving plenty of writing pads, shaving soap and toothpaste for the others. After repeated and indignant protests, the canteen authorities put eatables on issue to regimental quartermasters, who dealt with them on usual lines, except that they exacted cash payment.

It was then that some genius in the Bushman's troop thought of a troop mess. A cookhouse was built, a cook appointed, and all resources, canteen and regimental, were pooled. The mess ran a president, treasurer and committee, and the cook, working for his own pals, dished it up to them hot. They invited the Bushman to breakfast one morning and asked him what he thought of it. After a plentiful feed of sausages and bacon, he decided that the war was as good as won. Before many days passed the squadron had four cookhouses in full swing; but, like all great reforms, troop cooking didn't get through without a struggle.

The chief opposition came from the M.O. He wasn't a bad sort as M.O.'s went, but he held the view that four cookhouses in one line made proper sanitation doubtful if not impossible, and he couldn't see why what was being done for four troops separately couldn't be done for the squadron collectively. He had never been through the ranks, and the mental processes of the rankers were beyond him. Luckily for the squadron, every officer it had, including the leader, had begun the war as a trooper. They put up such a fight that the M.O. climbed down. The fame of the squadron's new enterprise spread; soon every troop in the Regiment had its own mess, and everything was merry and bright, especially when it became known that the brigade was going to Solomon's Pools for a fortnight's rest.

"I've some pleasant news for you, gentlemen," said the adjutant. "There will be an inspection at 1400 this afternoon. Men will shave and wear bandoliers. They don't need to kiwi up specially. The whole brigade will parade on the flat ground near B.H.Q."

A small group of officers heard him in stunned silence. The Regiment had arrived at Talaat-ed-Dumm a few days previously on its way to the two weeks' precious rest near Bethlehem. It had had seven continuous weeks on the Mellahah, and it was rotten with malaria. It was to ride through to Solomon's Pools that night. A major asked a question for the others as well as himself.

"Has he gone stone mad?"

The adjutant spoke reprovingly.

"My dear fellow," he said, "if you were a general commanding such gallant troops as these and properly concerned about their health, wouldn't you give them the tonic of seeing and hearing you as often as you could?"

"It's all right for you to be sarcastic," the major retorted. "It means waiting about all the afternoon in the broiling sun and getting back to the lines just before saddle up. Why couldn't he have waited till we'd had a week at Solomon's Pools if he *must* have a look at us?"

"Well, there it is," replied the adjutant. "You can have my sympathy, if it's any use to you. The squadrons will leave their lines at 1330. You'd better break the news to them now, gently."

The Bushman, as Senior Loot in his squadron, was temporarily in charge of it, his major being away. He went across to the lines at once. An all-night ride following on the heels of the inspection would settle what little guts the men had in them, and he cursed the shortsightedness of a general who couldn't or wouldn't see it.

The worst of it was that there was a lot of truth in the adjutant's sarcasm. The general was concerned about the men, but unfortunately he occasionally showed that concern at times, and in places, and in ways which made rankers doubt its existence. As a result the less they saw of him the better they liked him. The fact that he was an able soldier only made matters worse. It showed how simply a man, who was otherwise a clever tactician, could defeat his own ends.

The type wasn't confined to generals; it existed right down the scale, even unto lance-jacks. During his passage up to commissioned rank the Bushman had had plenty of chances to study if. He came early to the conclusion that the best results, the winning of the war being the objective, were obtained by a commonsense use of the blind eye and a judicious amount of kid. And, if it did become necessary to hit, to hit hard.

The squadron took the news with resignation, since most of its cursing powers had been sapped by Mellahah mosquitoes. Men shaved, put on tunics and bandoliers, gave their boots the once over, and marched across to B.H.Q.

The parade formed up at 1400 in hollow square. That looked ominous; it meant that inspection would almost certainly be followed by an address. Like most poor speakers, the general had a voice to match, and he was long-winded into the bargain. The prospect of hearing once again what most of the horsemen already knew by heart was the last straw. They had one consolation: a strong wind was blowing and only those at close quarters would be able to hear.

Time passed, but no dust-cloud proclaimed the arrival of a staff car, and the men availed themselves gratefully of the permission to sit down. At last the general turned up—an hour late. He was staggered to learn that the parade had been waiting; the time should have been fixed for three o'clock, not two. The Horsemen might have forgiven the blunder, and even taken back some of the curses they had been calling down on the general's head, if he had been satisfied to thank them briefly for their service and let them go. A few optimists thought he might, for once.

It was a vain hope. Followed by his staff and the brigadier, the general made a leisurely tour. He looked at every man, he spoke to one or two he knew personally, and he shook hands with the wearers of South African ribbons, Long before he completed his inspection silent prayers were going up that, since the land had a record of being one of miracles, the earth beneath his feet might open suddenly and close slowly.

The inspection over, the general took up a central position and began his address. Most of it was blown away on the wind, but the Bushman could hear movements in the ranks behind him, and he knew well enough what was happening. Men were collapsing and being helped to the rear.

At last the ordeal ended. The general intimated that he wished the R.S.M.'s to march their respective units away, and all officers to remain. He gave them a further quarter of an hour; but the Bushman, for one, was long past listening. He came to his senses fully while strolling back to camp with the two colonels, half a-dozen majors and twenty captains and loots. They were all talking at once—it was well that the rocks of Talaat-ed-Dumm were unable to echo their words back to B.H.Q., where the brigadier was getting his personal issue.

Just before dark the brigade moved off along the narrow road leading up the mountains. The night was sweltering, and the breeze which might have given some relief dropped at sundown. Many men slept as they rode, and during the halts lay in a stupor in front of their horses. The Bushman had never been able to sleep in the saddle, but during this night The craving overpowered him. He could not sleep, nor could he keep awake. During the halts he dared not sit down—he could not risk missing an order. Once he fell. At last, in desperation he swallowed a mouthful of rum, neat, and its sting drove the pain of sleep-craving from his brain and body. At intervals during that long night he took sips from his bottle and held the spirit in his mouth until it burnt. He rode into the camp at Solomon's Pools next morning feeling almost fresh, but thirty men of the brigade were evacuated that day to hospital.

The field-ambulance colonel was ropeable. He used language which should have put him in front of a firing squad, and he swore he would take the matter through to the C.-in-C. himself; but he didn't. It was explained to him that the one sure result of his representations would be his own return to Australia. Then, discipline had to be considered. Such action could only undermine the confidence of the rank and file in its leaders, and that might easily mean losing the war! After a while the ambulance colonel was able to join with the most disgruntled trooper in seeing the joke.

For two precious weeks the Horsemen rested. They lived

largely on grapes, tomatoes and pure air. Early in August they descended into hell once more—but for the last time. As they rode down the last foothills in the forenoon's breathless heat, spiral whirlwinds of dust rose to greet their return to the Dead World.

On the first of September the Regiment moved across the Jordan. Any change from the Mellahah was welcome, and the Bushman got away from it with nothing worse than Jericho sores. For three years he had not been troubled by so much as a headache and he began to believe he was 'malaria-proof', but the mosquitoes near Ghoraniyeh did what those in the Mellahah couldn't. They put him in hospital. His last day's work was to take his troop on the Nimrin patrol, but he spent most of it in the shade of a bamboo clump with a raging temperature. Somehow in the evening he managed to ride to camp and the M.O. promptly evacuated him.

He did not miss much, for the end of Jacko was close at hand. The thrust in Northern Palestine succeeded even more thoroughly than the third battle of Gaza, and it left the army holding the east Jordan foothills with no option but speedy retreat.

There was no chance of repeating the Jaffa drive this time. The rugged mountain country prevented flanking, and Jacko was in full retreat along the three existing roads before his movements were suspected. Once more the Regiment climbed the Number Four road through empty camps and deserted dumps which told a complete story of enemy demoralisation. The few parties the Horsemen overtook surrendered freely, and two days after leaving the valley the Horsemen were once more threatening Amman. Its defence was half-hearted, and by evening the Regiment was camped in the centre of the-town. Its final casualty list was one killed and two wounded.

Still, the Horsemen had a few more shots to fire—but not at Jacko. At Aziza, twenty miles southward, several thousands—the remnant of the Mecca army—were being dogged by Arabs in much the way that a pack of dingoes follows a crippled bullock. When a couple of mounted squadrons appeared Jacko surrendered to them in mass formation on one condition, that he should be protected against his cutthroat co-religionists. Allah went into the background when an Arab could see a harvest of blood and loot ready for the taking. The Horsemen were only too delighted to go to Jacko's rescue, and the order to fire on anything appearing on the skyline was most welcome.

The Regiment was ordered down to take part in this last variation of the war. It arrived in time to see most of the fun and to fire a few shots on behalf of its enemies against its allies! Jacko had outposts on the ridges surrounding his camp, and the Regiment did its last there, side by side with the men against whom it had warred for over three years. When the work of collecting prisoners began, a new problem arose. They had to be marched to the valley, somehow, and until they got there they would still need protection from the gentlemen of Arabia. The Jacko army marched out of Aziza still in possession of its rifles, and it did not pile arms for the last time until it reached the prison camps already prepared for it.

There was nothing more for the Horsemen to do in the Trans-Jordan mountains. By slow stages the Regiment moved back, and once more it camped in the valley, but only for one night. During the long uphill ride to Jerusalem few men cared to look back.

Chapter Thirty-Six
Cairo - October 1918

Afternoon tea was in full swing at the Continental. Waiters in white robes and scarlet sashes hurried to and fro, and the band blared as usual. There was nothing to show that the day differed from any other. A few men in uniform sat amongst the civilian crowd. It was just ordinary Cairo.

The Bushman sat at a table with a couple of his brother officers. He had seen no one from the Regiment since his evacuation with malaria, and he had much to hear.

"We were able to identify most of them," one of the officers told him. "The Turks had buried them, but of course the Arabs had dug them up for their clothes. Anyway, everyone who was missing that day has been accounted for."

The Bushman asked: "Did any of them get near the machine-guns?"

"One or two. We had a good look at Jacko's possies, and there's no doubt he knew how to build them. Even shrapnel could not have done them any real damage. The squadron went to certain destruction when it left the hilltop, and the men knew it. They knew about the blunder too, just as the boys of Balaclava did. Still they went."

"You found Snow?"

"Yes. They've all been brought back. Blood, to the cemetery at Jerusalem."

"Where's the Regiment camped now?"

"Wadi Ianein. It's not the same since the 1914 men kit for home. A good few others have gone too—leave to England and Gawd knows where. They're making new N.C.O.'s every day. You'll see chaps troopers to-day and sergeants next week. It's not going to be easy, killing time, and with all the old non-coms gone, some of the 'jockeys' and 'judges' will soon begin to play up, I'm going to wangle leave home somehow. You ought to do the same."

The Bushman shook his head. He said: "I didn't come away with the Regiment, but I'm going back with it. It shouldn't take long now, I suppose they won't want us any more, even if this armistice isn't signed."

The band broke off in the middle of a bar and began the National Anthem. The men in uniform stood rigidly. They sat again unmoved, and after some moments' silence one said: "I suppose that means it's all over. Go and have a look at te notice board, someone."

The Bushman got up and passed through the swing doors into the main lounge. A few officers stood looking at the communique board. An official message stated badly that an armistice had been signed by Germany at eleven o'clock that morning. He returned to his pals.

"Yes, it's signed," he said. "They've given the order 'Cease fire.' And no one seems to care a damn."

He looked around him. Soldiers and civilians alike were carrying on as usual. There was no excitement, no congratulatory remarks; not even a handshake.

"Well, how do you feel about it?" asked one of his pals. "Have you got a cheer left in you? I haven't."

The Bushman admitted that he hadn't either. He said: "Of course, our show's been over for weeks. I expect the boys in France are feeling a relief from the strain."

"Yes," replied the other, "but they're not cheering. They'll leave that to the civvies. It'll be a proper 'maffick' in London or Sydney, but not here."

The Bushman laughed.

"The civvies here will be putting on mourning. I was in Alex the day Bulgaria pulled out, and there was such a hullaballoo in front of the Stock Exchange I thought a riot was on. So there was—inside the building. Prices were toppling at the first whisper of peace. Egypt'll have to get back to work now; it won't be able to live on baksheesh much longer."

"We won't, either. After all, there's always been some

comfort in the old pay-book with its seven days a week. I suppose the next thing a man'll have to do will be to think of what's going to happen to him when he's a civvy. What about you, Mac? Going back to wheat cockying?"

Mac shook his head energetically.

"Not on your life," he said; "I've given the army four years, it can do something for, me now. There'll be good jobs going. I'm damned if I'm going back to fight droughts and do a starve growing wheat to feed anti-conscriptionists. Blood'll go back to his patch of brigalow scrub, I suppose."

The Bushman answered:

"I don't know what I'll do yet. I'll start thinking of it when I put on civvies; not before."

"Well, someone ought to do something to celebrate the winning of the war. I suppose we have won it. Make a suggestion, Mac."

"All right. Let's fall in all the fellows on leave, and march 'em round to the Savoy and make Allenby shout. Or we might raid the pay-office."

"We might have done that once; there's not enough kick left in the boys nowadays."

The group broke up and the Bushman strolled off to the park in Opera Square. He found a quiet spot and sat down to think things out. He was on three weeks leave following his discharge from hospital, but he still felt shaky. The poison of the Jordan Valley had not quite left his body.

The war was over. He knew that most men would be like boys let out of school at the prospect of going home, but there would be a few, like himself, who could work up no special enthusiasm about it. On the day the Regiment broke up he would be spiritually homeless, and he had never been able to shake off a feeling of bitter resentment against his country. Perhaps a quarter of its people had been for the war, heart and soul no matter what it cost; another quarter had been as bitterly hostile as it dared. The remainder had been lukewarm, taking all it could get in return for lip-service. There would, of course, be fervent welcomes until the novelty of home-coming soldiers wore off, and those who had scabbed hardest would cheer loudest. He thought of the sergeant whose leave had been refused, lying in his Beersheba grave; of Snow, thrice wounded. Snow, whose body had been left to the jackals, animal and human, of Arabia, and he knew that while memory remained he would never forgive those of his countrymen who by their votes had stabbed the Australian army in the back. He silently vowed that he would never march through the streets of an Australian city and listen to the mocking lip-service of the anti-conscription mob.

He left the park and crossed Opera Square. The ending of the war had brought him a different problem, and as he walked slowly along the Sharia Madebegh he tried to work out its solution. He came co the door of a small clothes-cleaning establishment and went in. He rapped on the counter.

A girl came quickly from an inner room. She had dark hair, flashing eyes, and an olive skin with a healthy flush of colour in her cheeks. She was poorly dressed, her stockings had been darned in many places, and her dilapidated shoes were signs of honest poverty. The Bushman kissed her across the narrow counter.

"My tunic ready, Marika?" he asked.

She shook her head,

"I sorry," she said in halting: English. "No one hardly work to-day. Ze war is fineesh."

He smiled. "And aren't you glad?"

She did not reply.

He continued: "Come, little Marika, surely you're glad it's over? You've always told me you were afraid I'd get killed."

Still she ignored his question. She asked: "When you go home?"

He laughed rather uneasily. "So that's what's the matter? Not for months and months yet."

She insisted. "But you go—some day."

"Yes, of course."

"And you leave Marika?"

"Well, I could hardly take you to Australia, could I?"

"Why you not take me?"

"You wouldn't like it out there, Marika. It's not like Cairo. Besides, what about your sister? You wouldn't want to leave her, and I couldn't take you both, could I?"

Her pleading mood changed to one of anger. She said; "I not care what she do. She think I bad girl. One day she say to me, 'Why you go with Australian officer in motor-car? You bad girl, you prostitute,' and we quarrel. I say, 'If I prostitute I not wear rags, I buy new dress and rings.'" She paused. "You know I not bad girl."

The Bushman spoke soothingly.

"Of course I do. Your sister's jealous because you're lovely. That's all."

She came quickly from behind the counter and seized his hand imploringly.

"If I lovely, why you not take me? You fond of me. I work for you, I die for you. If you leave me I wish you killed: I kill myself. No woman ever love you like Marika love."

She threw her arms about him and hid her face. He disengaged them gently.

"We'll talk about it to-night. I'll bring a car and we'll go for a drive first. Where shall I pick you up?"

She named a street corner in Esbekieh. He said: "All right, then—at nine o'clock. Now I must go."

He had time to kill after dinner, so he hired a car and drove out to Mena. For awhile he sat in the shadow of the Sphinx, but he thought more of the Regiment than of Marika, It meant more to him than any woman ever had or ever would, and already what was left of it was beginning to dissolve. The 1914 men had gone, and others were going. There would be difficult times ahead; ail he could do would be to help keep its record intact.

Suddenly he remembered Marika, and looked at his watch.

It was late. He returned to his car and told the driver to hurry. As it turned the corner near Shepheard's the Bushman thought that he had come to a revival of old days in the Wazir. The street was packed with excited Gyppos and shrieks sounded from the road leading to Esbekieh. The driver summed up the situation in three words: "Esbekieh finish, Effendim."

It certainly looked like it. The jeweller's shop on the corner nearest Shepheard's was a wreck. Slabs of glass from its windows lay shattered on the pavement, and the inside array of jewels had gone. Shutters from shops on either side had been wrenched off in more or less wanton destruction. The Bushman paid off his car, and from the din in the side street he concluded that the rioters, whoever they were, were meeting with some resistance. He hurried to the outskirts of the disturbance, thankful that for once, at least, Australia couldn't be blamed for it. He saw one plumed hat and recognised an N.C.O. from his own brigade.

"What's happening. Corporal?"

"There's hell to pay, sir. That wild mob camped near Heliopolis has broken loose. They burnt down their picture show and looted a canteen last night, so they gave 'em all leave to-night. They cleaned up the shops near Shepheard's in two ticks, and they're taking the street in a face."

"None of our fellows mixed up in it?"

"Haven't seen any."

"That's good. Perhaps this show'll make up for the Wazir. It may convince English residents here that we're not the only undisciplined mob in Egypt."

The corporal grinned. He was a 1914 man. He said: "Strooth! Listen to those screams! They must be rough-housing some of the bints."

The Bushman gave a start as he remembered Marika. The corner where he was to have met her was dangerously near the storm centre. Still—

He said: "Let's get down a bit closer. Corporal; there might be some of our fellows—"

As they reached the fringe of the struggling crowd two

hatless men with bleeding faces burst from it. They saw the officer's uniform and hurried to where the Bushman stood.

"They've murdered a bint down there," one exclaimed breathlessly. "Me and my mate tried to stop it, and a mob of the curs got to us."

The other took up the tale.

"She was standing on the comer when they came along, and wouldn't clear out, but hung on to a lamp-post. One big swine grabbed her, and she smacked him over the face. He tore most of her clothes off and hoisted her on his shoulder, and she kicked him in the mouth. Then he chucked her on her head in the gutter and poured the boot in."

"We went to try and help her and they nearly kicked our guts in," continued the first. "She's dead all right. By Gawd, she was a bonzer looking girl, too."

The Bushman's voice shook slightly as he said: "Come on, you fellows; let's see if we can do anything. Get back to back if they try to interfere with us."

They were joined by several others, and they pushed their way through the crowd to where a circle of Gyppos stood round a bleeding and half-naked body lying in the gutter.

At midnight two horsemen turned into the Sharia Madebegh and made for Rossmore House. One said suddenly:

"I believe he knew that bint."

The other replied: "Garn! What makes you think that?"

"Well, why should the sight of a dead bint make him stagger and call out, 'Oh, my Gawd' the way he did? He knew her all right."

"Not him. I know that officer—he's in our brigade. Just come out of hospital after malaria. His nerve's gone, that's all, and he's like plenty more. It lasted a bit too long for some of 'em, old son. Bloody good job it's over."

Chapter Thirty-Seven
Egypt - December 1918

Once more the Bushman crossed Sinai—on his way this time to a peace camp. He found the Regiment camped near Wadi Hanein, killing time as best it could with football and bridge and an occasional race meeting. He took over his troop again, but it was some time before he could memorise its new names and faces. Both his sergeants had been troopers when he had seen them last, and in the mess, he found that most of his particular pals had departed! with the 1914 leave men.

The mess tents stood on a hillside overlooking the village of Surafend. On the night the Bushman returned, two staff men from D.H.Q. were guests at dinner, and the murder of an Enzed the previous night was the main topic of conversation. One of the visitors supplied details.

"He woke and made a spring at the Arab, and got in full charge of slugs straight through the guts. The Arab dropped the blunderbuss and bolted, and some of the fellows nearly got him as he tripped over the tent rope but he was too slippery to hold. They tracked him to the village later on. I was down in the Enzed lines this morning. I didn't hear much, but the look on some of the fellows' faces was quite enough. I wouldn't like to be one of the Arabs in that village to-night. There'll be Rafferty's rules there unless I'm much mistaken."

Someone said: "I heard a rumour that they've been round the lines recruiting. Isn't D.H.Q. doing anything?"

The staff man shrugged his shoulders. He said: "D.H.Q.'s done all it could. A cordon was put round the village as soon as the murder was reported, and it would have been there now if G.H.Q. hadn't ordered its removal. Unluckily we're in G.H.Q. territory. If anything happens in that village—and something will—don't blame Division. There! What did I tell you!"

The silence in the hollow where the village lay broke with startling suddenness. Screams, loud shouting and yells of "Knock him! Knock him." rang out continuously. Then, at successive points, smoke shot up, and the glow of flame soon followed it.

The colonel gave an instant order for a roll-call. Groups of men stood about the lines watching, listening and speculating. The uproar was soon at its height, and the glow from the burning village lit the hollow sufficiently to show the cordon surrounding it and the fleeing Arabs being turned back by the ugly rush of men armed with cudgels. The roll-call accounted for every man in the Regiment but three, and everyone knew where they were.

As the Bushman was leaving the mess three mornings later he was stopped by the cook. He was orderly officer for the day.

"Any chance of getting me an off-sider, Sir?" he said.

"I can't manage the dixies and everything on my pat."

"No sign of Mahmoud?" the Bushman asked.

"No, the black 'kelp's' still A.W.L. I s'pose he was down in the village and got knocked on the head like the rest of the ... By Gawd! I believe that's him coming now!"

An Arab was slowly approaching the cookhouse. His hesitation suggested that he would have run the other way for choice, but something even more powerful than fear lured him on. The cook greeted him cordially.

"You bloody black bastard, where th' hell have you been the last three days? Here, get busy on those dixies, or not a skerrick of mungeree will you get."

The Arab took no notice of him. He sneaked up to the galley and squatted down against its wall, his gaze downwards. His hands shook and his teeth chattered. The cook took pity on him.

"Windy, ain't he, Sir?" he said. "He must've been in the village all right. Wonder how he got away? Here, Mahmoud, tell us how you dodged the 'Askaris'?"

Not a word could they get from Mahmoud. He glanced furtively at the ground beside him, but made no move.

The cook threw him a tin of bully beef.

"P'raps he'll talk better on a full gut. I'd like to know what happened. You might be able to get the yarn out of him, Sir."

The Bushman said he'd try. He had an idea that Mahmoud would tell the story of his own creation for five piastres.

Some months previously Mahmoud had hung about the camp for days, drawn by the magnet of "mungeree keteer." In a rash moment he had ventured into the lines, but had been promptly pelted out of them with volleys of clods and horse-dung. His line of flight had taken him past the officers' mess at a moment when the cook was carrying in a roast. The smell was irresistible. Mahmoud circled the cookhouse, and since the ground was bare of ammunition, he finally mustered enough courage to allow him to approach a greasy-looking individual wearing a singlet, breeches without leggings, and boots without socks. They came to an amicable arrangement. In return for scrubbing the dixies and scavenging generally, Mahmoud could fill himself daily on "bulla."

Mahmoud worked so well that the cook even slung him & few piastres occasionally, as well as fatherly advice to keep out of the horse-lines, and particularly not to go near another camp of Askaris just over the hill if he valued his proofs of masculinity—to say nothing of his life. He found a "bint" in the village with whom he spent most of his leisure hours, but the attractions of Delilah took him there once too often.

Mahmoud heard the fatal shot fircd in the camp over the hill, and he knew from the subsequent suppressed excitement in the village that it might become unhealthy at any moment, so he left promptly for his camp behind the cook-house; but since nothing happened that night, he took a chance on the one following. This time his reception by the villagers was so hostile that he left early. Before he went a hundred yards from the most outlying mud hut, he saved his life by a quick sidestep.

Two figures rose suddenly and silently from the ground and dashed at him with uplifted clubs.

Mahmoud wheeled and raced back to the village. He had barely reached it when the uproar began. He tried to escape on the farther side, but was driven back by a rush even more difficult to escape than the first one. The village was surrounded.

His fleetness of foot saved him more than once, but the Askaris seemed to be everywhere. Again and again he heard a sound that increased his terror—the sickening thud of a club on a skull. Several times he ran into the arms of the Askaris, but escaped minus most of his clothes. He saw men dragged to the village well and hurled headlong downwards.

At last, completely exhausted, he staggered into a hut which had escaped the firestick, and in one corner he saw a pile of women's clothing. During his ducking and dodging he had kept his wits sufficiently to notice that no harm was being done to women and children, and the knowledge saved his life. In the few seconds left him Mahmoud disguised himself as a bint, effectively, and cowered in a corner of the hut. He was soon discovered and dragged to a compound where some of the Askaris were mounting guard over a number of women and children.

He lay quaking in their midst until the tumult died down. Then, along with the others, he was taken to the outskirts of the village, shown the road to Enab, and told to "Imshi." He obeyed the order too eagerly. His speed aroused immediate suspicion, and some Askaris gave chase; but Mahmoud had a few yards start and that was quite enough.

"And where did you go?" asked the Bushman.

Mahmoud had no idea. He only knew that he had run until he dropped, and had spent two days hidden in an orchard. The Bushman wondered why he had come back, but Mahmoud didn't tell him that his little hoard of piastres was hidden in a tin behind the cookhouse, and he was only waiting for a chance to unearth it.

The chance came a few minutes later when their backs were

turned. A cheer from the cook brought everyone out of the mess to see what had happened.

"Gawd! Can't he sprint? Good-bye, Mahmoud. First stop Akaba. Did he tell you what happened, Sir?"

The Bushman retailed Mahmoud's story. He added that he wished the Regiment had got going in the same way before the sacking of Surafend. There would be hell to pay, and the fact that the Regiment could prove an alibi would make no difference. It was on the spot, and that would be enough. The whole division, absent or present, would get it in the neck. The cook listened in silence. Then he delivered judgement with a dixie lid in each hand.

"Well, Sir," he said, "I'm not sayin' that it wasn't plain murder, but you can bank on this, that there won't be any more fellers shot through the guts with a fistful of slugs. What would you have felt like doin' if it had been one of your pals? Anyhow, Surafend's been a nest of thieves since before Abraham. They tell me that the Jews in Richon held a special thanksgiving service the day after it was cleaned up."

A few days later three regiments paraded at a spot not far from the ruins of the silent village. The balance of the division was scattered far and wide, but each brigade was represented on the parade.

The parade stood easy whilst waiting for the Commander-in-Chief of the front. Amongst the men then; was a tenseness, a silence which showed that this was no ordinary gathering, and many of them as well as their officers prayed that nothing might happen to make matters worse. The war was over, and the ranks included many "rainbows" to whom regimental records meant nothing. There was a definite risk that even the Commander-in-Chief might be counted out if he overdid it.

The divisional commander stood at the entrance to the parade square. He and his supporting staff looked far from happy, and with good reason. When the general rode up he made no acknowledgment of any salutes. He looked at the parade and rapped out an order;

"I want the New Zealand regiment brought closer," A few moments sufficed to bring the Enzeds into the more direct line of the fire to come. When the general spoke every man heard him, and years passed before many of them forgot or forgave the bitter injustice of his words. Some never did.

He said: "For four years, as a division, you have steadily made a good name, a great name; but in one night you have washed it out. You have proved yourselves at heart to be cowards and murderers. Those of you who could beat unarmed men to death are both; those who know where the guilt lies and will not say are merely cowards. I would have no mercy on that guilt if I could sheet it home. I cannot; therefore I will not punish the innocent for the crimes of the guilty." He paused for a moment to give dramatic effect to the thunder of his final sentence. "I was proud of you once; I am proud of you no longer." Again he ignored the salute of the divisional commander as he wheeled his horse and rode swiftly away.

At the words "cowards and murderers" a murmur rippled through the ranks, but it quickly died away. For that small relief the Bushman, for one, felt grateful as he marched his troop back to camp.

The bridge players put down their cards as the adjutant came into the mess. They guessed that he had a bomb to drop.

"Leave is stopped indefinitely for all officers in the division, and all recommendations for decorations are cancelled. That applies to all ranks."

Someone murmured: "This practice must cease. Anything else, Mac?"

"No—at least that's all G.H.Q. can think of at the moment."

"Well, convey our respects to the C.-in-C. and tell him we like the way he keeps his word not to lump the innocent with the guilty."

"He's thought better of it. This is where we collect."

"But what about the other regiments? They're scattered

from here to Gallipoli. Do you mean to say they're included?"

"Certainly. It's a divisional crime."

"But D.H.Q.'s enquiry proved that there were fellows there from the battery and G.H.Q. itself. What's the C.-in-C. got to say about that?"

The adjutant laughed. "Better ask him."

"Well, we're all well branded now; What he should have done on that parade was to have given the order. 'Cowards and murderers, two paces step forward. March!' We could all have moved, and satisfied him."

"Oh, well, we're playing bridge. Come on, you cowards and murderers, let's finish this rubber. Your call Norm."

"My call? Certainly. Three 'Surafends.'"

Chapter Thirty-Eight
Egypt - December 1918

On Christmas morning the Bushman woke with a headache, but it wasn't due to malaria. He joined the adjutant and orderly officer at breakfast, but everyone else slept it off, The good work had begun on the previous afternoon. Supplies were obtainable without difficulty and the officers' mess handed out an additional case of whisky per squadron "buchshee." Later in the evening the mess was surrounded and serenaded, but by midnight the lines were deserted. There was a mass movement towards the headquarters of another brigade for the purpose of making "Old Charlie" shout. A few got there safely and succeeded. The next objective was a popular officer on division, but D.H.Q, was too far away. The would-be serenaders collapsed in their tracks.

After breakfast the Bushman went to see how the horses were getting on. They had been fed, but the picquets had gone back to bed. The tents were silent, the cookhouses cold. He found the orderly officer trying to solve the problem of getting several hundred horses to water. There was not a man to be seen, and, most unprecedented of all, there were live marines lying at more than one tent doorway. For once the supply had more than equalled the demand.

"By Gawd, Blood, how are we going to get these horses to water? There's not a man in the squadron sober enough to sit on one."

The Bushman doubted him. He could remember a few of his old pals who had kept as sober as judges during the wildest nights.

"All right," said the orderly officer. "Tell you what I'll do. You give me a fiver, and I'll give you back a quid for every sober man you can find. Is it a bet?"

The Bushman pulled out a wad of notes and began to peel off five, but at that moment two of the old section he had led in his lance-jack days staggered out of a tent. For a few moments they held each other up, then they collapsed. The Bushman was well satisfied that if they were in such a state everyone else in the squadron would be unconscious. He put the wad of notes back into his pocket.

"No, you don't," he said. "You win easily."

Soon after New Year every unit on the front seemed to be camped at Rafa, partly to simplify administration and partly for demobilisation purposes. In the circumstances it was a dangerous move. The backbone of every unit, the N.C.O.'s, who carried more weight than any officers, had gone. They had acquired their status during four years of service and they could not be replaced. The ranks held a large percentage of "peace delegates," and the gospel in the camps at Rafa was simple. The war was over. Before long civilian life would put everyone on the same footing, and to hell with those who seemed to think the show was beginning instead of ending.

Men had to have occupation, even the worst camp outlaw admitted that. The programme was reasonable enough—mornings were allotted to the parade ground, and afternoons to football, with race meetings at the week-ends. Killing time in the morning parades was the chief difficulty, and most officers racked their brains every night thinking of something fresh for the following day. For awhile the Bushman kept his troop amused by promoting the latest comers to the rank of temporary-acting-lance-jacks and, letting them try out their drilling powers. Then after an issue of that he would march the troop to a spot where it could sit down unseen by the wrong eyes and invite questions about the many incidents of the campaign for which no one had been able to find a reason. He gave short lectures, but like most junior officers he kept his ear well to the ground and he learnt enough to make him hope fervently that something would happen to scatter the units of

205

the Rafa camp before it was too late.

Nothing very serious happened until the weather took a hand. The rainy season set in and brought violent wind and bitter cold with it at a time when mounted parades were the order of the day. Brigade-majors urged their cancellation in vain. The climax came when squadron-leaders refused to ask men to drill in driving rain and took them back to camp.

At last it came to the holding of mass meetings, to the delivery of inflammatory speeches and threats of inflammatory action, and conciliatory action by those in authority was hailed by the chief trouble-makers merely as evidence of weakness. There were firebrands loose amongst the men whose last intention was conciliation, and while officers might have easily handled their respective units had they been camped apart, they were helpless against mass suggestion.

Relief did come, and next to instant demobilisation it came in the best way. Riots broke out. in the Egyptian delta, and the Horsemen were ordered to a new front. The camp at Rafa was broken up in time, but only just. A plot had been hatched to burn down D.H.Q. by a handful of criminals who had spent most of the war years in military prisons and who had drifted back to their units as soon as danger passed.

Horsemen! With the exception of a few officers' hacks there wasn't a horse on the lines. They had all been graded, and all unfit for further service found a grave in the sandhills between Rafa and the coast. Morally that slaughter was pitilessly inhuman; actually it was merciful. The repatriation of horses that had spent years in a disease-ridden land was impossible, and the alternative to a painless death was slavery at the hands of an Arab. More than one horse passed as fit was shot quietly by its owner rather than allow it to run that risk. The Bushman was amongst the few officers who held on to their horses until the last. He had his reward later when he watched his fatten on the green berseem of the delta. It was a mare that had belonged to a pal who fell at Amman.

Chapter Thirty-Nine
Egypt - February 1919 to June 1919

The Regiment spent some days on the Canal while it re-equipped for the new campaign. When it tried its luck at a remount depot there were not enough horses to go round, and mules were placed on issue. That looked like rubbing it in after four years on horseback, but there was no choice. Squadrons were marched in single file to a remount shed and each man halted opposite a rump in a stall. If the rump happened to belong to a mule, that was that. One man at least was blessed with luck. He halted behind the horse he had handed in some months previously.

When the Regiment rode out on its way to the train it only needed Alexander's band to complete the picture of a ragtime army. Still, a few horses whose breeding was obvious found their way into the trucks. They had been got by Moonlight out of Remount Depot.

The delta patrols were something new, and the Regiment welcomed a camp to itself. From Quesna it patrolled the surrounding country and did police duty at the railway station. It found squadrons for detached work at other centres, but its activities were mainly peaceful. The worst of the rioting and destruction took place further north, but the reprisal which followed the murder of two horsemen put a stop to the general sabotage.

This time the reprisal was official. The two horsemen were shot dead from across a deep canal during a night patrol. Their bodies were taken back to camp, and at daylight there was a general go-as-you-please towards the village held responsible. Machine-guns, bombs and petrol took the place of clubs as weapons, but G.H.Q. had learned something from Surafend and took instant action. Long before daylight the village was surrounded by a battalion of infantry, and the colonel commanding the sector was waiting on its outskirts to meet the invading Horsemen. He told them that his instructions from G.H.Q. were to assemble and flog the entire male population, and he suggested that they should send along a few representatives to take a hand in the game if they felt that way. A few took him at his word, the rest of the expedition returned to camp.

There was no triangle in the village, but a window in the courtyard used as a guillotine made a suitable substitute. Over a hundred men were mustered, stripped, and dragged one by one to the window. The sentence was twelve strokes each from a sjambok, but the count was not kept with any special accuracy until the loggers tired. Long before the last man was dealt with, even the pals of the murdered horsemen were satisfied. If the Arab version can be believed, a dozen of those who were flogged never needed correction again—in this world.

Towards the end of the Regiment's stay in Quesna it took part in a stunt known as the "Turkey Trot," and no man was ever heard to growl when his sergeant warned him for it. The fellahin had to be paid for fodder supplies, and by way of adding to the popularity of the army it was formally identified with the handing out of several thousand pounds daily. An officer and a section accompanied the officials who did the paying, and the Bushman got the job for a solid fortnight. By the end of that time he couldn't look a turkey in the flesh.

On an average the pay-clerks got through three villages a day. They travelled by gharri, shepherded by the Horsemen, and they knew enough to make the midday halt at a village where the Omdah was rich. Their approach was heralded by excited shouting, and the Horsemen shared in the general welcome. As soon as they dismounted, horses were led away to heaps of green berseem, and riders lounged about waiting impatiently for midday.

Before the paying out began, the Bushman was formally presented to the Omdah as the personal representative of His

Majesty the King. The Omdah assured him that everything in his poor house was his for the asking, and the Bushman was sorry he couldn't take him at his word, for the clerk who interpreted had already informed him that the Omdah's Income ran into six figures and that his harem was stocked with houris from Paradise.

He contented himself by replying that the privilege of being there was sufficient, and that he would personally convey to the King his delight in being thus honoured by so distinguished a representative of the great Egyptian nation. At midday he was told that the Omdah wished to know if he would honour him with his presence at lunch. He said he would be overwhelmed by the honour. And his men? Would they also deign to eat? The Bushman told the Omdah that he would do his best to persuade them.

The feast was set in the vestibule of the Omdah's dwelling, and before it began a slave brought soap and water and washed the hands of everyone about to partake. One table accommodated the Omdah, the Bushman and the clerks, but nothing could be seen of plates, knives or forks. When the clerks explained to the Omdah something of the foreigners' quaint custom, an eating outfit was produced for the Bushman, possibly from the Omdah's private museum.

The table was circular and the flanged brass tray which topped it was covered by a spotless linen cloth. The first course was soup, and the tureen held a chicken intact. With a courtly bow the Omdah placed it on the Bushman's plate and invited him with a gesture to help himself to soup.

Then, the others taking turns with him, he dipped into the dish and the soup followed the bread bridge to their mouths as fluently as rice following a chopstick. When the tureen was empty there was scarcely a drop on the cloth.

Next came a turkey; then a goose; then a dish of pigeons with lamb cutlets to follow; and lastly sweets.

The Omdah pulled the poultry to pieces with his fingers as neatly as any chef with a carver. He handed round legs, wings, and portions of breast and seasoning with the courtesy of a true host. When the goose appeared, the Bushman glanced across at the "bob" table where his four men were polishing the bones of what had been an outsize in turkeys. They had been assured by others already on the job that the supply of turkey exceeded the demand. They laughed at the idea, but the Omdah's kitchen was ready for them. A second bird was placed before them, one even larger, browner, and fatter than the first. They reduced it to bones nobly, but they could only pick at the goose that followed, and they admitted that the Omdah won. Through the interpreter the Omdah asked the Bushman anxiously if his men had enough to eat.

The camp at Quesna was situated in a desert on the oasis, several acres of sandhills as bare as any part of Sinai. They were part of the property of an Armenian who owned a fair slice of the surrounding delta country, Egypt was unhealthy at the time for any breed of foreigner, so he welcomed the Regiment and its protection. He begged the officers to use part of his house as their mess, and he was delighted when the horse-lines were pitched close to the walls of his compound. He told such harrowing tales of the suffering of his unfortunate countrymen at the hands of the barbarous Turk that the Horsemen began to feel that they had done righteous work in making the world safe from Jacko.

A light truck line, ran past the compound and in crossing it the limbers damaged some points. A careless driver backed his waggon into the wall and knocked down a few hundredweights of bricks. A big heap of broad beans, dry in the shell, lay inside the compound, and most of them found their way into the nosebags. It was considered that, as the horses were helping to make Quesna safe for an Armenian, he would scarcely grudge them a few beans.

The Armenian said nothing about the points, the bricks, or even the beans, until the day before the Regiment departed. Then he presented his bill. A temporary committee was appointed to examine his claims before passing them on to brigade.

It seemed that beans were scarce in Egypt and that the horses had eaten a small fortune. He claimed not only their value as seed, but also that of the crop he would have harvested from them the following year! The Horsmen came to the conclusion that, after all, Jacko knew more about Armenians than they did.

As soon as the date of a Regiment's sailing became known, its camp was invaded by Tommy officers. They came for miles looking for hacks, and particularly for something with a turn of speed. Most of the regimental sprinters had found new owners that way, when the original outfit was handed in at Rafa. At least it was certain that they would be well cared for until their days of active service ended.

The day before the Regiment left Quesna, the Bushman saddled up for the last time. The quartermaster of an infantry battalion wanted a steady hack, and they had arranged a swap. He rode very slowly over the sandhills on his way to the infantry camp.

The quartermaster was delighted with the old mare, and promised faithfully that he would take her with him to India, and end her days in the active service way when she was no longer fit for duty.

The Bushman took off his saddle and bridle and put them on to something with three legs. He led it away without a backward look, then suddenly he tied it to the lines and walked quickly back to where he had left the mare. He rubbed her head and neck and kissed her nose softly.

Poor patient, trusting thing! For four years, through times good and bad, she had carried men in the service of the land that had bred her, and her reward was—desertion.

The Bushman walked the two miles back to Quesna.

The midsummer's night was hot. The Bushman lay on his ground-sheet, but he could not sleep. He smoked restlessly, and at last, just before midnight, he pulled on his boots and climbed to the top of a little sand dune overlooking the camp.

The tents had been struck for the last time and the Horsemen lay in the open on a slope by the Canal, waiting embarkation on the morrow. They had one more short stage to do, the last stride back to civilian life, and they were taking with them—memories.

The Bushman looked at the still figures and wondered what fate had in store for them. Most of them would pick up the threads of life again where they had let them go, better men. The war would become merely an interlude, its features a blur. They would meet again and yarn happily; they would remember the good times and forget the bad, but how many of them would look on their days, of service as something about which there was everything to remember and nothing to forget?

The Long Patrol was ending close to where it had begun. The Bushman turned his back on the Canal, a silver streak through the barren sand, and faced eastwards.

A light breeze blew from the desert and the Polestar shone faintly.

He went over it all again, track by track, camp by camp, battle by battle, and faces crowded for remembrance—the faces of men who were staying behind.

No. They were the Regiment; those who, on the morrow, would board the transport, a leave party. They would come back when their leave was over, and those who mattered would take their old places in the Patrol that would be unending. There would be awaiting them a Welcome Home such as nothing in civilian life could give, the grip of the hands of Men.

The Bushman lay back on the sand and slept happily. He dreamed of his home-coming.

Chapter Forty
The Bushman's Dream - 1939

There are Shadows at midnight on the sandhill near Kantara, but only the Polestar and the Desert Wind know their meaning. They can hear the faint stamping of impatient hooves, the jingle of bit and stirrup. When the Shadows are joined by Others the Wind blows less fiercely, the Star shines more brightly over the reunion of the Souls of Men.

The Bushman climbed slowly up the sandhill. He paused half-way, for he had forgotten how to walk through ankle-deep sand, and he shaded his eyes to accustom them again to the night light of the desert. His heart beat hard with suspense. He knew that he was close to the end of his long journey, and he was sure that Snow would be there to meet him. He saw the Shadows and he knew that his troubles were over. He was Home.

The Horseholder moved a few steps-forward. His face wore the same broad grin, his voice was the same old drawl.

"So it is you, Blood. The old mare knew something. She kicked up a hell of a row, stamping and whinnying, when I went to saddle up. You've made it pretty hot, haven't you, taking twenty years' leave? You old lead-swinger, how are you?"

He held out his hand, and the Bushman gripped it. Something came back to him then, something that he had never found in twenty years of civilian struggle—the meaning of manhood.

"Didn't you know I was coming home?" he asked.

Snow shook his head.

"We always know when someone's coming, but not who it is. It's a popular fatigue meeting the Long Leave fellows. The chaps growl if they don't get it, and tell the sergeant he's not running his 'roster' properly."

"How often do you have to send a horseholder?"

"Pretty nearly every night now. They're coming back thick and heavy; we get quite a decent little draft sometimes. A few came back soon after you all went. They reckoned Leave was no use to them. Blood, what did the fellows do with it? I s'pose a man wouldn't know most of 'em now."

The Bushman chuckled.

"Too right you wouldn't. A lot of them are bald and grey, and fat as tubs."

"Their wives must keep plenty of good mungeree up to them. Do the kids ask, 'What did you do in the great war, Daddy?'"

"That was a great gag, wasn't it? The kids don't care if their daddy's got enough feathers to fill a pillow. And the civvies don't, either."

"But the fellows? Have they forgotten?"

The Bushman replied slowly:

"A lot of them have, but some of us still get together twice a year, at the reunion and at the march on Anzac Day."

"But, do you march? You always swore you wouldn't."

"I didn't for a long time, but things got anyhow. There's still the same dirty crowd of 'antis' out there, and they began to get nasty. It was up to the Leave men to let 'em see that we were still there if it came to a show-down. There's always a few drop out of the march every year now; their leave's nearly up. And it's hard to keep a decent step when a man sees the old, old women standing by, the mothers of you fellows, wearing your medals. You have to bite your lip hard, Snow, when you see them crying and hear them say, 'God bless you, men.'"

"Blood, do any of the malingerers turn up at the re-union?"

"A few. Their hides were always pretty thick."

"Wonder what they think of it all now?"

"Some of them wish they had the chance to do it all over again, differently. I asked a chap not long ago if he was coming to the march—you'd remember him well enough, he was in

Frank's section. He said no, and I asked him why? He said, 'I played a rotten game and I know it. The Anzac march is no place for me.' Where is the Regiment now?"

"It's waiting just over the hill. We're finding the Long Patrol to-night."

"How far do we go?"

"Right through to Aziza."

"You're magnoon," protested the Bushman. "Why, it took us three years to do it."

"Yes, but we walked. It's gallop march now, always, Besides, Jacko used to block us sometimes."

"Where's Jacko now, then?"

"You'll see him, mobs of him, camped all along the track. He guards the railways and pipelines, and keeps an eye on the Bedouins, but we're good cobbers since he's learned to drink beer and play two-up."

"And I suppose you rob him?"

Snow grinned.

"Too right we do. He's always broke the day after pay, but we only play to keep our hands in. 'Feloos' is no use to us. There's no leave, and no one would take it if there was."

"Snow, I've still got your cheque, the one you gave me when I went up to the school. I never cashed it."

"Well, you can tear it up. Serves you right for having twenty notes and not spending 'em. Come and have a look at the Regiment."

They moved to the top of the sandhill. At first all that the Bushman could see on the plain below was an irregular line. Then slowly it took shape. Horses stood motionless with lowered heads, and men lay around and beneath them with reins over their arms.

The Bushman said:

"The Regiment's still a long way below, strength. Look at the broken sections."

"We could've been full strength long ago, but we don't take back the lead-swingers or the hospital kings."

"What becomes of them?"

Snow grinned.

"They go to Moascar. They send up a draft of them now and again to clean up the lines, and the rest of them do slope arms for the duration. What bloody fools they were! They know it now."

"And who leads the column?"

"Old Tommo- He was the senior of the officers who never took leave. You'll have to ride at the tail to-night, Blood. All the leave men do when they come back, gets them used to the pace. When we get to Aziza you join the old troop. They're going to blanket you for making such a welter of long leave."

"Any orders about smoking?"

Snow laughed. "A man can't smoke at the gallop, you old fool. We get issues of cigarette smoke, and sleep too, as we pass Hill 70. Pity they didn't invent that in the old days, isn't it? A man wouldn't have had to wait with his tongue out till someone passed the order back."

The shadow line in the hollow began to stir. Men rose from the ground and threw their reins over the horses heads.

"They'll be off in a minute or two," said Snow. "We'll go and report to Tommo."

They mounted and rode to the head of the column. Snow reported: "Old Blood is back, Captain, from Long Leave."

The Bushman heard a murmur passing along the line— "Old Blood is back." "Old Blood is back"—and a well-remembered voice muttered: "Some say 'Good old Blood,' but I say, 'Halt! while Sergeant Blood rolls a fag.'"

Then the order came, 'Gallop march!' and they wheeled in behind the column as it flashed by. With a horse beneath him. and galloping knee to knee with Snow, the Bushman felt a strange thrill of happiness. He only needed a cigarette to make it complete. He tried to roll one and failed. Snow laughed at him.

"I told you we'd get an issue at Hill 70. Here we are—we're coming to it now. Get a good gutful. The Q.M.'s are just as tight with it as they used to be with the rum."

They rode through a scented cloud. The Bushman drew

several long breaths and at once his craving for a smoke left him. He felt wide awake, and when he looked behind he saw that the cloud had disappeared.

"We don't waste any of it," said Snow; "but we've still got a few greedy cows who get in for more than their cut. How'd you like a feed of dates, Blood?"

They were passing between giant sand dunes with palms clustering thickly at their bases. The Bushman caught a glimpse of Romani, Katia, and Bir-el-Abd, and at each place shadows massed by the roadside. He heard hoarse shouts of "Australia Quice," and on the rushing wind an answering cheer went back—"Good old Jacko. Jacko— Australia—Soa-soa."

Then the pace grew harder as the Horsemen crossed ground firm and grass-covered, where the sheen of young wheat glistened in the starlight. They thundered across a dead river and into a thick fog on the scaly hillsides beyond it. When loud shouting again broke the night air the Bushman's hand rose in salute—to the Welshmen who fell at Gaza.

Over hill and hollow, through timbered land and sleeping village the Horsemen galloped on. The desert air lay far behind; instead they breathed the scent of orange grove and almond tree. Suddenly the column wheeled half-right and slowed as it climbed upwards. On the mountain top it passed through an old city, and it halted in reverent silence beside a garden beyond its walls.

Onward, then, and downward to the Dead World. On the ranges beyond the column wheeled again, and halted suddenly inside a circle of low hills. The Bushman heard the click of bolts and saw streaks of light in the sky.

"It's only that windy old fool Jacko." Snow told him.

"He always will fire flares here; thinks the Arabs are waiting to cut his throat."

"When do we join the old troop?"

"As soon as the trumpeter sounds the call. There it goes now. Listen!"

217

The Bushman smiled happily in his sleep. The fragment of a soldier's song floated through his dream: "I'm calling them Home—Come Home—Come Home."

The End